PAINT AN
INCH THICK

PAINT AN INCH THICK

ADAM DOMPIERRE

SMILODON SUN
PUBLISHING

To Riley.

And still the box isn't full.

"Tell her, let her paint an inch thick, to this favor she must come. Make her laugh at that."

-Shakespeare's Hamlet

1

Out, Damned Spot

I stood balancing precariously on a chair in my home office when an unexpected visitor knocked on the door. "Come in," I said, pushing myself upward on my left leg and stretching my right arm out as high as I could. Still, I ended up a little short of what I was after.

The door opened behind me and I heard a woman's voice say, "Oh my!" Not what she expected to see when she entered the office of a private eye for hire I guessed, but that was only fair. I turned my head back towards her, which sent my equilibrium spinning even further awry. That was all it took and I felt my feet go skittering across the chair beneath me. A second later, my arms and legs spun wildly, like windmill blades in overdrive. The chair going one way and my out of control body the other, I collapsed with a cacophonous crash.

The landing came suddenly, a far cry from gymnast-like. But I at least ended up on my back and not my neck, with no rogue limbs bent or broken out of shape. The paper towel I had been swiping with fluttered down and landed over my eyes, leaving me in what must have appeared to my new guest as an altogether undignified state.

She rushed to my side. "Oh no! Are you ok?"

"Completely," I said, surprised to find that I almost meant it. "More of a startle than anything."

"You're telling me."

I steadied the chair I had just sent careening and accepted a hand getting up. Just as I settled into my seat, one of the chair's legs buckled and gave out underneath me. I was sitting crookedly now, but I took the paper towel off my head and tried to look as competent as I could under the circumstances.

"What can I do for you?" I asked in my best attempt at a professional voice.

"What," she looked around the room, "what were you doing just now?"

I sank down in my now-lopsided seat and pointed at the chair across the desk, but she looked at me cautiously and chose to stay standing.

"There's a smudge on one of those windows," I said pointing behind me. "Right up in the top corner. I can't tell for the life of me if it's on the inside or the outside, and I've had a heck of a time getting at it."

That relaxed her some and she decided to sit after all. "You're a professional detective and you can't tell which side of the window a streak is on?"

"More of a smudge than a streak," I said, "but I suppose that's beside the point."

"Yes, I suppose it is." She hesitated. "You know, maybe my coming here was a mistake."

She rose to her feet, but I implored her to stay. "Ok, not

the best first impression. But obviously you've come here for help."

"I did," she said. "And it occurs to me now that maybe I should seek it from someone who can tell the inside of a window from the outside." Tough but fair.

I rebounded. "Do you want a window washer or a detective?"

We looked each other over more closely. I put her at about forty-five years old, well-dressed and well-made up. Her dark hair fell over a red blouse and cold, even eyes. In her left arm she held a folder. Whatever it was she deduced about me, she apparently decided I was worth taking a chance on. For the moment, anyway.

"I'm here about my husband," she said by way of opening.

"You'll have to give me more than that," I answered.

"He's missing, and I want him found."

"Missing for how long?"

"Two days," she said.

I nodded. "Unusual?"

"Absolutely."

"Any guesses what happened?"

"No idea."

"Well, that does complicate things. And what of the police?"

"That's why I'm here," she said. "My husband, Thomas Lawrence, well... He makes an extraordinary amount of money, you see. But the way he makes it..."

"Not strictly legal," I guessed.

"Nothing bad," she assured me. "But that amount of money tends to attract the dangerous types, doesn't it?"

"So I've heard. And you think some of these dangerous types are involved in his disappearance?"

"Disappearance or worse, yes."

Seemed pretty straightforward so far. "So, what is it Mr. Lawrence does for all this money?"

"He paints houses."

I laughed out loud, an involuntary reaction, before apologizing. "Not quite what I had in mind."

"That's all I'd like to say for now."

"Concealing information only serves to delay me," I said, "but as you like it. What do we have to go on?"

She slid an unlabeled manila folder across the desk to me. "You should start with these three. They're all connected to Thomas's business."

"The business you're refusing to tell me anything about," I said, leafing through the documents.

She smiled. "That's the one."

I read the names on the files she had given me. Patrick Raymond. Jake Crossley. Warren Hyde. "No women?"

Her eyes sharpened. "What do you mean?"

It was a rather blind hunch but I started down the path to see where it would lead. "You're sure there were no other women in Mr. Lawrence's life? No judgements. Believe me, in this business it's practically prerequisite."

Mrs. Lawrence shot up from the chair, gathering her purse as she rose. "How dare you!" she cried. "You don't know the first thing about my husband, or me for that matter, and yet you're going to sit here and..." She went on like that awhile, which was all the confirmation I needed.

"Easy, easy," I said and found myself apologizing for the second time before lunch. When the storm abated I continued. "How many?"

The question surprised her, and for a moment she lowered her guard. "How many what?"

"How many other women?"

Turned out that was the wrong thing to say, so I got yelled at again. She ended it with, "Are you the worst detective in the entire city?"

It was certainly possible, but on the other hand, Summerport was a pretty big city. I decided to play it cool. "Seems unlikely," I said. "A town of this size..." Probably could have been more forceful in my defense there, so I kept it moving and hoped she wouldn't notice. "You're the one who hired me," I reminded her.

"Not yet I haven't."

I had to admit she had me there. "Well, what are you doing here if I'm so lousy?"

"Maybe I'm casting a wide net," she said brusquely.

"Maybe." I could feel her patience fading. "Look, if you won't tell me what he does for a living and you won't tell me about the people closest to him—pardon the expression—what exactly do you expect me to go on here?"

"The three men." She tapped on the folder on my desk. "One of them is responsible. Forget your other ideas, none of your business anyway. You'll find the answer in here."

"One of these three. You're sure?"

"Yes," she said. "This could be quite the opportunity for a nice-looking young man like yourself, just starting out... the chance to build yourself a reputation. Show them you're more than just another pretty face." I didn't know who "them" were, and in fact I already had more than one successful missing pet case under my belt, but I resisted the urge to boast. She continued, "The money doesn't matter."

"In my experience," I said, "the money always matters. But I get your meaning. If you mean to say that you're willing to pay whatever it takes."

"Whatever it takes as long as the case gets solved."

"The case will get solved," I promised. "By me," I added

just in case there was any confusion.

"I don't know what your daily rate is, but I trust this will suffice," she said, pulling out her checkbook. "Any other expenses you accrue will of course be covered as well." That was pure Handel to my ears.

I paused, thinking over everything that had just transpired between us. And try as I might, I couldn't resist looking this particular gift horse in the mouth.

"Well, hold on now," I said. "Five minutes ago you had 'no idea'—your words, ma'am—what happened to your husband. Now you're sure one of these three men has taken him. You can understand my confusion."

"Read the files," she said and handed me a check big enough to cover me for a month, at three times my usual asking rate. "My phone number is in there as well; I'm Veronica. Call me when you have something to go on." With that she was out the door.

"Well," I said to the empty room. "Good day to you too."

2

As it Happened, I Did

I leaned back in what remained of my chair and looked up to the spinning ceiling fan. Its five blades rotated lazily in the half-light of the office. They didn't provide much of a breeze but that was fine by me. High heat is good thinking weather; something about the humid, heavy air that sharpens the senses and makes abstract facts feel more real and immediate. I smiled an easy smile and opened the folder Veronica Lawrence had laid on my desk.

The organization of its contents was immaculate; the accumulation and presentation of that much data would have been no quick job. Probably took more than the two days since Thomas had supposedly gone missing to put together by the way I figured it, but maybe she just worked fast. Each of the three suspects, if that's what they were, were binder clipped together. I spread them out across the desk and flipped through them one by one.

Patrick Raymond was first. If I didn't know better, I

would have said his picture came from one of those old west novelty photo shoots. But frayed and faded as it was, I took this to be the genuine article. My eyes were drawn to the most prodigious handlebar mustache I had ever seen, like the handlebars belonged to a 1200cc Harley Davidson. Raymond's stern eyes glowered out from above the mustache, dark against the lighter red and brown sepia tones. I could see from his expression that he wasn't the type of guy I'd go to with any hope of borrowing a dollar.

His outfit suggested something between cowboy and adventurer-general. He wore a wide-brimmed hat, lined with exotic-looking flowers around the edges. Below that, a tan duster was open enough to offer a glimpse of an ornate vest and a revolver in a shoulder holster. The anachronous getup made it hard to approximate his age, but I felt safe saying he was at least forty anyway. Of course, if he were forty when this picture was taken, which had to be several decades ago, by now he must be... The math failed me, as it often did. Next to the picture Veronica had listed his place of business—something called Manticore Cooperative—but I didn't see anything else for me to go on.

Next up, Jake Crossley. This one came with a modern photo of a wide-shouldered man with a chiseled face, a bald head, and a countenance that seemed ready to sell me something. He wore a black polo adorned with some prestigious-looking logo I didn't recognize and what I took to be an expensive watch. Stately presentation, but his million-dollar smile didn't reach his eyes. Someone less generous might have said there was something soulless in those eyes, but not me. The ensuing pages had pictures of his house, business, a couple of whatever the plural of Mercedes is, and even a sizable boat—*The Premiership*.

I did my best not to be impressed by Mr. Crossley's

lifestyle but came up short. A cursory glance over the supplemental materials showed he held a position at Raymond's company, although what an Operations Manager was, I could only guess. Business and residential addresses followed here, adding to the substantial amount of information Mrs. Lawrence had collected for me. *Definitely not a two-day job*, I thought.

The third name was Warren Hyde. The sum of Hyde's information amounted to a single page. The picture quality was a significant step down as well, noticeably smaller with a resolution on the grainy side. What I could see of his face was remarkably unremarkable, generic even. Dark hair hung over his eyes, which were concealed by a pair of black Wayfarer sunglasses. A scraggly mustache completed the ensemble. Apparently not much was known about this last guy. Or if there was, Veronica didn't know about it. No addresses, vehicles, or even known associates; just the name of a bar—The Silver Rabbit. Not much, but something of a starting place anyway, I figured.

After the scant offering on Hyde, she had included a dossier on her husband. Would have been worth starting with, I thought, but at least it was there. The first page was all pictures, a veritable collage, largely solo shots, some with his wife, some with other people. One of them seized my attention. I flipped back a few pages to confirm, and sure enough, one of the photos was Thomas Lawrence and Jake Crossley. Except in this picture Crossley had a full head of hair. There was a resemblance between the two men. Both were sharply-dressed, with stylized coiffures and mirror-rehearsed grins.

"A painter, huh?" I asked the picture. He didn't look like the type to me, but then I didn't know the guy either.

Beyond the photo display the usual information

followed, as it had with the others. More answers than questions at the outset; I'd have to call that unusual. But the central questions loomed heavily: What happened to Thomas Lawrence, and where was he now? I went over the papers again, committing as much of the information as I could to memory, then closed the file. I had a mountain of data in front of me and had to figure out where to begin my climb.

Given its connection to two of my primaries, I decided to find out what I could about whatever the hell Manticore Cooperative was. Here is where the bigger firms or more experienced independents would have tapped into their resources, either technological or contacts on the ground. I didn't have any of either; that simplified things. With my path forward clear, I set off for the bus stop.

People complain about public transportation, but I've always loved it. No two rides are ever the same, and you just can't beat the clientele. I found all strangers waiting when I arrived at the bus stop, but a minute and a half later I heard a friendly voice call out, "Hey there, pardner!"

Turning to my left, I spotted Old Leonard ambling towards me, leaning on his shabby wooden cane for support. He smiled at me through a thick gray beard and waved as he approached.

"Leonard, my man!" I clapped my hand on his shoulder. "What brings you out today?"

"Overdue for groceries," he said. "Bus hasn't come yet, has it?"

I looked around at the other people waiting with us as though that might suffice for an answer, but apparently it didn't. "Well, no, Leonard. That's why we're all still standing here."

Leonard thought that over awhile. "That checks out," he finally decided.

"Well, I'm glad we cleared that up," I said. "Here comes the bus now."

I hung back and let the other passengers get on first. When they had all boarded, I climbed the steps and nodded to the driver. The front few rows were all spoken for so I took the first open seat some five, six rows back. The air brakes hissed and the bus pulled slowly away from the curb. I took out my map of the city and checked it against the address I had, reasoning out the best place to disembark. With that decided, I passed the time looking out the window and watching the city blocks pass by evenly. Sunlight came shining in and a sliver of it landed across my face, but that didn't bother me any. I closed my eyes and felt the warmth blanket my eyelids.

As it turned out, that was a mistake, because by the time I opened my eyes I had missed my stop by a good half hour. I awoke with a scramble to alertness, limbs jerking every which way. The movement had all the dignity of a baby giraffe on ice. That accomplished, I rubbed the sleep from my eyes and tried to get my bearings. I was a long walk from Manticore now, but it would have been an even longer bus ride. I pulled at the cord, trying to make it look like that had been my plan all along. It's not easy to look cool while pulling a bus cord, but I managed what I could given the circumstances.

The heat wrapped me in its arms as I stepped off the bus. I was a solid eight or nine blocks from the Manticore building, and the sweat on my forehead built steadily as I navigated the streets. About halfway I stopped off for a food cart hot dog and water on the art museum steps, and they tasted just fine. Fifteen minutes later I came upon a black office building with mirrored windows and a sign in a stylish red font out in front. I pulled at one of the heavy exterior doors and felt a cool rush of air hit me with my first step inside. A pretty blonde woman sat behind a large black desk some thirty feet beyond the entrance, talking into a phone and jotting down notes on a pad of paper.

It was only then that I realized I probably should have done even a modicum of research on what this place was before I just showed up. Because as I approached the receptionist's desk, I didn't have the slightest idea what I was going to say or do. But honestly, that's how I operate a lot of the time, and if nothing else I know it keeps my adversaries off guard. Luckily, the woman behind the desk was busy with what seemed to be a convoluted conversation, which allowed me to scope out my surroundings while she carried on with the caller.

I stood on a reflective dark floor that looked like highly-polished marble to my eye. High-backed black leather chairs rested on either side of me, and behind them the walls were smooth and black with occasional red and gold accents. Somewhere running water sounded pleasantly, and the air had a refreshing smell of something close to cucumber. All of this is to say it was a classy joint.

While I'm on the subject of things I wished I'd done before coming, I can add dressing nicer to that list. My worn-out running shoes/cargo shorts ensemble just wasn't cutting it and, comfortable though it was, I found myself wishing my t-shirt didn't have a cartoon stegosaurus on it. But that's hindsight for you.

To my left was a stainless steel drinking fountain, and that was ultimately what saved me. Not the fountain, exactly, but the flyer posted above it. A giant dollar sign in the center of it seized my attention (I've found giant dollar signs have a way of doing that). The tête-à-tête at the desk didn't seem to be any closer to a conclusion, so I let myself wander over to get a better look at the advertisement.

"Do you like MONEY???" it asked in electric green letters. As it happened, I did, so I read on. "Manticore Cooperative is holding open interviews for sales positions. September 2nd - September 16th, 8:00 - 3:00. Inquire at the front desk." The pitch continued from there but I already had everything I needed. September sixteenth. I had made it in on the last day. It had to be afternoon by now given my delays, but I hoped I was still on the right side of three o'clock. A quick glance at my watch showed I had almost an hour to spare. A few steps away the receptionist was saying her goodbyes to whoever was on the other end of the line. I saw my chance and sidled up to the desk.

"Hello," I introduced myself, "my name is Eddie London. I'm here for the open sales interview." The look on her face told me what she thought of my initial impression (not much), and I could see the word "open" would be doing a lot of the heavy lifting in this opportunity. What she didn't know was that I didn't care about the sales position one bit. I was here to find out what I could about Manticore—and hey, if a few greenbacks found their way into my pocket along the way, all the better.

"Are you aware of the requirements of this position?" she asked in a tone that suggested she was certain I wasn't.

"Naturally," I lied. "Which way to the interview?"

I caught a moment's hesitation before she smiled without warmth and said, "Why don't you let me arrange you an escort? One moment, please." I nodded and leaned my elbows on the desk, pawing at the top of my shoe with the opposite foot. "Mr. Crossley to the lobby," she said into an intercom. "Mr. Crossley to the lobby. Thank you."

My back to the receptionist, I allowed myself an unseen smile. No better way to draw out the muscle than the old fish out of water routine. It wasn't as good as the head man, Patrick Raymond, but a face to face with the second name on my list was solid consolation.

"So how do you like working here?" I asked after she hung up the phone.

"Oh, I love it here," she said and smiled again. Either she was an awfully good actress or this one was genuine; I favored the latter. "We're doing some really amazing things. Really amazing things."

"I'd love to hear about some of them," I said, but I never got the chance.

"Something you need, Hannah?" asked a voice from above and behind my left ear. I turned around to find myself staring into the chest of the man I took to be Jake Crossley. Craning my neck up to his face confirmed it. Target sighted.

"He's here about the open sales interview," Hannah said and pointed at me. "I didn't know if I should send him back or..."

Crossley took a step back and sized me up. "Of course!" he said and reached out a big paw to shake my hand. "Jake Crossley, good to meet you." His grip was an iron vise but I managed to get through the interaction without visibly wincing.

I let my right hand fall to my side and flexed it a time or two to get the blood going back through it. "Good to meet you, Mr. Crossley. Eddie London. I'm here about the open interview for a sales position."

"So I've heard," Crossley said good-naturedly. "Come

on, follow me." He winked at Hannah as we left her desk, but I didn't think I was meant to see that so I left it unacknowledged.

"You know we mostly get suit and tie types in here," he said with a laugh. "What am I saying 'mostly'? It's all suit and tie types. This," he waved a hand at my getup, "this is a first for sure."

"Yeah, stegosaurus," I said, and he laughed again. "So what can you tell me about the position?"

"We're right in here," he said, ignoring the question and directing me into a conference room to our left.

Inside four women and two men were seated along a wide wooden table. Opposite the table a plain wood chair sat alone; I took this to be my charge. Crossley corroborated as much with a point of his hand, then took his place at the center of the table. Fourteen eyes were trained on me now, and I felt much like I imagined I would have at a firing squad.

Crossley introduced his six colleagues and I forgot all of their names immediately. "Welcome," he said. "I'd like to start with a question."

"Makes sense," I agreed.

"Do you know what a manticore is?"

I did, vaguely, but I was more interested in his explanation. "Tell me."

"It is a beast," he began, "with the body of a lion, the wings and tail of a dragon, and the face of a man."

I nodded. "Sounds pretty impressive. A little anticlimactic at the end there, but—"

"Quick," Crossley interrupted, "what's the first thing you think of when you hear the word 'Lion'?"

I started to say, "The Cowardly," but he was already answering his own question.

"That's right, you think of strength. And 'Dragon'?"

"Enter the."

"Fearlessness," Crossley continued. That made me zero for two. "And," he had learned not to give me any more guesses, "the man is intelligence. Put it all together and what have you got?"

"A manticore, I guess."

"Strength, fearlessness, and intelligence. That's who we are here. That's what we're bringing to the table. So my next question is what do we stand to gain by bringing you aboard? Convince me."

I laid out my qualifications as I saw them, most of them tied to my punctuality. Not the world's finest selling point I'll admit, but you have to work with what you have.

The firing squad regarded me apathetically. "Well," one of the women said, "we certainly thank you for coming in. Take a right outside that door and you'll find your way back to the lobby."

Crossley shot her a severe look and held up a hand. He returned his look to me with a smile. "Not so fast, Emily," he said. "There's something I like about this guy. Do you have any idea how much confidence it takes to walk into a building like this dressed like... that?"

"An unconventional look for an unconventional candidate," I said.

Crossley beamed, like the turn of phrase really impressed him. "I think you've hit it on the head right there," he said. "We're asking this guy to sell, right, recruit? That's not about being some stuffy shirt. It's about connecting with people."

One of the other men spoke up. "With all due respect, isn't that what an interview is for? I don't think he's sold us at all. I'm certain he's not the best we've seen and I'm pretty sure he's actually the worst. No offense," the man added to me.

I waved that away graciously.

"It doesn't matter if he's sold you," said Crossley. "He's sold me. So he's in. I'll leave the other candidates to you. Keep who you want, cut the others loose. I'm going to get our new hire acquainted."

Life sure moves fast sometimes, I thought. A few hours earlier I had never heard of Veronica Lawrence, her missing husband, Raymond, Crossley, Hyde, or any of the rest. Now I found myself working for Manticore Cooperative. I still didn't have the faintest idea of what they did, or what they had just hired me to do, so I thought I should probably get on that.

"Thank you for the opportunity, Mr. Crossley," I said when we were back in the hallway. "Can you tell me about what I'll be doing here?"

"Don't worry about the others in there," he said, which was nice but didn't get me any closer to an answer on my question. "They mean well, but you know how it is."

I didn't, but I thought it best to keep that to myself. "I sure do."

"I'll tell you what, let's go talk to Hannah, get you set up with all the paperwork. You good to start Monday?"

"Monday's good, yeah." That would give me the weekend to take in all that had happened over the past several hours.

Hannah was at her desk doodling some unicorn-looking thing on a notepad when we approached. "Hannah, I'd like you to help me welcome Eddie to the team. He's going to be working for us in sales," Crossley said.

She looked up from the paper and initially couldn't hide her surprise. "Him?" she said. "Really?" But she recovered quickly and gave me a friendly look. "Welcome to the team!"

"Let's get him set up with the standard introductory

packet. He'll be starting with us Monday." Crossley patted me on the back and I managed to not get knocked off balance. "Well, I'll leave you two to it. Really glad you came in today, Eddie. See you soon."

"He seems impressed," Hannah said as Crossley left us. "That doesn't happen often. You must have really done a number on them in there."

"Can I be honest with you?" I leaned in closer. "I'm as surprised as you are. I didn't even know what this place was, I just came down here—" She looked at me amiably and I noticed for the first time the soft green color of her eyes. A sudden urge struck me to tell her the whole story as it happened, and was happening, and lay all my conceits bare. But I pulled myself out of it and stood back up. "I guess it's all in the packet, hey?"

"Sure," she said. "But take this too." She tore a piece of paper off the notepad and wrote down her number. "Reach out if you have any questions," she said, sticking the paper into the folder she handed me. "Sometimes these packets can get pretty confusing, you know."

3

White Fang, Tony

I made it through the bus ride home without sleeping through my stop (progress not perfection, as they say). When I got back to the office I went over the material Hannah had given me. Standard payroll-looking forms, then a Gardner's Multiple Intelligences Inventory, and finally some brief personality tests. Saving the higher-thinking for last, I went about jumping through the personnel hoops.

I picked up the phone and put a call into my guy Tony at the docks. Two rings and he picked up. We said our hellos and I got right to the point.

"Tony, calling for an ID."

"Sure thing," Tony said. "What name did you give them?"

"Eddie London."

"London, huh?"

"No good? It was either that or Paris."

"It'll do. Same address and all the rest?

"I don't see why not."

"Sure thing," Tony said again. "Come see me Tuesday."

"No good," I said. "I'm due to start Monday. Meet you Sunday?"

"Sunday..." I heard him sigh. "Gonna be tough. Gonna cost you extra."

"Money won't be a problem. My client's words, not mine."

"Sunday then. Come by around four."

"Appreciate it, Tony. See you soon." I hung up and mentally crossed that task off my to-do list.

The supplemental forms from Manticore Cooperative remained, but I had a couple days to think on that. My in with the company was secured, and though I hadn't made contact with the boss yet, I felt I was well on my way to accomplishing that. Which left only the third name from Mrs. Lawrence's list, Warren Hyde. Where Raymond and Crossley seemingly lived the high lives as businessmen, Hyde was the mysterious wildcard. All I had on him was the low-res photograph and the name of a bar.

I looked at his picture again. Something there was about that face, kind of made me feel like I had already forgotten it as soon as I looked away from the photo. My rendezvous at Manticore had taken up the larger part of my afternoon and night was fast approaching. Friday night besides, which struck me as the perfect opportunity to take a trip down to The Silver Rabbit and see what I could discover there, if anything. I carefully slipped the picture into my pocket and headed back to the bus stop.

The sun was setting behind me and I took in the lengthening shadows as I walked the streets. Not as balmy as when the

sun had been at the height of its powers hours earlier, but the heat hadn't altogether dissipated either. The concrete and asphalt were vengeful like that, and when the dying summer's sun baked them, they held to their warmth long after its source disappeared below the horizon.

Lights came on across the cityscape and I could feel the energy of the night coiling like a viper about to strike. Inside houses and apartments, people were getting ready for the night ahead and I couldn't resist looking into the windows as I passed, imagining the thousand different lives they led. The air was heavy but I felt light, grateful to have a clear objective in front of me and, from that, a reason to be traversing the streets. Better anyway than to be holed up in a house alone, which is where I would have been otherwise. A smile came to my lips unexpectedly and I realized I'd been doing a lot of it that day. "Eddie London," the purpose-driven professional.

Different bus crowd on Friday nights. It skewed younger, more affluent, less of the charming eccentricity I had come to appreciate. But they were fun in their own way, their positive energy contagious, and I enjoyed the ride that brought us deeper into the downtown district. The Silver Rabbit was a short walk from where I stepped off the bus, across the railroad tracks that always felt like an all-too-tangible border between the good and bad parts of town. My destination lay three blocks beyond the tracks.

The Silver Rabbit was roughly square shaped, a little better than thirty feet to each side. Two dingy windows flanked a black door that stood salient against the pale gray paint chipping away on the rest of the exterior. Loud music poured out into the night, driving guitars, pounding drums, and a singer who obviously didn't list Sinatra among his influences. A group of three stepped to the door ahead of me, two men and a woman. A short but burly bouncer with a graying crew cut at the door waved them through after a cursory glance. I attempted to follow in their wake but the doorman threw an arm across the entrance before I could step through.

"Need to see some ID, boss."

I looked to the people who had just passed by and back to the bouncer. "They just..." I said, but if he found that argument convincing, he sure didn't show any sign of it. ID was an inconvenience but not dramatically so, so I reached back and fished my driver's license out of my wallet. The man produced a black light from his pocket and ran it over the license once, twice, three times. He looked it over, then up to me, back down, and up to me one last time before nodding and handing it back to me.

"Young face I guess, huh?" I said.

"Something like that."

I waited for some confirmation of permission but none came, so I opened the door and walked in with a swagger in my step.

At least that's what I had intended to do. What actually happened was that the door was far heavier than I expected. I tried to pull it open and slide in all with one cool motion; instead the door didn't budge and I swaggered straight into it. The bouncer let out a sympathetic wince, but by then I was already in recovery mode.

"Heavier than I remember," I quipped, which didn't really make any sense, so I hurried inside before anyone else could notice my clumsy entrance.

The Rabbit is hopping tonight, I thought, and then I thought that thought was very clever, but unfortunately I didn't have anyone to lay the line on. I kept it in my back pocket in case the opportunity presented itself at some point in the future (it didn't). The crowd was about an equal mix of haggard-looking bikers and skinny youngsters dressed like they were still mourning the death of punk rock. It was the kind of place a tattoo artist or piercing practitioner could really clean up. The density of people was highest near the bar, but I could hardly stand around without a drink, so I turned my shoulders sideways and angled my way through.

A couple ducks and weaves and a few elbows in the ribs later, I was leaning on the mahogany. The two bartenders were both frenetically filling orders so I bided my time scanning the sea of faces in the hopes of finding one that was familiar. Lots of faces, unique and memorable ones besides, but I didn't see the floppy hair of Warren Hyde anywhere. By then the line at the bar had ceded an opening so I took it.

"Seven and seven," I said, hailing one of the bartenders like a cab across town. She nodded and whirled away like a top. I used the moment to take Hyde's picture from my pocket and tried to recommit the face to memory.

"Seven and seven," she said, placing the drink on a napkin in front of me.

"Thanks," I said and handed her a bill. "Hey, one more thing while I've got you." She looked away like she had other places to be, but I continued before she had the chance to go. "You know if Warren Hyde has been around here lately?" I got a blank stare in return. "This help?" I showed her the picture.

"No, sorry," she said.

"Wait," I said, "does that mean you don't know if he's been around or that he hasn't been around?" But by then she was gone. Me and my inelegant questions.

The bartenders passed by each other and now the other

one was a few feet from me so I reached out and grabbed him by the arm. "Hey, buddy," I said, "I'm looking for Warren Hyde." I held up the picture but he just shook his head and broke free of my grip. Well, I wasn't too clear on what that meant either. I was back at square one, except somehow worse, because at least when I walked into the bar I had a possible path forward. Now I was deprived of even that, and I hadn't even had a chance to touch my drink yet.

"Who the hell wants to know?" a voice behind my left shoulder bellowed. I turned and found myself eye to eye with a bald man with a graying goatee.

"Well," I looked around, "me, obviously."

"And who the hell is me?" he snarled.

"Me am—" that wasn't right. I started again. "I am asking on behalf of Thomas Lawrence. That name mean anything to you?"

"Lawrence," he repeated the name. "Warren don't want nothing to do with those people no more. He's out. Maybe you need me to show you to the door."

The commotion had drawn a few bystanders into our orbit. If something went down between me and Baldy, I knew whose side they would be on. And it wasn't mine.

"Well, good, 'cause I'm done with them too," I said, matching the ire in his voice. "Bunch of no good bastards!" I added for effect. "Listen, you've got me all wrong. It sounds like we're on the same side of this thing. Buy you a drink?" That appeased the crowd that had gathered.

He eyed me suspiciously but decided the risk was worth the reward. "Something with whiskey in it," he said.

I reached back to the bar and grabbed my drink for the first time. "Can't beat that service," I said as I handed it to him.

The tables were all spoken for so we found a patch of

unoccupied wall to lean against. I had given my drink away so I grabbed an empty beer bottle off one of the tables just to have something to hold. Helps a guy look natural.

"So how does someone like Warren get messed up with all this Lawrence business anyway?" I asked, trying to seem like I knew more than I did.

My new friend gulped his drink greedily, clearly not his first or even third of the evening. "Now you're asking the right questions," he said. "The way I see it—"

I could tell this train would be a lot harder to stop once it got rolling, so I jumped in front of it while I could. "Didn't catch your name, friend."

That threw a hitch in his thinking and it took him a moment to recover. "They used to call me Curly," he said. The shine of the bar lights on his bald head showed why they stopped. "Now the way I see it, they were using him all along. And Warren was no dummy, but these people start waving their fancy houses and cars in front of you, promise you the world, right?"

I had to interrupt again. "Was?"

"Huh?"

"You said Warren was no dummy."

"He wasn't. But listen—"

"You miss my meaning," I said more forcefully. "Why not 'Warren is no dummy'? Why past tense?"

"You're exactly right," Curly agreed. "Warren is no dummy." I made a mental note to stop analyzing each individual word and instead wait till I had Curly's story in full. He continued. "But they say, 'Hey, you want a piece of this action?', right? And sure, who doesn't want some of that? I mean, would you say no? I don't know, maybe you would. I wouldn't though, pal, and that's me telling you the truth."

Apparently I was going to need to redirect this runaway

train after all. "Right, right," I said. "I'm with you. What about those things they expected him to do to get all those promised riches?"

"Well, hell," Curly said, "same thing he had always done, right?"

"Isn't that the truth?" I nodded, feeling more lost than ever.

"But then again, Warren was really good at it, you know?"

"That he was," I said. "Damn shame in some ways." How to word the next part? "And when you think of all that stuff they had him doing, probably the most dangerous part of all was the..."

I passed the baton but my relay partner wasn't interested in carrying it forward. In fact, he looked closer to falling asleep. "That's right," he said, his words coming out like watercolors.

"Let's get you some air, Curly," I said and maneuvered him towards the exit.

"Could use another drink," he said, but he followed me without protesting.

"Sure, sure, Curly. Outside, though." I still hadn't had a drop of alcohol, but I was starting to feel like I could use one, or several.

The humid air hit us as we stepped into the dark arms of the night. Not the eye-opener I had been hoping for, but it seemed better than inside the loud and crowded Rabbit anyway. Curly looked washed out leaning against the gray building, a ghost in the fog. Then his legs went soft and he slid down into a sitting position on the dry grass. I felt sorry for the man and pretty lousy about how I had tried to manipulate him, noble intentions or not.

"Do you have a ride home tonight, Curly?" I asked.

The next words he spoke from his place on the ground were cogent and came through clearly. "The most dangerous part of all," he said, "of course was the robberies."

I dropped the schtick. "Who was he robbing?"

"Not who," Curly corrected. "What."

More talking in riddles. "Listen Curly, how about a number I can reach Warren at, straighten this whole thing out?"

"Warren doesn't want to be *reached*," he said, injecting venom into the last syllable. "Not these days."

A modest breeze kicked up and brought a little relief to the gravity of our conversation. Just a little, though. I got down on Curly's eye level, resting on the balls of my feet like a major league catcher. "I'll leave my number with you then. Fair enough?" He didn't return my eye contact but I continued. "You talked about danger. I have reason to believe he's still in danger, maybe more than ever. Lawrence has gone missing. It's my job to find out who did it, and if he and Warren were tied in this thing together, they could be after your friend too."

Curly raised his head and met my eyes. He studied my face, and finally, even through the haze of alcohol, my earnestness won out. "What'd you say your name was anyway?" he said. "Hell, we've been talking for I don't know how long and you never even told me your name."

"Only because you never asked." I handed him a business card. "Remember, we're on the same side and I'm here to help. Will you pass that along to Warren?"

"Sure, pal, I'll pass it along," Curly said. "Doubt it'll do you any good, though."

4

The Fish and the Fisherman

I slept late into Saturday. No word from Warren, but then I hadn't expected any. Not so soon at least. I wanted to get through my Manticore paperwork so I would have Sunday free to retrieve my fake ID from Tony and anything else that might come up. But that consisted of all of about four sheets of paper, so no rush on that. More sleep probably should leave a person feeling more rested, but I've always found just the opposite. I passed what was left of the morning in a grogginess that carried over into early afternoon besides.

Around one-thirty I gathered up the papers from Manticore to see what I could make of them. It occurred to me that they didn't know me at all, so I could respond to the questions any way I wanted and bias the answers in my favor. Then, upon further reflection, I decided that was too much work. Plus, if I did, I would be responsible for matching my behavior to my answers. I didn't much like the idea of pretending to be someone I wasn't (any more than I had to), which was good because I wasn't much of an actor.

Answer them straight, I told myself and sat down with the questions and a pen. The Multiple Intelligence Inventory was first and took only a few minutes. There was a key at the bottom, so I added up my columns and checked the results. Logical rated the highest, Musical the lowest, which seemed to check out. One down, three to go. Nothing to it.

The personality tests were less scrutable in terms of what exactly they were measuring. Their questions were largely tinged with a certain bleakness, apparently designed to draw out personal doubt and insecurities. Examples: "Do you ever think back to negative events from your past?" "Are there things about yourself you would like to change?" I checked Yes for both of them, though I couldn't imagine how any sane person wouldn't. The forms went on like that, and I diligently made my way through all of them.

Just over twenty-four hours had passed since Veronica Lawrence showed up at my office, and I didn't feel too bad about the progress I had made. Nothing on Patrick Raymond, and that was the first name she had given me. But I had hit it off with Jake Crossley and would see him again Monday, hopefully the first step towards landing a meeting with Mr. Raymond. Warren Hyde's status was somewhere between the other two. For as rough as our start had been, I felt Curly and I achieved a certain rapport by the end of the night. He hadn't given me any assurances that Warren would come through (quite the opposite), but nonetheless, something gave me a good feeling about where we left things. Call it intuition.

I thought I'd ring up Mrs. Lawrence and let her in on the good news. She sounded surprised to be hearing from me.

"Is this the detective? You've found him already?"

"Hello, ma'am," I said. After a pause I realized she wasn't going to return the courtesy so I went ahead without it. "No, no, of course not. But I do have some good news."

"I told you not to contact me until you found my husband," she bristled. That didn't sound right to me, but memories are slippery things.

"I've been busy," I said. "I have a job at Manticore now, starts Monday."

"You have a job? What on earth does that mean, you have a job? You already had a job, the one I hired you for!" Each sentence sounded angrier than the last so I cut her off before they could escalate any further.

"You wanted me to investigate Raymond and Crossley, yeah? Well, this is how I'm doing it. I'll be working directly under Crossley, in sales, whatever that entails, and from there I can start working on getting some information on Raymond." Silence from the other end of the line. "I thought you'd be happier to hear it," I confessed.

"Manticore, Crossley, Raymond... fine. But you haven't told me anything about what happened to my husband, which is what I'm paying you for."

"Only because I don't know anything. But," I reminded her, "Rome wasn't built in a day."

"So I've heard. They didn't hold a ribbon cutting ceremony after laying the first brick either."

"Ribbons?" I said, but perhaps I had missed the metaphor. She was upset enough about my Manticore news, so I decided to withhold my non-news on the Hyde angle. Instead I pressed her for more information on the missing man. "Tell me about the outlaw house painter."

"Outlaw," she laughed. "I told you, it's nothing bad. Victimless crimes."

"The legal system just calls those crimes."

"Actually," she corrected herself, "it's even better than that. There are victims, financially anyway, but they've got it coming. Don't waste your tears on them."

"I wouldn't dream of it," I said. "And this is all tied into Manticore, or Warren Hyde somehow?"

"Yes," she said. "Obviously yes, or why else would I have—" Frustration got the better of her before she could finish her sentence, which was probably for the best as far as I was concerned. After a moment to compose herself, she returned. "Listen, don't call me anymore. I'll call you for updates from now on. Once a week, ok?"

That seemed awfully clinical for a woman whose love of her life had gone missing, but at that point I was happy to get off the call with whatever professional dignity I had left intact. "You're the boss," I said. "I'll speak to you in a week." Veronica hung up without saying goodbye.

Feeling a little dejected, I looked over the Manticore paperwork again, mostly to have something to do. Hannah's number was still in there; I had forgotten about it in all the excitement at The Silver Rabbit. I was struck by an urge to call her, but I talked myself out of it. That seemed needy, and I would be immersing myself in that world soon enough anyway. Waiting another two days wouldn't hurt.

I pushed the folder aside, found a stray piece of paper, and set about scrawling lazily with my pen. The drawing didn't have any particular shape at first, but soon legs and a body were apparent and I realized what I was doing. Sketching wasn't anywhere near my wheelhouse but I was usually good enough to make things look like the things they looked like. I let my hand travel of its own volition, allowing my mind some time to think.

Strength, fearlessness, and intelligence. That's what

Crossley had said Manticore Cooperative stood for. Their headquarters represented as much. That black and shining building, opulent but somehow sinister. The people inside were immediately impressive, too. Attractive, affluent, and highly-polished. But something felt off about that, I thought. Crossley had gone to bat for me too easily, and Hannah had gone from dubious to enamored on the strength of his endorsement alone.

I didn't like any part of it. There was obviously significant capital behind the operation, but that only made it all the more suspicious. Money could buy a lot of favors in this town, and I imagined that was true of all towns. More would reveal itself with time, but I resolved to go into Monday with open eyes and a skeptical mind. Either one just might be enough to save me if things turned bad.

Introspection session complete, I looked down at the sketch I ended up with. Four powerful legs supported a trunk-like body that gave way to a winding serpent's tail. Massive wings sprung from its back, spanning the length of the page, and its human head wore an ugly countenance encircled by a mane of mangy hair. It was a manticore all right. There was nothing majestic or regal about that creature, though. It was a twisted, evil beast and difficult to look upon. I couldn't remember ever drawing something that affected me in such a way, but I forced myself to meet its eyes.

The room felt cold around me, in spite of the typical summer heat. Suddenly I no longer wanted to look at the picture, so I flipped the paper over and set the Manticore materials on top of it. Bringing the monster to life (as it were) had changed something, and I didn't want to think about Manticore at all anymore. I had another twenty-four hours until I needed to meet Tony to pick up my new ID, and I resolved to spend them on anything unrelated to the case. I passed the remainder of the day running errands and finished it with a vampire movie. The errands were dull and the movie was worse.

The next day I caught a bus down to the waterfront. A brisk wind sailed in off the bay, carrying the cries of gulls across the shoreline. The afternoon sun was high in the sky and the area was well-populated with people out for a Sunday stroll, though not to the point where it felt crowded. I slipped down past the walkways and picked out where Tony set up shop. I nodded a hello to some dock workers who looked vaguely familiar and announced my presence with three sharp knocks on the trailer door. Footsteps sounded from inside and soon the door swung open to reveal a barrel-chested man with a big mustache and a bigger smile.

"So good to see you again!" my friend said, welcoming me inside. "You never come around here lately. Why is that anyway?"

"Been lighting the candle at both ends," I said. That wasn't really true, strictly speaking or otherwise. The next time I double-lit any candles would be the first. But it was polite, and sometimes that has to be good enough.

"Always so busy," Tony said. "You're something else, you know that? You have my money, yes?"

"I do and I do." I handed him an envelope, sealed and unmarked. He could have counted it, it was all there, but Tony didn't even bother. By now he knew I was honest and, just as importantly, he knew I was smart enough not to risk the consequences of trying to pull one over on him.

"Well, anyway, let me get you that ID, Mr. Jack London," he said with a wink.

That wasn't right. "Jack London? Tony, I said Eddie London."

He frowned. "Jack, Eddie, Steve. Who cares, hey?"

"What? No, Tony, I care. That's like asking me to go undercover as Edgar Allen Poe."

"Edgar Allen? What the hell are you talking about?" The mustache was still there all right, but the smile was long gone. "You tell me Jack London, I make you Jack London."

I took a moment to compose myself. "Tony, listen, Jack London, he's a writer. A very famous writer, one whose name is sure to draw attention. Attention I don't want. And," as though further justification were even required, "I told my employers my name was Eddie London."

He looked at me without speaking. Finally he said, "So maybe Eddie is a nickname, hey? Like your real name is Jack, but everybody calls you Eddie. I'll get the ID."

I was running out of options, but walking into Manticore as Jack London wasn't going to be one of them. "Listen, Tony," I said, "amigo. I'm trying not to draw any undue notice, you understand? And the name Jack London is going to get me noticed. *Call of the Wild.*" I tried to get it together but failed. "*White Fang,* Tony! This is a very well-known name." That argument seemed to sway him a little, but not yet to the point of acquiescence. "And," I threaded the needle carefully, "if—or when—this ruse falls apart under the scrutiny that extra notice brings, they're going to ask questions about who helped a guy like me commit financial fraud.

"Now that's not a threat Tony, that's just the truth. I know you're a very resourceful man and I'm grateful for this mutually beneficial business arrangement we've struck up. Even more, I'm grateful for your friendship. I am. And I hope I've earned the privilege to speak candidly enough to say, as your friend, that going about it your way is sloppy. Just sloppy enough to get us," I allowed some space after that word, "caught."

Tony looked at the ID in his hand. My picture, address, and license number, all under the name Jack London. Before I could react, he grabbed me by the back of the neck and pulled me towards him. With an expressive laugh, he kissed my cheek and rumpled my hair.

"You are a good friend," he said with a big smile. "I should have seen it myself. You know sometimes I get to the way, people, they don't want to tell me the truth. Like they're scared of me, hey?"

"Always looking out for you," I said. "I'll still need that by the end of the day, though."

"No problem," he said. "Small fix, take me twenty minutes."

A "small fix" after all that arguing. Well, I wasn't going to press the issue. I wanted to get out of there before he could change his mind. "That's great, Tony, you're the best. I'm going to take a walk over by the water. I'll be back in half an hour. Just in case you don't work as quickly as you used to."

"This guy with the jokes," Tony said, wrenching my neck again. "See you in twenty minutes."

The fresh air was a welcome respite from the cramped quarters of Tony's trailer. I breathed deeply, feeling I had just dodged a bullet or two inside, maybe literally. A clean ID that wouldn't raise suspicion was my ticket through the gates of Manticore. I still couldn't figure out why Crossley had championed me so stridently in front of the others, but that was a problem for another day. I baked in the sun for a while and stared into the purifying calm of all that deep blue water. When twenty minutes had passed I made my way back to the trailer.

"Eddie London!" Tony called out as he saw me approaching.

"And don't call me Jack," I said with a grin.

Tony handed me the ID. "Ah, you're a good kid," he said. "You know better than to ever get smart with me, don't you?"

"I do."

He leaned in close and said quietly, "Anything goes sideways here, you've never heard of me. Got it?" I nodded. He patted my cheek and sent me on my way. "Yeah, you're a good kid. You need anything, you give me a call, hey? Remember that!"

Come Monday morning I was on the bus early and didn't even sleep through my stop. I had dressed a lot better than on my initial visit too, black dress pants and a pale blue tie over a white button up shirt. With my messenger bag slung over my shoulder I looked downright presentable. Crossley hadn't told me what time to show up so I settled on eight o'clock sharp. I made my way through the now-familiar black doors and found Hannah already sitting at her desk.

"Mr. London!" she said as I came through. She wore a yellow dress, and between that and her flowing blonde hair, she looked to me like a ray of sun. Her smile was unaffected and if I allowed myself the thought, I might have even said she looked happy to see me.

"Good to see you again," I said. "I filled out all that paperwork you gave me." I unzipped my bag and handed her the file.

"Oh, perfect," she said. "I'll let Mr. Crossley know you're here." She tapped a few buttons on the phone. "Mr. London for you, sir... Uh-huh... He did, yes... Very good. Ok, we'll see you shortly." She hung up the phone and returned her attention to me. "He's on his way."

"Obliged." I expected she would get back to her work then but there must not have been anything too pressing.

"So," she said, leaning her elbows on the desk, "you do anything fun last weekend?"

I should have been cagier, but she was easy to talk to, and I found myself wanting to be able to give her a good answer. The truth was on its way out before I even realized it. "Yeah—well, depending on your definition of fun, I suppose. Ever hear of a place called The Silver Rabbit?"

She shook her head. "What's that, like a pet store?"

"Not really." I caught myself before I gave away anything more about my investigation. "Closer to a zoo. How about you?" I never got closure on that question because before Hannah could answer, Crossley came into the lobby.

"There's my guy!" he said, extending his hand in my direction. I steeled myself for the vise grip I knew was coming but it still hurt like the dickens.

"Are you doing grip exercises with that thing, or what?" I said, rubbing at my hand after he had let it go.

"Grip exercises!" he laughed. "Hey," to Hannah, "get a load of this guy, am I right?" She smiled politely and raised her eyebrows slightly at me. Crossley took the folder with my paperwork from her hand. "Well, come on back," he continued. "Day one on the most important job of your life!"

That sounded like straight corporate puffery, but I realized he might have been right. Manticore Cooperative would be only the second job I'd ever held, the first being trying to get this one-man fledgling of a detective agency off the ground. There was also my lemonade stand empire every summer between the ages of seven and ten, but that probably didn't count, strictly speaking.

We left the lobby and were about to head down the hallway when I turned back to wave to my new friend at the desk. She had been watching after us and gave me a smile and a thumbs up when I looked back.

"Good luck!" she said. Formality or not, it made me feel a lot better about the whole operation and my feet got a bit lighter.

"I see you found an adult to dress you this time," Crossley said as we stepped into one of the offices. "Can I get you some coffee?"

"Never touch the stuff," I told him.

He laughed again, shorter than before. "You know there are times I don't know if you're messing with me or just genuinely that weird a dude."

"That's two insults in the space of about ten seconds," I wanted to say, but it seemed a little early in my career to be mouthing off to the boss. Instead I deescalated. "I mean, if you have tea..."

"Forget the tea. Let's take a look at your personality surveys." He motioned for me to sit down and opened the folder as he took a seat of his own.

I sat back and studied him as he went over the papers. Line by line I watched him furrow his brow, clucking his tongue intermittently. At one point he said "oof" and at another he shook his head as with great dismay. Finally, he set the papers back on the desk, ready to give me his final verdict.

"Are you serious with this?" he said.

"Problem?"

"Eddie, listen man. I'm in your corner, you know that." He looked to me for a response but I just waited on the next line. "But these inventories, you have some problems here. Do you realize that?"

"Some problems? Of course, sure."

Crossley sighed. "Maybe I'm underselling this. These results; I'm concerned, ok? But listen, you've come to the right place. We can help you."

A smirk threatened my lips but I didn't let it get that far. "Oh?"

"Don't worry, I still want you for the job. Like I said, you've come to the right place. If I can be candid... Are you a religious man?"

"Not especially," I said.

"Ok. So, what I would like to give you is a set of tools to get your life back on track. We have a distinguished record of doing exactly that for people just like you. Now I won't lie to you, these services do not come cheap. But they're more than worth the cost, believe me."

The line of conversation was beginning to bore me. "What is it you've hired me for, Mr. Crossley? Job duties, hours, salary. Lay it on me."

"Sure, sure. One at a time then. Job duties: Like I told you before, you're in sales. Recruiting for the company. We can get more into the details later. Hours: Eight to five. So far so good?"

"I follow."

"Salary is what I wanted to talk to you about. Let me ask you something. Would you rather be given a fish or learn how to become a master fisherman?"

"I would rather be given a fish," I said. "For sure."

"What?" Crossley hadn't expected that. "No, no one takes the one fish. You want me to teach you how to be the master fisherman."

"Seems a lot easier for both of us if you just give me the fish."

He gave me a look that told me he was sure I was an idiot.

"But if you learn the skills needed to fish, you'll have a lifetime of fish."

"Listen Crossley," I said, "I don't even like fish. Maybe a tuna melt once in a great while but—"

"Dammit man, it's not about the fish!" he said, as though he wasn't the one who brought up the fish in the first place. "It's a metaphor for..." He trailed off, unsure of where to go from there.

"Do you offer any kind of stock options?" I asked. Always good to get stock options if you can.

Crossley raised his hand to his face, closed his eyes, and squeezed the bridge of his nose. I had never seen someone do that outside of cartoons, but it looked like it hurt a lot. He held it there a while before he spoke again.

"No. We do not offer stock options. What I can offer you is this: Enlightenment. Oneness. Complete and total consciousness." When he had finished, he looked at me with fevered eyes.

"Consciousness, huh?" I pondered that. I was already conscious as far as I could tell, but I was getting the feeling Manticore Cooperative wasn't the typical corporate offering I had thought it was.

"We can unlock your ultimate, truest potential," Crossley said. "Make you more than you ever dreamed possible. It's a proven system, personally developed by our Leadership Guru, Mr. Raymond." The name drop caught my attention in a major way, but I tried not to show any outward sign of it. "And," he went on, "it will cost you nothing. This is our gift to you in exchange for working for us in recruiting. You have nothing to lose by accepting this opportunity. Eddie, I promise you: Manticore will change your life."

He was safe in that promise, because in fact it already had. I was no dummy (not totally anyway), but Crossley was one heck of a salesman, and I could see how his pitch had worked on so many others in the past. Still, when I put some space between that natural charisma and my logical thinking, the ideas themselves sounded like a whole lot of malarkey. The new hire in me knew a scam when he saw one; the detective in me knew the value of playing along to gather more information.

"I've heard enough," I said. "Sign me up!"

5

A Searchlight Moon

Crossley shot me one of his billboard-sized smiles. "Well, let's get started then! So, what questions do you have for me?"

Where to even begin? "What is this place? You sell, like..." I wasn't even sure how to finish that sentence, so I hoped trailing off would serve as a suitable replacement. But it didn't, and Crossley just stared at me waiting for me to finish my non-thought. I rephrased. "What is it we even do here?"

Still he stared at me, something like confusion coming over his face. "You mean to tell me you've never heard of Manticore?"

"Sure, I remember Manticore. The dragon-man-lion thing. Fearlessness, all that good stuff. But as to the business model, you know, the day to day..." I redirected again. "How can I help?"

"Well, first of all, don't call it a business," Crossley said.

"Ever again. Manticore Cooperative is a lifestyle. A path by which one enters into a realm of higher understanding, of higher being."

"Hmm, ok. I guess I had thought more like... warehousing, or real estate speculation," I admitted. "And less like entering a realm of higher being."

That wasn't what he wanted to hear. "If you weren't interested in what we offer, what brought you here in the first place?"

"The open interviews," I said. Of course, I only noticed the flier after I was already inside the building, so that answer wasn't going to hold up to any scrutiny. And I certainly wasn't going to tell him anything about Veronica Lawrence or her missing house painter.

I could see he wanted to talk more about this philosophy kick he was on, so I handed him an open invitation before he could poke any holes in my cover story. "You know what? Doesn't matter. Lay this higher consciousness pitch on me. I'm all ears."

"All right then, sure. Well, you may not know it yet Eddie, but you have just joined the most elite group of thinkers on the planet. Forget the life you knew before. That was less than a shadow of your true existence. We are, each of us, unlimited possibility. But I ask you, how many ever achieve their true potential? One in ten, one in a hundred?"

"Fewer," I wagered, and I meant it.

Crossley nodded. "Far fewer, Eddie. What we do here—you asked me what we sell, such a ridiculous question—is we unlock all the dormant capabilities residing inside you. Think of it," and here he paused. "*Really* think of it. If I offered you the ability to achieve a hundred percent—sometimes more!—of what lies unrecognized inside of you, you would seize that opportunity, wouldn't you, Eddie?"

He had piqued my interest. Not in reclaiming any invisible latent potential; that part was surely nonsense. But I was interested in where the con went from here. I implored him onward. "Of course. But how?"

"Of course you would, that's right. I'll tell you, it all started with a young man from England."

"Richard the Lionheart." It was a shot in the dark, but imagine the look on his face if I guessed it right. And then keep on imagining, because I didn't.

"Richard the... No, what? No. That man was Mr. Raymond. If you were paying attention, you've heard me mention him before. He started Manticore, although it wasn't yet Manticore at that time, naturally. Would you like to hear his story?"

By that point I was genuinely interested, in spite of whatever flaky hidden potential treacle he had led off with.

"Yes."

"Mr. Raymond was born poor, just outside of Blackpool."

"Starting at the very beginning, I see," I said.

"Don't interrupt." I held up my hands as a mea culpa. "His father was a sailor, a cruel man, and Mr. Raymond's mother raised him and his three brothers largely on her own. Times were hard; far harder than you or I can imagine, I'm sure. By the time he turned sixteen, two of Mr. Raymond's brothers, sadly, had already died. The only survivor was the oldest who, like his father before him, had gone off to a life at sea, never to be heard from again." Pathos, tragedy, and mystery. Crossley spun a pretty good yarn, I had to admit.

"When Mr. Raymond's mother fell ill, it was up to him to support her. He abandoned his schooling and worked any job he could find then. Inevitably these were the loudest, hottest, and most back-breaking. When the sickness finally took his mother, Mr. Raymond was truly, undeniably, alone. Entirely alone in the world, Eddie, for his endless working hours had left him with precious scant time to build any of the social relationships you or I may take for granted."

"Well," I put on my most enlightened-sounded voice, "they say everything happens for a reason."

"Hogwash."

"Hogwash?"

"Defeatist hogwash."

I winced. That was the worst kind of hogwash.

"I know where this story ends," I said, "and I know it ends happily. But I'll admit, you've got me wondering how we get from Point A to Point Z."

Apparently flattering interruptions were allowed, because Crossley didn't snap at me after that one. He continued his story. "Although he was on his own, and lacking a formal education besides, these hard-won experiences provided Mr. Raymond with skills that would take him far from the dismal streets of his backwater home. He saved what he could of his wages and, when he finally had enough, he bought a one-way ticket to the United States."

"The land of opportunity."

"Mr. Raymond was relentless in his pursuit of personal improvement. He was still young, remember, with a mind and body that were sharp and lean, both honed by years of arduous survival under brutal conditions. His resilience served him well, and he tested his mettle in a myriad different ways. He rode the rails for a time, later put together a sterling record as a bare-knuckle boxer fighting out of Boston, and helped Mexican lawmen retake a homestead from a crew of bandits."

"Quite the resume," I said, and it was. Whether or not

any of it was true was another question.

"There are other stories from these years as well, too many to tell," Crossley assured me. "After two decades in America, Mr. Raymond had found much of what he never had back home in England. But then England wasn't home anymore, not in any real sense. He finally settled here in California, where he won the love of others. Nearly everyone he met was affected by him, in an almost supernatural way. If, when—" he paused (the first hitch in his near-soliloquy extolling the virtues of the great Patrick Raymond), then decided he favored his initial word choice. "If you get the chance to meet him, you will see what I mean. I'm sure of it."

"I look forward to it."

"The caterpillar wasn't yet a butterfly, but very nearly so. Mr. Raymond impressed a wide range of people with his accomplishments, as I said. Many of these people were great themselves; he was no longer alone, and what's more he was a man of influence and a man of means. From this seed, the Manticore Cooperative sprouted."

I wasn't sure I followed his metaphor. "Raymond was the seed?"

"And the sun, and the water, and the soil," Crossley said. "There is no Manticore without Mr. Raymond, and he leads us to this day. But you've gotten me off track. One of these men that recognized his genius was Micah Lennox. You can forget the name, it's not important. What is important is Lennox's wealth, and his passion: big game hunting. Specifically, the pursuit of the Big Five. Are you familiar?"

"With the Big Five? I'd say not."

"I didn't think so, no offense. You just don't look like the type."

I found the second half of that way more offensive than

the half he apologized for, but what did I care about the Big Five? "Some enlightenment thing?" I guessed.

"No," he said, as though that were ridiculous. "Although some would see it that way, yes." Not such a stupid guess after all, then. "Elephant, rhinoceros, leopard, buffalo... the most prized trophies. Completing the Big Five is the high-water mark for any big game hunter."

"Elephant, rhinoceros, leopard, buffalo," I repeated. But that only made four. "You're missing one."

Crossley smiled. "So was Micah Lennox. He had beaten the first four, but one more remained to kill. The lion."

"King of the jungle." I liked lions, from a distance. What I didn't much like was bored rich men going to where those lions lived and killing them in some misguided attempt to fill a hole they didn't have the skills to otherwise address. Discretion told me to keep my mouth shut regarding my feelings on trophy hunting.

"By that time Lennox was an older man. The first four hunts had taken their toll on him—financially, physically, and spiritually. But, close as he was, he couldn't very well stop one prize short."

"I suppose not."

"Lennox resolved to take one final run at bagging himself a lion. Enter Mr. Raymond. Thirty years Lennox's junior, he had already built a prodigious reputation. In the prime of his physicality and cunning, he was a skilled marksman besides. Lennox reasoned that a venture with a hunter the quality of Mr. Raymond couldn't possibly fail. Together they set off for the plains—not the jungle, Eddie—" he added with a hint of condescension, "of Tanzania.

"There they met up with Lennox's local guides, and for three days and nights they tracked a pride, waiting patiently for their opportunity." Crossley paused, seemingly for effect.

"On the third night, a puff adder crawled into the tent where Mr. Raymond and Lennox were sleeping. Lennox just so happened to be closer to the entrance that night, which proved to be a critical stroke of bad luck for him. The snake moved slowly, silently, over the sleeping man. Initially there was little danger; the sleeping bag may have been enough to save him, but the snake crept steadily along, and soon it was flicking its forked tongue out at the only part of Lennox that peeked out from under cover: his face."

I didn't much like where this was going for Lennox.

"Something must have startled the snake, because it struck, sinking its venomous fangs into the exposed flesh. Lennox cried out then, which woke Mr. Raymond. Reacting with preternatural reflexes and calm, he reached for a nearby machete and brought it down with fearsome force. The attacker was dead, but its damage had been done. Their guides were alerted by then, and the whole party came together in the tent. Lennox lay conscious but unresponsive, the snake head still buried in his cheek. The Africans removed it delicately, but they knew he was unlikely to live long; a day perhaps. There was no chance of reaching medical care in time."

That was all a lot to take in, but the story continued.

"As it turned out, Lennox never spoke again. His condition steadily worsened, and on the second day he slipped into unconsciousness and then, finally, the release of death. He had made it to the very verge of achieving his dream, but in the end, nature won out. One short, as you said. At that point Mr. Raymond was left with a choice: He could press onward and secure the kill, thereby maybe winning for his friend some vicarious brand of redemption. Or he could turn back and return to his life in the States."

Crossley looked me in the eye. "What would you have

done?"

"I wouldn't have been there in the first place," I told him. "But if you mean in his position, in the moment, I would've turned back."

"I thought so," Crossley said. "Maybe I would have too. But I guess you know by now, Mr. Raymond was made of sterner stuff. He resolved to see Lennox's plan through, no matter the cost. The next day they closed in on the target. And it's funny about lions. You called them the King of the Jungle, and it's a common mistake. But do you realize they climb trees?" I didn't. "The second largest cat on earth, many of the males are over five-hundred pounds, and they sometimes sleep in the high limbs. Do you believe that?"

I had a hard time picturing it, but I had just made the jungle/plains mistake and he seemed to know what he was talking about. "Sure," I said. "Not that I knew it, I didn't. But if you say it's true, then sure, I believe it."

"The guides knew that, they must have, but Mr. Raymond didn't. So when he snuck away from camp that night, he had no one to warn him about the trees. Female lions do ninety percent of the hunting. Not a lot of people know that." I was beginning to think Crossley had recently read a very thorough encyclopedia entry on lions. Either that or he had performed this speech so many times he knew every twist, turn, fact, and figure cold. The latter seemed more likely, and I wondered how many people had sat in this chair before me, getting the same pitch on The Wonderous Adventures of Patrick Raymond and His Life-Changing Manticore Cooperative.

"The male lions protect the pride, protect its territory from intruders," Crossley continued. "Mr. Raymond had made himself just that as he crept under the wide, black skies of the Serengeti. He had his rifle with him, a Rigby double barrel, and that was all. No artificial light brightened his way, only the cold, clear shine of the faroff moon and stars. He would've kept that rifle ready, you can be sure, but his eyes were trained on the horizon. Relatively inexperienced in that terrain, he thought he would see his prey from a distance, leaving him plenty of time to formulate a plan of attack. In this way, he passed carelessly under a series of Acacia trees.

"I mentioned before about Mr. Raymond's incredible reflexes, bordering on precognition. I suppose he must have had something to react to, perhaps a shifting in the branches high above his head. The sound was a fully-grown male lion springing forth, down onto Mr. Raymond, with lethal intent. Later, he would say time slowed in that moment, to an almost glacial crawl. His eyes rose synchronistically with the barrel of his gun, and he felt his finger resting on the trigger. The lion came at him so slowly, at least that was how Mr. Raymond perceived it, like a feather drifting down to the earth.

"He estimated its length at seven feet. It came down through the air with a deep, dreadful roar, all four legs at full extension." He paused again. "What happened next was a peculiar thing."

"What happened next was a peculiar thing?" I felt like we had crossed that bridge some time ago.

Crossley ignored my interjection. "Because Mr. Raymond looked up and he saw two great wings coming off the back of the lion."

"Impossible," I said. "I'm a pretty suggestible guy, any number of telemarketers can testify to that, but winged lions are too much, even for me."

"Quite right," Crossley said, "that such a thing is impossible. The lion didn't have wings, of course not. But have you ever seen the leaves of an Acacia tree at night?

Especially when they're backlit by a searchlight moon in the wild dark of the African plains?"

"Well, not a searchlight moon, no."

He took the dig in stride and continued his delivery without hesitation. "The leaves were spread out on either side of the lion, enormous and black. These were the 'wings' Mr. Raymond saw. In the light and safety of day, we know they were Acacia leaves. To Mr. Raymond, a couple yards and fractions of a second from being mauled and devoured, they appeared as dragon wings. And they might as well have been. But it wasn't the puncturing claws, the razor-sharp teeth, or the rippling muscles powering them that made Mr. Raymond freeze up. It wasn't even the black dragon wings."

I thought I could see where this was going. "The manticore holds up pretty well so far, but Crossley, you're not going to tell me this lion had the face of a man. I don't care what kind of moon it was or how spooky the leaves looked."

"What made Mr. Raymond freeze up was in the eyes of the lion. A sort of orange-brown they were, but not feline. Human, Eddie."

"What's the difference?" I asked, but I realized it was a stupid question even before I finished it.

"The windows to the soul, isn't that what they say? Even in the dark, and with the surprise terror on him, Mr. Raymond assessed in those eyes a humanity beyond that which could exist in the mind—heart, soul, whatever you want to call it—of a mere beast. This was a lion, certainly, but also more than that. Something... irreplaceable in those eyes. So, a crossroads: Take this life, knowing that refusal would likely ensure the end of his own? Or trust the manticore that would momentarily be at his throat? Remember, there was not even time to think here. Only to react."

It didn't seem like much of a dilemma to me, but then I thought of what Crossley had said about the eyes, and I felt I could almost see them myself.

"That was Shakespeare," I said. Crossley looked confused and I had to remind myself he couldn't have very well followed my unspoken train of thought. "Who said the eyes are the windows to the soul. People are always stealing his words to try to sound smart. Sometimes it even works." Actually, it might have been the Bible, but I was on a roll and not much interested in turning back.

"Would I have shot it? Hell yes, I would have shot it. What jumped out of those trees wasn't a manticore, or a unicorn, or a weremermaid. Because none of those things exist, not even a little bit. It was a lion. And that lion would have torn him apart if he didn't kill it. But it obviously didn't tear him apart, because this guy is still alive. So what's the point?"

I had built up a pretty good head of steam, but then it occurred to me that somewhere a twist or ironic ending to the story must be coming, because those types of moralisms always have twists or ironic endings. "Wait, don't tell me. Mr. Raymond, long may he reign, spared the noble creature and it... Oh, I don't know. It revealed to him the true meaning of life, or the path of light, or some such gibberish." I had to pull myself back then, because I was supposed to be there on a mission to get in good with Manticore Cooperative and learn what I could about the heads of its power structure. Instead, I had dialed the sardonicism up to eleven.

"I'm sorry," I said. I wasn't sincere, but I tried to fake sincerity. "Please tell me what happened next." Crossley sat with that a while. He didn't want to tell me after my little outburst, I could tell; but I could also tell that his need to see the story through to a conclusion was stronger than his desire to punish me by withholding it.

I pushed a little further. "Mr. Raymond spared the lion."

"No," Crossley finally said. "He shot it through the face. At which point the rest of the pride all scattered. The safari guides heard the shot, and when they came upon Mr. Raymond, he was standing over the dead body of a lion. No wings of a dragon, no face of a man. Mr. Raymond had conquered the manticore."

6

Mr. Available

The hagiography went on like that over the course of several hours. A lot of that time was spent on Crossley feeding me more stories on the unrivaled genius of Mr. Patrick Raymond, polymath to the stars, though no story stayed with me half as much as the alleged manticore descending from the darkness of the trees. I learned that over the course of his wide-ranging travels, Raymond had discovered, or maybe amalgamated, a system of living that would solve all the earthly troubles flesh is heir to. Since I had joined up with the Manticore Cooperative, Crossley explained, I would have the tremendous fortune of being educated in the way of Raymond's doctrine.

I played the enthusiastic part, and truth be told, he had piqued my curiosity about this explorer of the mind/guru extraordinaire. Not because I thought he actually possessed any hidden secrets of the universe, but more to find out what I could about how he had built such a successful business (for that's what it was, it seemed to me) on nothing more than bluster and obvious trickery. There was the case I was supposed to be working on besides. Wouldn't be much of a detective if I lost sight of that.

The indoctrination session wore on, with Crossley laying ever more laurels at his captain's feet. I weathered an endless rundown of Raymond's satisfied clients. These began with a healthy dose of the pedestrian—careers elevated, marriages saved, hitherto hidden potentials suddenly realized. From there, the names built up to a veritable who's who of the rich and famous. Business tycoons, movie stars, the elite of the sporting world... Name after renowned name, and all of them had been lifted to such stations by their progression through the Manticore Cooperative's program, or so Crossley said. Naturally, this wasn't all out in the open, he explained, for the sake of appearances. Furthermore, I had no way of knowing how many (if any) of these stories were actually true, which struck me as pretty convenient for the Cooperative.

I didn't actually buy a bit of what he was selling, but by the end of Crossley's production, I could see why others had. The whole operation was impeccably polished and he spoke with a compelling charisma. Three or four hours had passed, and when I convinced him I was sufficiently excited about the opportunities Manticore presented for me, we broke for lunch. Like everything else in that building, this was a high-class affair; Crossley and I ate beef tenderloin, mashed potatoes, and green beans covered in some buttery-type of sauce that I couldn't place but appreciated nonetheless. He asked if I had any wine requests, and then, seeing that question had me hopelessly out of my depth, told his employee to bring us something I couldn't pronounce. When it came, I had the courtesy to pretend to be very impressed.

"I imagine you'd like to meet some of the people you'll be working with," Crossley said when we had finished.

"That sounds great," I said. To my surprise, I found it actually did. I wasn't going to be committing myself to whatever culty organization they were running, but I had been treated well so far, and I saw no problem with more of the same. "Am I going to meet Mr. Raymond?"

"Not just now." Crossley walked me around, introducing me to various people in various offices and the like. Some of the employees I recognized from my initial interview. I couldn't tell what any of them did exactly, and I forgot most of their names again, but at least I was starting to get my bearings. Each of them spoke glowingly about Manticore Cooperative, how happy they were to be a part of it, and how lucky I was to be joining up. The over-niceness of it all came over me, and I was caught between the allure of such a warm welcome and a nagging insistence in my gut that everything wasn't quite what it seemed.

"Any questions?" Crossley asked after we finished our thorough tour of the headquarters.

"A couple, yeah. I still don't know what it is that I've been hired to do here."

"Sure, sure. Ok, so basically you'll be an ambassador, or a recruiter. And trust me Eddie, you're selling the best product on the market: A chance for people to improve their lives immeasurably. Immeasurably," he said again. "And that's going to be the hardest part of the job, to help them see that, because it all sounds too good to be true, doesn't it? I know! I was there, just like you. But you're starting to get it, aren't you?"

Just the opposite, actually. I stayed quiet, hoping that question was rhetorical, but the silence that fell between us suggested it wasn't. "I am, yes," I said finally.

"That's right. And just a couple days ago you didn't even know we existed. Amazing, isn't it?" That one was rhetorical. "So, you bring us new people. Because we want to do as much good as we possibly can. We want to save the planet. And we're going to, Eddie, with your help. You're stepping into a much larger world."

"Another question, if I might: How does Manticore make its money?"

"Well, that's easy. We have a very valuable product here. Maybe the most valuable product on Earth, in fact. And when people see that, they're happy to pay market rate for it. We could charge a whole lot more, Eddie, and that's the truth. But it's not about the money. We just need enough to cover our operating expenses, the salaries of people like yourself, and of course the home office here."

Nobody who was concerned with just covering expenses operated out of a building like that, but Crossley made it sound downright ascetic. "I see now," I said.

"You haven't even heard the best part yet. As an employee of Manticore, you're entitled to all these same mind training services at a greatly reduced rate. I trust you can't wait to get started."

"Well, hold on now," I said. "I'll be paying you?"

"You'll be buying training services," Crossley corrected, as though that was any kind of contradiction. "I mean, why wouldn't you after everything I told you today? Of course you will. But you know what? It's almost quitting time. Why don't you go ahead and cut out a little early? Give you a chance to get a headstart on bringing us some names of potential new recruits."

I was in no hurry to get on that, headstart or otherwise. But I did want out of that building and away from Jake Crossley and the rest of them. I needed time to think.

"I certainly thank you for your hospitality," I told him. And then, so there were no misunderstandings, I added, "I look forward to seeing you again tomorrow."

"Great, great. Except you won't be seeing me tomorrow. This is an awfully big operation—and growing—to be second in command of, so I'm afraid my attentions will be needed elsewhere. But I think you have what you need to get started. Let Hannah know when you have your leads and she'll put them on my calendar. We'll be in touch about your future training sessions. Good seeing you, Eddie, and glad to have you aboard." He shook my hand brusquely and disappeared down the hallway.

I made my way back to the lobby, but Hannah wasn't behind the desk. In her place sat a dark-haired young man with a face like a pigeon. He gave me a friendly nod and saluted towards me with some hand signal that I wasn't quick enough to catch. Some secret sign they hadn't covered in my orientation? I did my best to return it, botching the particulars I'm sure. He seemed satisfied enough with that, so I pushed my way through the big black doors and out into the street.

Traffic whirred by, sounds of engines and horns mingling with a river of voices from the sidewalks. By then I knew the neighborhood, more or less, and was able to find the nearest bus stop without consulting my map. Forever forward. It was a short wait before the bus pulled up over the hill. I climbed aboard, taking another shot at the strange hand signal the secretary had flashed me on the way out of Manticore. After a moment of confusion, the driver recovered enough to give me a thumbs up in return.

The bus wheels spun below me, cruising through the city streets and stopping intermittently to let passengers on or off. Crossley had tasked me with recruiting members for the Cooperative. His directive didn't go much beyond that; apparently, I should accomplish this by delivering the thirdhand gospel of Patrick Raymond and his conquests of both the natural world and the mind. Except I didn't have the first ounce of respect for either, and I didn't trust my ability to pretend to. I set about thinking of other ways I could get them some names, buy myself some time, and maybe even start to work my way up the organizational ladder.

I disembarked not at my usual stop, but near a park I knew. The atmosphere was better there, more conducive to thinking. Birdcalls and friendly-looking people walking their friendly-looking dogs replaced the crawl of traffic and that uniquely urban sense of claustrophobia. I leaned back on a wooden bench, spread my arms along the top of it, and laid my legs out far in front of me. It wasn't especially comfortable, and I probably looked a little ridiculous, but the physical act helped me get in the right headspace. Like if I stretched my body out, my thoughts would follow.

Objective: I had to give Crossley names of people interested in joining the Manticore Cooperative cult. "Cult" was maybe too harsh a word, but that was how I had come to think of it. Obstacle: I didn't know anyone who would go for that, and I wasn't willing to send them into that winged lion's den even if (especially if) they were. Resolution: Well, that's what I was working on.

I tried to rearrange the principal pieces, see if the reshuffling would make a way forward any clearer. Maybe I had misstated the objective a moment earlier. Crossley had not asked for names of people interested in joining

Manticore. That was not what he had said at all. He said he wanted names. That opened up a nice little loophole for myself. I didn't actually have to find people who wanted to join up. All I had to do was to get him names, and names were easy to come by.

Then it occurred to me that at some point these names would be expected to show up for an interview, if that's what it was, with Crossley. That complicated things. I didn't have many people I was willing to entrust with an undercover operation when my case depended on it, but there were a couple. I filed the thought away for later and tried to let myself enjoy the bus ride home unburdened by the sinister feeling this Manticore operation left me with. Alas, my best efforts fell short.

It was Monday evening and I was due back at Manticore Tuesday morning. Doing what specifically, I didn't know. That was becoming a recurring theme with these Manticore people, and I didn't much appreciate it. I didn't think they would expect me to have a name already, but if they did, I wanted to have one ready. And even if they didn't, I would get our working relationship off on the right foot. I needed someone I could trust and who had some experience being less-than-truthful under pressure. One name came to mind, so I put in a call.

"You've got Tony," my friend said, answering the phone.

"Tony, need you to do something for me."

"This related to the ID thing?" he asked.

"Yes, sir."

"That's the one with the expense account, yeah?" There were times it seemed Tony couldn't tell me what day it was if I spotted him two guesses, but his memory was always clear where business was concerned.

"Yes, sir," I said again.

"I like the sounds of that. What do you need me to do?"

"Kind of a long story," I said. "Can I come by?"

"Now?" he said. "Getting kind of late, isn't it?"

It was. "Name your price."

He did, which made me regret saying that. But it's not like it was my money. "Ok," I agreed. "See you shortly."

Tony's shaggy lawn was in need of a trim, I saw as I made my way up towards his house. But then he was a busy guy. His house was a squat, one-story affair, white with navy shutters on either side of a large living room window. The window had no curtains or blinds and I could see through to the inside where Tony slouched on a recliner. I knocked three times, then heard his footsteps approach.

"Jack London! What can I do for you?" Tony said as he opened the door and welcomed me inside.

"Eddie London," I corrected him. "Jack was the writer."

"Sure, sure. You got the money?"

"Not this time, Tony, I have to expense it. But you know I'm good for it."

"Ahhhhh," he said, drawing out his protest. "I know, I know. Still, would have been nice to come over with the money." He sank back down into his recliner and I found my way to a nearby couch.

"I don't have the money, Tony, not yet. But listen. You ever hear of a place called Manticore? Manticore Cooperative, they've got a place down on Seventh Street."

He shook his head. "What's a manticore?"

"Sort of like a lion, but with..." I could see the answer would only lead to more questions that I didn't much feel like answering. "It doesn't matter. They're this group, or business I guess, and that's just the name they've given themselves."

Tony's eyes sharpened. "What kind of business are they in?"

"Boy," I said, "I wish I knew. The thing is, I'm working for them now."

"You're working for them and you don't know what kind of business they're in? What are you, stupid?"

"Take it easy," I said. "I'm not really working for them, just pretending to. For the case."

"Hmm, ok," Tony said, deciding that was acceptable enough. "So I'll say again, what can I do for you?"

"So my job, if you want to call it that, is to recruit people to join this organization. Except I'm not going to do that, because something feels off about the whole operation."

"Like what?'

"Like it's a cult," I said, finally voicing the word I had been avoiding saying out loud.

"Woah," Tony said. Not the direction he had been thinking in.

"But I have to bring them people, right? Because that's my job, to recruit. So, in my infinite wisdom, I figure I'll bring them someone who can play the part without actually joining up with the crazy thing. What you can do for me is this: You go in for an interview with this guy Crossley, act like you're interested, and make me look good to the bosses. But you give them a fake name, address, all that, so when they try to find you to follow-up, you're in the wind. Free and clear."

"Fake names are my specialty," Tony said, proud as could be.

"Sure, they are, Tony. Just remember, William Shakespeare is already taken."

"You better watch yourself," he said, raising his hand like he was getting ready to smack me. Then he laughed a big, unrestrained laugh. "You're a funny guy sometimes. William Shakespeare... I'm going to tell them my name is Billy Shakes."

"Sure, why not?"

I could see Tony working through the plan in his head, testing it for any weak spots. Eventually he decided he was satisfied. "Sounds like my kind of gig," he said. "And it pays well, right?"

"It sure does. Now I don't know when I'm going to need to bring you in, so just be available, ok?"

"That's me, Mr. Available," Tony said, and he got up to pat me on the back enthusiastically. "You just tell me when you need me and I'll go have some fun with those folks over at the Monstercore."

Part of me wanted to correct him, but the larger part was content to let him have his moment. "That sounds great, Tony. I appreciate you, and I'll be in touch."

Night had fallen by the time I got home, which was good because I was tired and no good at sleeping while it was still light outside. I slid my key into the lock and pushed the door open. I switched the lights on, but they flickered briefly then died. *A problem for another day*, I thought, and shrugged off the inconvenience. Locking the door behind me, I found my way through the dark of the house to the bathroom to brush my teeth, then to the bedroom to rest my eyes. As I moved towards the bed, it seemed I caught a glimpse of a figure outside my bedroom window. *Really should check that out*, I thought, but my body was already finding its way to the mattress. A moment after my head hit the pillow, I was fast asleep.

7

The Bullpen

Hannah greeted me as I came through the door at Manticore Cooperative the next morning. As much as I was starting to hate that place, I didn't hate her. Not by a long shot.

"Eddie!" she beamed. "Mr. Crossley told me yesterday went well. So, you're all set up for client enlistment?" Was that what they were calling it? Sounded suitably Orwellian to me.

"I am," I said. "Except it was all very vague, you know? I don't know where I'll be working or to whom I report—Crossley pretty much said he would be too busy to work with me one on one."

"He is," Hannah said sympathetically. "It takes so much work to keep this place going, keep helping all these people. If you could only see what goes on behind the scenes here." There was something in that last line. We locked eyes after she said it, and I felt a transfer of understanding that went beyond words, though to what end, I couldn't yet say.

"I'll bet." I tried to read her further but the moment had passed. "So where do they want me during working hours?"

"You'll start off in the bullpen, third floor. Ask for Miss Jones. Actually," she added, "you won't have to ask for her. You'll pick her out. You can make phone calls there, or set up off-site drives. Probably the best place to pick up tips from the more experienced recruiters too."

"How long have you been here?" I realized I was stalling, looking for ways not only to avoid the bullpen, but to extend our conversation.

"Two months," she said after some thought. "Or it will be in about ten days." Our eyes met again and I was sure of it then, something beneath the extroverted cheerfulness that she wore on the outside. Something deeper.

"That's a pretty long time," I said, although it definitely wasn't. "Are you willing to show me the ropes a bit?"

Hannah shot a quick glance over either shoulder. "What are you doing for lunch today?"

I shrugged. "No plans."

She leaned ever-so-slightly closer. "I know a place. Meet here at noon?" There was a weight to those green eyes now, as though this were about anything but lunch.

"Noon it is," I said.

I stepped out of the elevator on the third floor and was greeted with a sign that said "Bullpen" with an arrow to the left. It wasn't long before I heard the commotion of the recruiters working the phones. I entered the room to find about twenty work stations spread across the large floor, maybe half of them occupied. The desk jockeys were a mix of young go-getters and an older, more tired-looking set. Both groups exuded tenacity, which I chalked up to eagerness in the former and desperation in the latter. Between the rows, pacing like a chain gang supervisor, I saw the woman who could only be Miss Jones.

She was every bit of six feet tall and lean, covering ground in long, graceful strides. Her keen eyes peered out from behind a pair of horned-rimmed glasses. This Miss Jones projected intimidation without saying a word. But hey, if Raymond could stare down his manticore, I could face up to my new boss.

"I'm looking for Miss Jones," I announced as I entered the bullpen. Every head in the place turned towards me, including the boss's.

"I am Miss Jones. And who are you?"

"New hire," I said, extending my hand. She didn't reciprocate, so I lowered it unceremoniously. "Eddie London."

She looked me over. "One of Mr. Crossley's?"

"That's right. Crossley—"

"Mr. Crossley," she interrupted.

"That guy, yeah. He wants me in recruiting." I wasn't sure if I should mention the new potential client I had enlisted, but I decided to save that bit of information until I needed it.

"You?"

"Me."

"Well," she said, as though a great weight had been added to her shoulders, "go ahead and get started. I'll expect a confirmed appointment by the end of the week." She turned away from me and resumed stalking the floor. "Let's go, people! There will be no slacking on my watch!"

I scanned the place and decided to try my luck at a desk between two of the older-looking recruiters. Maybe pick up on some of that experience Hannah mentioned. To my left was a woman I put at about fifty, and to my right a man who was probably a decade older. I greeted them with a friendly nod as I sat down but didn't get much in the way of return.

The woman was on the phone, pitching somebody about improving their focus, energy, and general well-being. Casting a real wide net there. On my right side, the man was poring over a series of names and numbers he had scrawled in a notebook. I took my shot with the less busy of the two.

"How's the day going so far?" I asked him.

"Can't really talk now," he said without looking up from his page of figures.

I persisted. "How do you like working at Manticore?"

This time he looked up, not at me, but to locate Jones. She was on the other end of the room, and my new coworker decided that was a sufficiently safe distance.

"I'll tell you the truth," he said, which would be a rare commodity in this building. "The work is not always easy. Don't expect it to be. But the mind training is worth it. We're saving the planet, one person at a time. It's very important you remember that. Some days it's the only thing that gets me through."

That answer was a lot more sobering than I expected, and it threw off any idea of a script I had planned. I wanted to follow up, but by that time Jones was on her way back towards us. Waiting for another window of opportunity seemed the more prudent move. As she came closer, I picked up a phone and faked my way through a conversation.

"Well, that's the great thing about Manticore, sir," I said into the dial tone. Jones passed by and I gave her a wink. All I got back was a frown, but she didn't hassle me any further and that felt like a win. When she was out of earshot again I tried to pick our conversation back up.

"Give me something I can work into my pitch, will you? How does Manticore save the planet?"

By that time my colleague was reaching for the phone to make a call of his own. "Not now," he said. "Just remember the big picture. Your job is to get them in the door. Mr. Raymond, Mr. Crossley, and the others will handle the rest."

I guess that was supposed to sound encouraging, but the effect was more chilling as far as I was concerned. Without a chance to follow up, I directed my attention to the woman on my left who had just completed her call, unsuccessfully by the looks of things. This time I skipped the perfunctory opening.

"How do you like working at Manticore?"

She looked over as though noticing me for the first time. "It's important work we're doing here," she said. "We're saving the planet."

"So I've heard. Remind me, how are we doing that, exactly?"

She brought her voice down. "You're a new hire, right?"

I nodded.

"So you haven't gone through any of the mind training sessions yet?" I shook my head. "That explains it," she said. "You just haven't seen the Manticore training in action yet. But you will."

Again, she seemed to mean that kindly, but it sounded for all the world like a hell of a threat. I wanted to follow up, press her for more, but our sentry was making her way back towards us. I could see how she stayed so thin, logging that many steps in a day. She was like a perpetual calorie burning machine, the way she moved up and down those rows unceasingly. I faked another phone call and wished it were closer to noon.

*　　*　　*

The morning passed like that, me trying to get information out of my workmates until they both got annoyed and took to ignoring me. I didn't find out anything of consequence; just that these two were completely devoted to the Cooperative, and that to them the daily pressure and rigid hierarchical structure was a fair trade for their access to the training sessions Manticore provided. We were dismissed for lunch at five minutes before noon and I was back at Hannah's desk by noon sharp. She was already packing up her things.

"You ready?" she said. "Let's go."

A minute later we were out on the street. The air was crisp but pleasantly so, and her green dress swayed in the breeze. Autumn was right around the corner.

"Feels good to get a change of scenery, doesn't it?"

"It does," I agreed as I followed her lead down the sidewalk. "So, the bullpen was interesting. What does your day to day look like?"

"Nothing interesting, I can promise you that. Managing schedules, some light paperwork, phone calls... It's a living."

"You don't sound as zealous as the other people I've talked to at Manticore," I said. "Saving the planet and all that."

"Oh yes, very much so," she said. "One person at a time. The coffee shop's just up here on our left. They make good sandwiches too."

We crossed the street and I held the door open for her as she stepped inside. The earthy colors and soft jazz soundtrack conveyed a relaxed atmosphere, with couples or small groups absorbed in their various conversations.

"How do you like your coffee?" Hannah asked.

"As far from me as possible," I said. "Crossley thought I

was kidding about that, but I hate the stuff. These sandwiches look good, though.”

I settled on a Reuben with peppermint tea and Hannah went for the turkey and Swiss and some coffee drink with a name I couldn't pronounce. When we found our table, she settled her eyes on me and asked a question that seemed to have been on her mind for a while.

“So, be honest now, what do you think of Manticore so far?”

I had lied to these Manticore people over and over, and in doing so I had become quite good at it. I had my story straight, my lines all memorized. It should have been easy to keep the ruse going. But suddenly I didn't want to lie anymore, not to her.

“It's been interesting.” I sipped at the tea.

Hannah shook her head. “That's no kind of answer at all.”

“Well, I know what you want me to say. You want me to say that it's been amazing, and everyone is so inspiring, and I can't wait to start my mind training sessions, whatever the hell those are. You want me to tell you that we're saving the planet—one person at a time!—and that I'm thrilled to be a part of it.”

“Oh?” She gave me that look again, the one that made me think there was more to her than I, and the others, had seen.

“Well, isn't it?” I said. “Do you remember the first time we met, at my open interview? You were so cold to me, like I didn't exist. That is until I came back with Crossley's seal of approval, and since then it's been nothing but interest. I wasn't good enough before? But now I've gone through the indoctrination, listened to stories about reclusive gurus, Mexican bandits, and winged lions attacking from African trees. On top of that, I have to recruit more strangers for your oh so noble cause. So now I'm worth coffee and a sandwich?" I had lost my temper but didn't care to find it. "And we're sharing all these glances that mean, I don't even know what. What's your angle here, anyway?"

Hannah looked at me calmly and said, "If I ask you a very important question, do you promise to answer it honestly?"

That sounded like we might be starting to get somewhere. "Shoot."

"Are you fully committed to Manticore?"

I kept my word and answered honestly. "I don't think I've ever been fully committed to anything in my life."

"That seems so sad," she said, and I could tell she meant it. Not as an insult. or even judgment, but simply as an acknowledgement of fact. Maybe she was right. She was past it quickly. "You're not a true believer then?" This time I didn't answer at all. She studied my face. Finally, she said, "Eddie, I'm going to take a chance here..."

I broke in and took a chance myself. "Hannah, I'll tell you what. I think the whole thing is rubbish. It's either a good old-fashioned grift or a zealotic cult, maybe both. Crossley paints a pretty picture, and maybe there is something to this Raymond guy, but there's a rottenness underneath it all. I'm sure of it."

What she said next surprised me, and not just because it wasn't something I often heard. "You're absolutely right."

"I just—Wait, what?"

She lowered her voice and went on confidentially. "It's exactly what you said. A cult, a grift, a mix of the two. It's a machine engineered to make money, no matter the human collateral damage. And the machine is very effective. Now I'm doing what I can to break the machine from the inside."

My thoughts jumped to Thomas Lawrence. Had he been

caught up in, then devoured by, the machine? That was certainly how Curly talked about Warren Hyde. Then I wondered why Hannah chose to get caught up with these people. Only after those two thoughts registered did the weight of what she had just said really hit me.

"You're not one of them? Like, you're secretly working undercover?" This was a revelation. "Yes, me too." That didn't quite make sense. Almost, though. "I mean, I'm undercover too. I'm working a case, on a man who's gone missing." I surprised even myself with how quickly I abandoned all pretenses of surreptitiousness. "Hannah, this is huge!"

"Quiet," she hissed, kicking my foot under the table. "You want to take out a billboard about it next?" Luckily none of the other patrons seemed to notice our exchange.

"Sorry, sorry, of course." She was right, but I was still having a heck of a time controlling my newfound excitement. "I have so many questions. How long have these people been around for? How did they get started? Ever hear of Thomas Lawrence?"

"Slow down, slow down. You're not just another new hire then either? I knew something felt off. What's this about a case?"

I noticed we had both relowered our voices. "I'm a P.I.," I said, "a private investigator. Just starting out really, but this woman comes to me looking for her husband. That's the Thomas Lawrence I mentioned. And one of the names she gives me as a person of interest is Jake Crossley. Patrick Raymond, too. So I get myself down to Manticore Cooperative to see what I can find out. There's a little more to the story, but those are highlights."

"Wow," she said, apparently just as surprised by my reveal as I had been by hers. "I mean, wow. I really didn't take you for the detective type."

"Not many do."

"I'm going to trust you, Eddie. And if you trust me, then we can work together." I told her I did. "That's good, very good. It was true what I said about only being on the job for two months. So I don't have nearly as much information to share as I'd like, but I'd be glad to tell you what I know so far."

Where to start? "So how do they make their money? They sure seem to have a lot of it."

"The members pay, like, a subscription you might call it. For the privilege of belonging to the Cooperative, and for the training."

Another reference to the mind training exercises. "What do those entail?"

"You'll enroll in them soon enough; they'll make you. The classes are harmless, so far anyway. Positive thinking, emotional regulation... It's nothing that couldn't be found in a dozen self-help books. Manticore just happens to charge exorbitant sums of money for the information."

"And people don't realize they're being scammed?"

"Some do," Hannah said. "Most do, maybe. But they can't just leave, or stop paying."

"Why not?"

"Manticore would ruin them. The people on the top—Mr. Raymond, Mr. Crossley, whoever it is, they're ruthless. And the members have seen what happens to people who try to leave. So, easier to just keep handing over the cash."

It was a pretty bleak picture. "You're not worried they'll try to do the same to you, whenever your true intentions come out?"

"Oh, I know they will," Hannah said. "And I know it won't matter. I have powerful friends; I'll be fine."

Powerful friends, huh? That meant one thing to me. "What are you, FBI? CIA?"

"It doesn't matter."

"NSA? NBA?"

"Something like that. The specifics aren't important, Eddie."

"Maybe not, but I'd still like to know. I take it your name's not really Hannah then."

She shrugged, neither affirmation nor denial. "In either case, it's better if you go on thinking of me that way. Leave it simple, less to keep track of."

I nodded. She didn't even bother asking about my name, but I guess that was all part of keeping it simple. It hurt a little, but I soldiered on.

"Why do I get the feeling your motivation for this war you plan on waging isn't limited to professional reasons? Why you, and why Manticore?"

Her eyes went kind of faraway then, like she was trying to decide how much to really let me in. For the moment she hedged her bets. "It's such a long story."

"The ones really worth telling usually are," I said.

"Ok. Well, baby steps. I grew up out east."

"We're in California," I said, at the risk of stating the obvious. "'Out east' covers a lot of ground."

She nodded and took a small drink of her coffee. "It does."

"Intentionally then." She met my eyes evenly but otherwise didn't respond. I let the silence linger until it became awkward, and then I let it linger some more.

I was just about to give up and try another angle when she said, "Kansas."

"Kansas, huh?" I avoided the obvious joke, but barely.

"A little town called... Well, you wouldn't know it."

"Don't presume to know my level of expertise when it comes to rural Kansan geography," I said, taking mock offense. "Marysville?"

"Hmm... No."

"Then I'm out of ideas." I pivoted. "What brought you out west?"

"I'm looking for someone."

"Aren't we all. Any chance he goes by the name of Lawrence?"

"No," Hannah said. "Caroline." Then, "She is my younger sister."

I put the pieces in the logical order. "Manticore got its claws into her?"

"If that's what you want to call it. Not like it was a kidnapping or anything. She joined of her own volition, like it was the greatest thing in the world."

I wasn't brave enough to ask Hannah's age, but mid-twenties seemed a safe bet, which would have made Caroline at least a couple years younger than that. I thought back to the charismatic Crossley, how impressive his operation must have seemed to someone more used to sputtering tractors and endless cornfields.

"Yes," I said, "I could see that."

Hannah smiled but there was no joy in it. "You think she was stupid to fall for it. It's ok, part of me does too."

"Not stupid, no. Whatever else Manticore is, they are obviously very effective at what they do."

She nodded. "Unfortunately so. But I'm not giving up on her."

"Of course not."

"You know, it's funny. I keep thinking back to this memory, from when we were younger."

"All your memories are from when you were younger," I

said.

A slight smile broke through her sadness. "Yes. Well. I was probably ten, so Caroline would've been five. And our parents bought us these toy planes, I don't even remember the occasion. The wooden kind, that you put together, and then they fly. Or sort of glide anyway. Maybe you know the kind."

I did.

"And the package they came in had all these bright colors, impressive-looking pictures of planes with shining steel wings, or dressed in intricate camouflage patterns. Real art, to a ten-year-old anyway."

"I remember those planes," I said, "or something like them."

"And the excitement, right?"

"And the excitement, yes. Like a world of possibilities lived inside that little box."

"These weren't even boxes. Like, pouches I guess, or thin little bags. But the imagination takes over, you know. So we opened them and inside there were these little slats of wood. Like... pine?"

"Balsa."

"Balsa, that's it. So, we put them together, Part A into Slot A or whatever it was, and you went along like that until the plane was finished. It was easy for me; at the time I probably thought myself too sophisticated for such a simple thing."

"A sagacious ten-year-old," I joked. "Wizened."

She laughed a little. "So it seemed at the time, I guess. But it was hard for Caroline. She was only five, right? So I helped her along, and soon we had a pair of identical balsa planes, ready for flight."

She stopped. "What time is it? You don't want to be late back to the bullpen."

"I don't care about the bullpen."

"But Samantha—that is, Miss Jones—"

"I don't care," I said. "Go on with your story."

"Ok," she said, and the worry that had been in her voice a moment before evaporated. "We had these two planes. So we went up to my bedroom on the second floor and opened up the window, ready for launch. There was a light breeze moving through the trees, perfect gliding weather. Caroline wanted to go first, but as the older sister, I pulled rank. Somehow that seemed very important to me at the time.

"I stepped up to the open window and waited for my moment, waited until the winds were just right. A decent gust kicked up and I gently sent the plane out into the world. I had timed it well; the air got under its wings and sent it soaring, up and then out away from the house. At one point it made a graceful loop, mid-flight. Caroline couldn't hide her excitement, bouncing around the room with a big smile on her face. 'Did you see that?' she kept saying. 'Did you see that?'" Hannah laughed again, momentarily transported back into the past. "'Yes,' I told her, 'I saw it. Your turn.'

"Then Caroline stepped to the window, but the finer points of the aerodynamics involved were lost on her. So she chucked the plane out of the window as hard as she could. Like you'd throw a baseball in from the outfield." I laughed a little myself, picturing the sight. "And her poor little plane just nosedived. No lift, no carry, just straight down. And you know how she reacted?"

"Tell me."

"Like it was every bit as cool as the fifty foot loop de loop my plane had done. Maybe even cooler, because it was her plane that had done it. She didn't care about the botched flight; she couldn't even conceive of any part of it being a disappointment. Instead, she sprinted down the stairs to retrieve her plane for another go. I followed behind and when I finally found my plane, it was just a piece of wood. The imagination, the wonder, that had gripped Caroline, I didn't feel it. But I was glad she did.

"We went back upstairs and I threw my plane one more time, the results relatively disappointing on the second flight. And then I was done with it. Caroline begged me to do it again, but I had grown bored of the little wooden toy. Ready for more grown up things, I guess. Sometimes I wish I could go back to the past, relive it as the person I am now."

"We all carry regrets," I said. I thought back over the story, trying to gather why she wanted to tell it to me and what she was really getting at. "You think that's why Caroline fell in with Manticore. The exuberance for new adventures, a fantastic conception of the possible."

"Some people would call that naiveté," Hannah said. "But yes, for good or bad, that's my sister. I could tell she had grown unhappy there, just little things she said when we'd talk on the phone, and then the communication cut off altogether. I had to come find her."

"I don't think a person can really be held responsible for mistakes they make before the age of twenty-five. Not in perpetuity, anyway. The brain not being fully developed yet and all, so they say."

She studied my face. "And how old are you?"

"I'll be hitting that deadline soon," I admitted.

"Guess you'll have to stop making mistakes then."

I shrugged. "Either that or raise the responsibility cut-off point. Keep it out ahead of me, like a horse leading a wagon. But hey, I wouldn't call it naiveté. We all need to believe in something to get through this life. Without that you're—"

"Samantha," Hannah said with a wry smile.

"I was going to say 'dead' actually. But Samantha joined

Manticore. So there must be something in her somewhere, don't you think?"

"Or was in her somewhere," she said. "I think evil exists, and that there are villains in the world, but not nearly so many as it would seem. No, I think most of the Manticore people started off with good intentions, the way Caroline did. But the Cooperative takes those intentions and changes them into something else."

"The Cooperative is just a building though, right? Or an organization? It takes people to carry out evil. People like Crossley, maybe."

"From what I can tell, Crossley's just a lackey," she said. "Patrick Raymond pulls all the strings around there."

"It always comes back around to the mysterious Patrick Raymond," I noted. "Have you ever met him?"

"I'm a secretary who's been there two months. No, I haven't met him."

"Do you know anyone who has?"

She thought that over. "Well, Crossley of course. And his little board of sycophants. Maybe Samantha? Which reminds me, we really do have to be going. She is going to expect you back and you can't be late on your first day of work, Eddie. You just can't."

"Samantha's not expecting me anywhere," I said. Hannah looked confused. "I told her I was going to an in-home appointment with a lead after lunch, all the way across the city. I won't be back till tomorrow as far as she knows."

"That was pretty clever," Hannah said. "Some foresight will serve you well with these people. But my lunch ends at one o'clock, and I need to be back."

"No you don't," I said, taking a big bite of my sandwich. "I told Samantha I might need you to come with me."

Her eyes widened. "What?"

"I said 'might.' You're free to go back there at your normal time if you want. But this gives us options."

"Did you say that to her, really?"

"I really did."

"And she just accepted it?"

"Well," I said, "it's not like I waited for a response. I said my bit and was on my way before she could argue. Better to ask forgiveness than permission, right?"

Hannah looked at me warmly. "I guess we're about to find out."

"I'm going to suggest something that's been on my mind for a while," I said. "And maybe it's nonsense, but maybe it's not." Deep breath. "What evidence do we have that this Raymond guy exists at all?"

"Beyond the words of known con artists? None, I guess."

"Doesn't that seem strange to you? Maybe he's a phantom figurehead, the Great and Powerful Oz behind the curtain."

"Maybe," she said. "But if we follow your thinking, who's actually in charge? Crossley?"

"Makes as much sense as anything else."

She tapped her empty coffee cup on the table. "But why create the Raymond character then? To what end?"

"The myth-making is a big part of the appeal, don't you think? 'Come learn the mind training secrets as discovered by the legendary Patrick Raymond—guru genius, world explorer, conqueror-at-large!' The pitch doesn't hit the same if the source of the lessons is some soulless corporate hegemony. And this way Crossley, or whoever, always has that indisputable trump card in his back pocket to play if needed."

Hannah considered that. "Maybe," she conceded. "I don't know if I'd go as far as probable, but I'll grant you it's possible. What's the plan for investigating your theory?"

"I'm flattered you think I have a plan. But I don't think that's the most pertinent question right now. Not as it applies to my missing guy anyway."

"What is the most pertinent question then?"

"The most pertinent question is, What happened to Thomas Lawrence? You've never heard the name?"

She shook her head. "Manticore has a lot of clients, and its reach is increasing. I could check through the files though, let you know if I find anything."

"That would be helpful," I said. "Most helpful. Thank you."

"Sure."

"And if there's anything I can do for you..."

"Thanks," she said. "Just keep me updated with whatever you uncover, I suppose. I don't know how you plan to go about getting your information, but for my part I've played the doting disciple. And I play it well."

"And that works?"

"You're asking if flattery works on egomaniacs? Yeah, it works. I'm getting closer—not as close as I'd like to be—but I'm getting there."

The sun angled in through the window, granting her hair a kind of golden luminescence. Her green eyes shone in the light and I saw there was much more to this woman that I had realized from the first impression. That first impression was pretty good itself, but this was better still.

"Veronica—that's Lawrence's wife—gave me three names," I said, thinking out loud. "Crossley and Raymond we've covered. The third one was Warren Hyde." Hannah's face showed no recognition, so I continued. "I met a friend of his at a dive bar across town. He said Warren was done with 'those people.' Didn't really make sense to me at the time, but I guess it does now, if he meant Manticore."

"They wouldn't have made it easy on him to be done, I can tell you that."

"That matches too. He's hiding out somewhere, which is good for him but bad for me. Seems he can't be found by anyone."

"Not yet anyway," Hannah said ominously.

"You think I have competition?"

"If he's trying to quit Manticore, or owes them money, yes. I can look into him too. What was the name again?"

"Warren Hyde. Like the good doctor's alter-ego. You know, I got close to finding him, maybe. I think I'll take another shot. My afternoon is free anyway, right?"

"Yes, I suppose it is. I'm going to head back in and see what I can find on your two names."

"And if Miss Jones asks about the in-home appointment we went on?"

"Then I will tell her it was a very productive afternoon," Hannah said.

We took the time to get our stories straight in case anyone at Manticore had a pop quiz for us upon our respective returns, then parted, off on our separate ways. Hannah went back to the office and I headed for the nearest bus stop.

When I arrived, I found a bus was already there, just idling like it had been waiting for me. As I stepped on board, the radio played all the same vapid, overworn hits I'd been enduring all summer through its tinny speaker. Except this time they sounded a fair deal better to my ear. And, though it might have been just my imagination, the sun seemed to shine a fair deal brighter.

8

A Little Excitement

My next stop was the Silver Rabbit, which looked a good deal more hospitable in the daylight. You couldn't quite call it welcoming, but at least this time I didn't go in half-expecting to catch a knife between my ribs. The door was unmanned, so I strolled right in and found the place mostly empty. The same bartenders I had seen a couple nights previous were working when I stepped up to the bar. They almost could have passed as siblings, both tall and dark. One was aggressively scrubbing at a beer mug while the other chewed her gum with all the subtlety of an air horn in a library.

"Good afternoon," I announced. The man behind the bar ignored me for his dishwashing duty, but the woman gave me a cursory smile so I tried my luck with her first. "Do you remember, I was in here a couple nights back? Looking for a man by the name of Warren Hyde."

"Got a picture?"

I retrieved the one Veronica had given me from my

pocket. If there was a lower quality photograph on Earth, I hadn't seen it. "Can't tell much here, can you?" she said, nonchalant.

"No, I guess not," I conceded. "How about the name, though? Warren Hyde."

At this the other bartender broke into our conversation. "Listen, buddy..." His tone made it clear I was anything but his buddy. "This might surprise you, but not many people give us their full name before ordering a drink around here. Weird, right?"

"Oh, give him a break, Brucie," the woman said. "Maybe he's lost a friend of his."

"Lost a friend and this is the best picture he's got? Use your head, Janie. The guy's a snoop."

"I'll have you know he is a friend of mine," I told him. "Sorry we don't take as many pictures as you'd like. How about when you check IDs? You must see people's names then, right? Think for me: Warren Hyde."

Bruce glared my way but Janie looked invested now. "We don't card as many people as you might think, mister," she said. "But hey, maybe he goes by a nickname. You ever think of that?"

I hadn't. "Sure, I thought of that," I said. "That was going to be my next question, in fact. Any guys around here go by nicknames?"

"Lots of guys around here go by nicknames," Bruce said coldly.

"Like who?"

"'Course, if it were me," he said, ignoring my question, "I would know my friend's nickname. I wouldn't have to be asking no bartenders about it."

"That's just the thing," I said. "So many nicknames out there these days. Who can keep them all straight?"

"Let's see," Janie said, counting on her fingers, "there's Smoky, Bozo, Curly, Rooster..."

"Enough," Bruce cut her off. Then, to me, "Order something or get the hell out of here."

"Sure, sure, I'll order something. Seven and seven, if you please."

Janie elbowed Bruce and started filling the drink. "You need to lighten up, Brucie. Too much stress can kill a man, you know."

"That's not all that can kill a man," Bruce said, looking at me.

"Hey, bartender!" a voice at the other end of the bar yelled. "You think I've been waiting all this time for my health?"

Bruce looked over in that direction. "All right, Donny, all right. Hold your damn horses." He shot me one more nasty look in parting and moved across the room. As he stepped away, Janie handed me the drink.

"Is he always so personable?" I asked.

She laughed. "Pretty much. Sorry I couldn't help, but I hope you find your friend."

"One of those names you mentioned," I said, "Curly. Tell me what you know about him."

Janie looked to the other end of the bar where Bruce was finishing up with the customer who had called for him.

"Don't think I should, darling. I've probably said enough. Good luck, though," she added kindly.

There wasn't much time to spare, but I hoped there was more behind that kindness that she had let on. "What time do you get off?"

She gave me a bashful smile. "What is this, a proposition?"

"No," I said. "Or yes, whichever." Bruce started on his

way back towards us. "Quickly, what time?"

"Four o'clock," she whispered, with Bruce just outside of earshot.

I nodded. The next moment he was upon us. "So I said to him, 'I'll be here,'" I said, continuing a story I had never started. "Well, this guy, he takes one look at me, and he decides he's going to let the dog off the leash, right?"

Bruce lingered awhile while I kept the ad-libbing up long enough to convince him I had given up on the Warren Hyde chase. But I noticed he didn't stray too far from either of us the whole time I was in the Rabbit. I finished my drink, checked my watch, and said my goodbyes. Just past three o'clock, which left me a little under an hour before my rendezvous with Janie.

My kingdom for a park within walking distance, but all that surrounded the Silver Rabbit was urban decay. I walked it anyway and found the September afternoon was enough to redeem the suboptimal environment. I spent most of the time trying to decide whether the neighborhood looked better in the daylight or the dark of night. As dangerous as the darkness had felt, it had the advantage of hiding the crumbling buildings and overgrown foliage. The sunlight provided no such cover, but by the end of my expedition, I decided there was a certain beauty in that too. All depended on how you wanted to look at it.

I bought a newspaper from a nearby stand and settled in at a bench across the street from the Rabbit. My watch read ten to three when I sat down, so I wasn't expecting Janie for another few minutes. The bar door swung open, but it was Bruce who stepped out. That's what the newspaper was for; I opened the paper wide and ducked my face behind it. After a minute or so I risked a glance over the pages. Bruce was standing on the steps, leaning against the railing with a cigarette in his mouth. Hard to tell if this was a routine smoke break or if he was searching the area for anything suspicious. I would have liked to keep my eyes on him, but that carried the risk of being spotted. Reluctantly, I brought the paper back up between us.

A few minutes later I heard the door open again and looked up to see Bruce had gone back inside. I looked at my watch; three minutes until Janie's shift ended. There didn't seem to be much interesting happening in the world, nothing I could find in the paper anyhow. I settled on an article about a team of dogs who had been trained to sniff out suspicious packages at train stations. It wasn't the worst three minutes I'd ever spent by a long shot.

A voice in the distance broke my concentration. "Ok, ok. Well, you take care Brucie, and I'll see you tomorrow."

I looked up and saw Janie leaving the Rabbit. She scanned up and down the street, looking for someone while trying to seem like she wasn't looking for someone. Sharp girl, I thought. She hung around the entrance for another minute or so, then decided that was enough and started walking due west in the direction of the sun. I gave her enough time to build a healthy head start, then set off to the south, with my back to any watchful eyes from inside the Silver Rabbit.

When I was out of sight I ditched the newspaper and traded my casual stroll for a brisk run. A block later I cut west and then north so I came up behind Janie. She was walking especially slowly, as though she had accounted for my needing to catch up. For the second time in as many minutes I was impressed with her canniness.

"Hey," I called out, "I found you!"

She turned around and gave me a cool look. "About time, Stranger."

I jogged up to where she was standing. "Eddie. So where were we?"

"I was at our agreed meeting place at our agreed meeting time. Didn't see you around."

"Well, that was by design, Janie," I said as we started walking together. "I wasn't hiding from you but, you know, the brute with the anger issues."

"Brute," she laughed. "That's what Bruce is all right. I guess the name fits pretty well."

"Like a glove."

"So, you've piqued my interest. What is it you're asking around about? And don't try that 'Looking for a friend' line."

"Ah, come on," I said. "It's a perfectly good line."

"Didn't work on me," she pointed out. "Didn't even work on the brute."

"And yet here we are. Listen, you mentioned Curly. What do you know about him?"

"Curly, yeah. Well, he's bald, right? But they call him Curly. I figured it was one of those ironic things. Like calling a big guy Tiny. Or else a nickname he got before he went bald."

"If he went bald."

She gave me a quizzical look. "No, I'm pretty sure he's bald, Eddie."

"Right. But maybe he just shaved his head."

"Bald, shaved head, what's it matter?"

"It might matter a whole lot," I said. "Anyway, just something I was thinking about."

"If you say so," Janie said, like I wasn't making much sense.

"What else can you tell me? How long has he been

coming around there?"

At my side Janie snapped her gum and contorted her face in concentration. "I don't know. Who can remember one face out of a hundred?"

"It's a tough question," I acknowledged.

"No," she said, "maybe it isn't. But I haven't been working at the Rabbit for very long. I know he's certainly been there since I started."

I felt I was getting close to something, but I couldn't yet tell what. "And you've known him as Curly that whole time?"

"That's what the other guys seem to call him, yeah. But always bald, like you said. I guess it never really bothered me, the contradiction. Pretty quiet guy. He has friends I guess, acquaintances anyway, but mostly keeps to himself. Nobody is as close to him as the whiskey. Anyway, we're coming up on my place pretty soon here. Anything else I can do for you?"

Maybe that was a hint and maybe it wasn't, but it didn't change my answer. "Honestly, I don't know why you've done as much as you have," I said.

"You just caught my interest is all." She spoke nonchalantly. "Figured I could use a little excitement. Life gets pretty boring around here sometimes. You know what I mean?"

"Not lately, no. Just one more thing before I let you go. You think Curly will be back tonight?"

"On a Tuesday? Nah, weekdays are slow. But if you want to take a shot this weekend, I'll be working Saturday night. Maybe come by, yeah?"

"Saturday," I said. "I'll keep that in mind. Thank you, Janie. For everything."

"Don't be a stranger, Stranger." She winked and departed off down some side street.

9

Two Truths and a Lie

Wednesday passed without much incident or consequence. Hannah greeted me just as she had done before, nothing to suggest that anything significant had passed between us at yesterday's lunch. That was smart; even a knowing smile or nod might be picked up upon and wasn't worth the risk. Samantha said she expected me to give her a name to come in for an interview with Crossley by the end of the week, preferably sooner. I already had that taken care of, so I sleepwalked through the day, unable to get any worthwhile information from the new coworkers I tried in the bullpen.

Back home, I took the opportunity to review the headway I had made over the past several days. In one sense, it felt like a lot. But in another, stronger sense, the puzzle looked as inscrutable as ever. I'd learned a little about Hyde, and more than a little about Manticore Cooperative. But the mystery of Patrick Raymond still eluded me, and I wasn't any closer to connecting any of it to Thomas Lawrence, which was the point of the whole operation. For that reason, I held off on calling Mrs. Lawrence, especially given the way that our last conversation had gone.

I reviewed the way forward on what I had come to think of as the two fronts of this war. My only connection to Hyde so far was Curly and his cryptic ramblings. That meant returning to the Silver Rabbit Saturday night, which seemed straightforward enough. And now I had the benefit of an asset on the inside, as it were.

Manticore lay on the more convoluted path. Despite my initial headway with Crossley, the walls of bureaucracy separated us now, and I had gone from his chosen one to another cog in the faceless machine. I would have to find a way to recapture his attention, but nothing came to mind at the moment. Then there was Samantha, and the sham of a client interview, which brought Tony into the scheme. And always the cypher of Raymond somewhere behind it all, playing the tune they all danced to. If he existed at all.

Reaching the limits of my own mind, I found myself wanting to talk the whole thing over with someone. Hannah was the obvious choice, and I still had her number somewhere. I pulled out the folder Veronica had given me, which had become a kind of aggregator for everything I had collected related to the case. The phone number was in there, but I set it aside for the moment and took another look over the Lawrence, Crossley, Raymond, and Hyde dossiers. I noticed again that the pictures of the first three men were much clearer and legible, that was obvious to see, but I picked up something else too.

The low quality wasn't the only noteworthy thing about Hyde's photo. Its age was, too. I had been hauling it around in my pocket, back and forth from the Rabbit, and it was starting to fray at the edges. It wasn't as ancient as Patrick

Raymond's picture but I knew Raymond's photo to be well out of date, even intentionally so. So maybe Hyde's was older as well. I came back to the idea of a bald man called Curly, and the possibility that he had not always been bald—the possibility that he once had hair like the man in that ragged and gloomy photo.

Samantha was waiting for me when I stepped off the elevator Thursday morning. "Your referrals," she said. "Mr. Crossley would like them today."

"Referrals? Plural? You said I had until Friday to find somebody. Singular."

"Take it up with Mr. Crossley. You are to be in his office in ten minutes."

"Ten minutes! Samantha—" I started.

"Miss Jones."

"Miss Jones, listen, I found someone who is interested in joining us. He's good to come in for an interview any time we need him. But that wasn't easy. If Crossley-"

"Mr. Crossley."

"If Mr. Crossley wants more than that, I need more time."

"I see it is three minutes after eight now," she said, making a production of looking at her watch. "You have seven more minutes, Eddie. There's your extra time. If you want my advice, anything fewer than three referrals will be a disappointment. And around here, disappointments lead to consequences. Actually, it's six minutes now," she said with a smile.

She marched off in the direction of the bullpen, leaving me dumbstruck in her wake. How on earth was I going to get him another two names? I could create them out of thin air and try to figure it out later, but it almost felt like Manticore was on to me, like that's the trap they wanted to spring. Or maybe that was paranoia. Three names. Billy Shakes and... beyond that, I had no idea. Down to five minutes until Crossley expected me. I started the walk to his office, determined to think of something on the way.

When I got to the top floor, Crossley's door was closed, and the sound of his voice came through in small snippets. The conversation was awfully one-sided, so he was either on the phone or berating a subordinate with no sign of respite. I was hoping for the former as I knocked on his door and stood back.

"Hold on," I heard him say. "Yeah... eight, maybe ten... not if... have to call you back." That last part at least was a relief. "Come in," he said louder, so I pushed the door open.

"Mr. Crossley," I said, extending my hand. "Good to see you again, sir."

"Eddie, have a seat. Fourth day on the job, I imagine you've been making a lot of progress. What have you got for me?"

"Well, sir, I—"

"Hold on." He held up a hand to silence me and I waited for further instruction. "Let me get you the paperwork." He opened a desk drawer and pulled out a stack of forms, peeling a page off the top. "Fill that out for me."

Crossley slid the paper across the desk and I looked it over. There was a line for the date, my name, and then some more standard information. Below that were three spots to list three referrals. First and last names, dates of contact, addresses, phone numbers, how I found them, and so on. I instinctively leaned back away from it in my chair, overwhelmed. I didn't much feel like completing any of that, so I tried to turn on the charm that won him over in my initial interview.

"So good news," I said. "There's this guy-"

Crossley didn't react one way or the other. "Just fill out the paperwork," he said dispassionately.

"Can we—"

"Eddie," he said, his voice now bordering on menace. "Just fill out the damn paperwork."

I looked across the desk at him, looked for something in those eyes, but they were icy and betrayed nothing. "Sure," I said. "Ok."

I worked my way through my name and the date, Crossley watching over me like a particularly-emotionless gargoyle. When I got to the referrals I hesitated, but only for an instant. Anything more than that would have drawn further scrutiny, and I had the feeling I was already on unstable ground. Billy Shakes was first, the easy one.

"I met this guy walking his dog at the park," I said. "I see him there regularly. Didn't get an address or phone number, but I can always contact him that way."

"Get that information from him this afternoon," Crossley said. "Two more."

Now I was stuck. My social circle wasn't that big to begin with, and the list of people I was willing to mix up with Manticore, even tangentially, was smaller still. There was one other friend I knew wouldn't mind, and that was my old bus stop buddy Leonard. We weren't close, but if I knew one thing about him, he was always up for an adventure, wherever it may lead. And anyway, good luck to those cultists finding him if it all went sideways.

"Second guy was at the park too," I said. "That was a productive afternoon." I smiled at Crossley but that didn't crack his neutral expression. "Dennis Markley."

"Get his information this afternoon. Who's your third?"

Showtime. You walked right into this one, Crossley, you fool, I thought. I wrote a name, address, and phone number on the third line, then slid the paper back across the desk.

Reading the third name broke through his preternatural calm. He looked up at me, back to the paper to confirm his eyes weren't playing tricks, and returned to me again.

"Let me guess. You didn't meet this one at the park."

"Why so surprised?" I asked, trying to sound genuine.

"I never said I was surprised," Crossley snapped.

That was a shot at intimidation, but I didn't flinch. "You didn't have to."

Crossley gave me what might have been an attempt at a smile, but he could only manage a grimace. "Ok Eddie," he said with saccharine sweetness, "how did you meet Thomas Lawrence then?"

"How does anyone meet?" I said. "Is there a problem?"

"No," Crossley said, his composure mostly recovered. "No problem at all. This Mr. Lawrence is interested in interviewing with the Cooperative then?"

"They tell me he paints houses," I said. "Quite well, they tell me."

"And when will Mr. Lawrence be in for his interview?" Crossley asked. We were both bluffing each other now. I would've been amused if I wasn't so busy watching for a sign that Crossley was going to come across the desk and start pummeling me. But no, so far, he had decided to play it cool. Or as near as he ever came to it anyway.

"Well, I suppose that's the complication," I said, drawing out the spaces between my words. "Thomas Lawrence—Mr. Lawrence, if you like, since you all seem to have this weird formality hang up—Mr. Lawrence has, quite unfortunately

I'm sure, gone missing."

I kept poking, but the bear wasn't taking the bait. "Quite unfortunate," Crossley said. "But you know, Eddie, I'm starting to wonder what you're implying. And while we're on the subject of poor fortunes, it strikes me that you might be having second thoughts about your relationship with Manticore. Which could be a dangerous position to be in, with you here in the jaws of the lion."

"What are you going to do, disappear me?" Enough with the subtlety. "Is that what you did with Thomas Lawrence?"

Crossley laughed out loud, loud enough to make me jump in my chair. "Is that what you think happened? Eddie, Eddie... Are you serious? We didn't 'disappear' Thomas. Of course not!"

"But he was a member of Manticore, and he disappeared. Is that right?"

"We have so many clients, surely you don't expect me to keep track of all of them. If he did, that's news to me and I am sorry to hear it. But there was no connection between Manticore and his disappearance."

"I don't believe in coincidences, Crossley," I said. What I didn't say, didn't dare say, is that my instincts told me he was telling the truth. The truth as he saw it anyhow, which left a lot of room for grays.

"Believe whatever you want. Thomas was a member here, it's true. We can try to reach him if you'd like, but..." He shrugged his shoulders. "Maybe he had some problems, or maybe sometimes people just want to move on somewhere new and get a fresh start. What more can you do?"

The way Hannah told it, no one ever just moved on from Manticore, but I wasn't going to give any part of her up to Crossley. "What do you do in a situation like that? Call the wife, I imagine, then the police?"

"The police?" Crossley scoffed. "Don't be ridiculous. Does a book club call the police when one of their members decides to drop out? Or a softball team when the third baseman quits?"

"No, no, that's not what you said a minute ago. You said he disappeared."

"I don't think I said that at all." Crossley leaned forward imposingly, his elbows resting on his desk. "Did I?"

"Yes."

"Well," he said, sitting back, "if I did it's only because you said it first and I followed your lead. Chalk it up to an imprecise phrase. I am a clumsy speaker at times." That was an obvious lie, and it felt good to banish the grays, even temporarily. "Anyway, it's immaterial, because that's not why you're sitting here this morning, is it? You're here because you owe me names. I'll be running the interviews first thing Monday morning."

Crossley was trying to wrestle the conversation back, but he was going about it stupidly. He was so concerned with retaking control that he was ready to abandon the revelation I had tip-toed up to the line of. For my part, I was content to let him do that. I slipped back into the role of browbeaten underling.

"Yes, sir. First thing."

"Tell Samantha to come see me."

That seemed to be what was going to pass for my dismissal, so I ducked out of the room before he could change his mind. A minute later I was back in the elevator heading down to the bullpen. I passed along Crossley's message, remembering to address Samantha as Miss Jones. I had come too close to blowing cover completely back in that office. A smarter man than Crossley would've seized on it for sure. I'd have to back off the impertinence for a while, which wasn't going to be easy. But my frustrations with Manticore needed to take second priority for the time being. I wasn't willing to risk erasing all the progress I had made so far.

The rest of the day was a return to the routine. I knew I'd have to get in touch with Tony and Leonard about coming in on Monday. That wouldn't be a problem for Tony, he'd already said as much, but Leonard would be trickier. I saw him only intermittently, never on any kind of a set schedule that I could discern. All I knew was he'd be at the bus stop from time to time, and whenever he was, we'd share a congenial chat. There was an understanding there. Never one that progressed beyond chance encounters, but I hoped I could count on him for the obligation I had just committed him to. If I couldn't... Well, I didn't much want to think about that.

I had harbored some small hope Leonard would be riding the bus I got on on my way home, but the next time I catch a lucky break like that will be the first. Instead, it was an amalgamation of strangers that greeted me. I played the problems over in my head and watched the landscape pass by my window. So, Crossley knew Thomas Lawrence. That wasn't exactly surprising, but it was still nice to have it confirmed. Getting his version of the story was nicer still. It would be easier to pull apart the lies once I knew what they were. The big lie, as far as I could tell, was this: Thomas was involved with Manticore but decided (for reasons unstated) that he wanted a change and departed amicably. Both Veronica and Manticore seemed to agree that he hadn't been seen since.

That move was the kind of thing I really should have run by Veronica, but our chats hadn't been all that productive as of late. On the other hand, it was her money keeping the whole operation afloat. I endeavored to reach out to her when I had more news to report. Then I thought of Hannah, and wondered if she had made any headway with her research into whatever files Manticore maintained on Thomas and Warren. Tomorrow would be a good day to finalize everything with Tony, which would leave me the weekend to try to track down Leonard and get him on board. That is, after my Saturday night date with the Silver Rabbit.

Some of that I could directly control, and some of it I couldn't. I thought it best to lead with the easiest task and start lightening my load. I put a call in to Tony telling him to expect me that evening.

"That sounds real good," Tony said. "Hey, how about you come and I grill us up a couple burgers? What do you say to that?"

"That sounds fine, Tony," I said. "Just fine."

10

Best Laid Schemes

I swung down to the corner store to pick up some chips and met Tony at his place. We found some shade from the sun and ate at a picnic table in his backyard. "You ready to talk strategy?" I asked.

"Who needs strategy? I go in there, tell them I'm Billy Shakes, listen to their BS, and walk out a free man, right?"

"I mean, that's the idea, yeah. But they asked for a few things I didn't anticipate. You'll need to give them an address, a phone number..."

Tony shrugged. "I got those."

"Right, but you don't want to use your actual information. Not with these people."

Tony waved that away. "What do I care? Some businessman gonna get mad at me?" He laughed at the absurdity. "They come after me, I'll bust their heads in. Pass me that ketchup, hey?"

I did as he asked. "You can do what you want, Tony."

"You got that right," he said through a mouthful of hamburger.

"I'm just telling you how I'd play it. So you can walk out of there a free man, like you said."

"Yeah, well, you play it your way, and I'll play it mine."

I still felt that was foolish, but I didn't want to push, lest he change his mind about our arrangement. "Ok Tony, like you said."

"So, Monday morning, hey? I don't like mornings, Eddie."

"Well, neither do—wait a minute. Eddie? You got the name right!"

"Sure did," he laughed. "I thought it would be good to practice, for when I see you at the Manticore." Manticore; that was two for two.

"Except you won't be seeing me there," I said. "At least I don't think so."

Tony paused mid-chew, his eyes expressing confusion. "How's that?"

"Well, I don't do the interviews, Tony. It's this guy Crossley. Fancies himself a tough guy, and I guess maybe he is."

Tony nodded. "Oh boy, I've seen enough of that type. They always find out the truth though, one way or another."

"If your experience is anything like mine was, he'll pump you up to the moon. Like he's doing you some great favor by welcoming you into their special little club, whether you deserve it or not. That's when he offered me that job, although it feels more like indentured servitude from the inside."

"I don't need no job," Tony said. "Busy enough around here as it is. You want another burger?"

"I'm set," I said, pushing my plate away. "Thank you,

though. Great job as ever."

"I've got a license to grill," he said proudly. "What kind of questions you think they'll ask at this interview?"

I tried to remember. "Just really general stuff, I think. Why you're interested in the Cooperative, what assets you bring to the organization. As I recall, it seems like most of their time was spent trying to impress me, rather than the other way around."

"Sounds like a goofy place." That was an astute observation. "They still don't know you're a spy?"

I laughed. "A spy? You make it sound like I'm 007, pulling explosives from my wristwatch. But no, they don't know I'm investigating a case. At least as I don't think they do. Crossley has some suspicions by now I'd bet. He caught me off-guard with a pop quiz yesterday. I wasn't as quick in my thinking as I should've been and played it kind of clumsy-like. But in the end, he's a glorified salesman. I don't think anyone's ever accused him of being the brains of any operation."

Tony was halfway through another hamburger, his third of the night if my count was accurate. "So who is?"

I sat with that question awhile, the sun progressing on its steady descent towards the distant western horizon. Those three small words suddenly carried a lot of weight. "Supposedly it's this guy Raymond. Patrick Raymond. But I'm not so sure about that anymore."

"Why not?"

"It's a long story," I said. "I guess you'll hear all about it on Monday. Eight o'clock. Tell them whatever you think you need to, but don't make any commitments, ok?"

"You worry too much," Tony said. "Relax, will you? I got this."

"I guess I'll be heading out then," I said and thanked him again. "Back at it bright and early tomorrow."

Thursday was behind me, and the day's wins and losses with it. Crossley had scored an early point with his impromptu morning meeting, but I felt I had gotten the better of that exchange by the end of it. I learned that Thomas was indeed involved with Manticore and then left for reasons that were not yet clear. Crossley denied any wrongdoing in between the two events, which is not to say he had entirely convinced me. I had prepped Tony for his Monday interview, which was all I could do on my end. The rest was up to him.

If Saturday was reserved for the Silver Rabbit, that left me Friday and Sunday to find Leonard, make my pitch, and get him on board. I didn't see any reason to put it off, so I wanted to start my search first thing Friday morning. I could use my work day for that, and I wouldn't even have to lie to Samantha or anyone else about how I was spending the time. Problem was, the park story was a lie; I would probably have to sell them on the idea that Leonard was going to be hard to find. Just my luck that the only time I was actually prepared to tell Manticore the truth, it would only complicate things. "*Oh, what a tangled web we weave...*" as the poet says.

The next morning, I called into Manticore and told Hannah I would be working outside the office. "Crossley wants names and addresses for my referrals, so I have to go track those down."

"Already?" The line fell into silence. Maybe someone from Manticore was nearby, or maybe she just treated all her work conversations like they were potentially being listened in on. I could imagine her carefully trying to select the right words, like diffusing some alien-looking bomb. "I will let Miss Jones know. Will you be in this afternoon?"

"Hard to say. Depends on how long it takes me to find the guy." To drag the conversation out much longer would have been suspicious, so I tried to find some exacting words of my own. "Hopefully I'll have some good news to share by lunchtime tomorrow."

"Understood," Hannah said. "Good luck and we look forward to seeing you."

It was possible, perhaps even likely, that all this cloak and dagger stuff was overkill, but I had a lot less to lose by playing it overly safe compared to the opposite. If Hannah picked up on my hint, she would meet me at the same coffee shop around noon the next day. And if she didn't, at least I didn't give Manticore another bit of evidence they could use to expose us. But I wanted to update her on my meeting with Crossley, and it sounded like she had more she wanted to tell me too.

That cleared my schedule to focus on the Leonard problem. I thought back on our conversations over the years, what I learned about the genial old man from them, and how that biographical information could help me go about finding him. Showing up at his place of employment was out. Old Leonard was long retired, I knew, from some vague job in the business arena he never seemed much interested in talking about. There was no family that he ever spoke of. I didn't even know the man's last name to look him up in the book.

What places had he mentioned with any kind of frequency? The library, different lakes, walking up and down the bike paths. It was all quickly adding up to a veritable goose chase. No way I could cover that much ground even if I had a week, let alone get lucky enough to find myself in the same place at the same time as my friend. The whole thing was pretty hopeless, and I started to think about who I could get instead as a replacement.

But then, no, I didn't need to run down all those different leads at all, because one central hub connected them all. An old man like Leonard wasn't making it out to any of those disparate locations without first going to the bus stop. That made it all so simple. The only thing I would have to do would be to wait at the bus stop. It might take all day, or even more than a day, but he was bound to show up there eventually. Then I could run the plan by him, and get him some cash for his trouble while I was at it.

I stepped out into the street in my t-shirt and made it about a block before wishing I had opted for something warmer. The weather was turning all right, the last days of summer losing their grip and falling off into the ether of the past. Under normal circumstances, I would've turned around for a coat, but I didn't want to lose the time that would take. So I forced myself forward, shivering all the while. At one point I broke into a jog, hoping that would warm me up. The wind whipping by me had just the opposite effect, but at least it would get me to my destination more quickly.

I could see from a distance that the bus stop was bereft of people waiting. I huddled under the spartan metal overhang that passed for a shelter. That didn't provide any warmth though, and sitting still only made me colder. I waited there like that, with nothing more to do than wait. *You could have at least brought a book,* I told myself too late. Between the antagonistic cold and the boredom that was somehow even worse, I made it an hour before I retreated back home.

Better to suffer the lost time that trek would require and come back more well-provisioned for a longer stay.

I retrieved a heavy black coat with fur trim from the back of my closet, pressing it into service a few weeks earlier than anticipated. Coastal weather can be funny like that. My bookshelf was in dire need of a refresh, and surveying it I didn't find much. I reached for the book I seemed to have been reading forever without much progress to show for it. A hopeless pursuit, probably, but the old man might yet get that whale one of these days. I tucked my heavy companion under my arm and set off back for the bus stop, where I hoped to find Leonard waiting.

He wasn't. I picked up the book where I had left off and passed the time more or less contently in the warmth of my jacket. A short time later it was noon and I found myself getting hungry (another bit of poor planning on my part), but I resisted the urge to leave my post for food. The hunger wasn't nearly so bad as the cold had been, and it somehow bolstered my mood to know I was in far better shape than those poor souls on the *Pequod*.

One hour went by, and then two, which rolled into three. A lot of people came and went in that time, but none of them were Leonard, not even a little bit. I had had all I could stand of whaling boats and had just about resigned myself to taking a short break at four o'clock before returning for a later shift. Of course, with my luck, that would be just before Leonard showed up for the only time that day. And if that were true, I reasoned, then I was sure to catch him if I stayed an extra half-hour. That didn't really make sense, I knew, but my rational side lost out, as it so often did.

That was fortunate for me, because it was just past four-fifteen when I heard a familiar voice call out, "Hey there, pardner!" For half a second I thought I'd dreamed it, but I looked to my left and, sure enough, there was the affable old man waving in my direction.

"Boy, am I glad to see you!" I said and greeted him with a big involuntary smile. "How have you been?"

"Oh, can't complain," Leonard said, easing himself down into his seat beside me on the cold steel bench. "And when I do, nobody listens anyway." He laughed generously at his own joke before finally catching his breath. "What's that you're reading there?"

"Something about a whale," I said, showing him the cover. "Most of it is lost on me, but something keeps me coming back to it."

"Melville! I know him well. *Bartleby* and *Typee* and all the rest." I didn't have a clue what those words meant, and I knew Leonard could talk circles around me in that arena if he wanted to.

"Oh yeah," I said, "all that stuff. What's on today's agenda?"

"Off to the library, as a matter of fact," he said. "I've got too many books as it is, but even I can't compete with that place." He laughed at his own joke again, and I laughed too. Not because the joke was funny, but because of how much he relished in performing for his audience of one. Leonard was a man who was well-practiced at extracting every bit of life from the moments he was given. That was probably a big part of the reason we got along as well as we did.

"They're going to start charging you rent, Leonard."

"They just might!" He chuckled at that too. "Where are you headed?"

"Nowhere," I said. "I came down here to see you, actually."

"Oh?"

"How would you like a job, Lenny?"

He shook his head. "No, I don't think I'd care for that at all. Heck, I'm an old man, pardner. Done my time, as they say. Now, could I use more money? Sure, I could. But the day-to-day freedom is worth more to me. I go where I want, when I want. See who I want, or don't see anyone at all, if that's what I want. You're asking me to trade all that in for a suit and tie every day? Thought you knew me better than that, pardner."

"You misunderstand," I said. "I'd never ask that of you, to trade in your freedom for a monkey suit. Of course not. I'm talking about an hour or two tops, one day and then it's over."

"Is that all?"

"That's all, I promise. And you would be well-compensated for your time. You know, could buy yourself something nice."

Leonard sat back and considered the proposition. "Not going to be having me dig ditches, are you, pardner? I don't think the old back's got the guff left in her."

"Digging ditches," I said, "don't be ridiculous... You'll be a matador." Leonard laughed like that was about the funniest thing he had ever heard, and I smiled myself, picturing the bearded old codger deftly dodging two-thousand pounds of horned fury.

Finally, he said, "Be real with me now, friend. What's this here job you've got in mind?"

I briefed Leonard much the same way I had done with Tony. Like Tony, his initial confusion gave way to a kind of excitement at the prospect of getting to play undercover agent for a day. The old man could use some excitement in his life, I figured. Stacks of dusty novels and duck ponds could only get you so far. He gave me a number where I could reach him, and his last name besides. I said I would be in touch and we parted ways, Leonard off to the library and me walking back home.

On the walk I wrestled with my decision to bring my friends into the scheme against Manticore. If they followed the directives I had given them, their part should be fairly low risk. I was less worried about Tony, but at least Leonard was sensible enough to heed my advice about not giving Manticore any of his real personal information. Ultimately, Leonard was smarter than Tony, if no match for the latter's swaggering braggadocio. It seemed a fair tradeoff.

Friday was dying as I turned the key in my lock and stepped through the door. The house was still, as it almost always was. Dusk threatened and I switched on a lamp, bathing the room in warm yellow. Another productive, if tiring, day. Tony and Leonard were now both confirmed for their interviews with Crossley, and I thought each would do well enough sparring with Crossley's mind games, albeit for different reasons. Saturday night at the Silver Rabbit loomed ahead of me.

There was one more thing I wanted to do before reporting back to Manticore on Monday, and that was to talk with Hannah again. I had a lot to catch her up on, and I was hoping she had some new information for me too. I wondered what she had found, if anything, on Thomas Lawrence at Manticore. Warren Hyde was a longer shot, and I didn't really expect anything there. But any information on Thomas would be extraordinarily helpful at that stage. Even the absence of anything would've been something. I was that kind of desperate.

11

Out of Somewhere

The next day I got to the coffee shop at ten minutes to noon and figured if Hannah didn't show by ten after, I would chalk it up as a miss. As it happened, I didn't have to wait that long, because she came through the door about five minutes after me.

"You made it," I said. "I wasn't sure my words conveyed my meaning."

"You were right to do it that way," she said, taking her seat across the table from me, coffee in hand. "Can't be too careful these days."

"That was my thought. Speaking of, maybe we should go someplace else?"

"I wouldn't worry about it. I didn't spot a tail, and even if they sent one, I'm sure I lost him."

"You know how to spot a tail?" I didn't even try to hide how impressed I was with that. "And how to lose one?"

"Sure," Hannah said casually. "I know how to do lots of

things."

"That seems like the sort of thing that could come in handy in my line of work," I said. "Maybe you can teach me some time."

"Maybe. For now we have more important things to discuss. What's this about Crossley and the referrals?"

"Surprised me with it first thing Thursday morning. Samantha tells me to go see Crossley and he's barking at me that he needs three names of potential clients I've recruited. Not just names either; he wants addresses, phone numbers, favorite pizza places, everything. It was all I could do to get out of there with my head still attached to my shoulders."

"That's not normal, Eddie. Seems like they usually give the new hires more of a honeymoon period."

"More good news," I said, when it was anything but. "You think they're on to me?"

"Could be. Suspicions anyway. What did you tell Crossley in your meeting?"

"I gave him two names, friends of mine who will cover for me. Then I told him I'd need some time to get their addresses and phone numbers and all that. Bought myself a couple days there."

"That's good," Hannah said. "But you said he wanted three names."

"That he did. The third name I gave him was Thomas Lawrence."

"That name you asked me to look into?"

"Right. Wanted to see how he'd react to it."

"And?"

"Well, it was a risk," I said. "I don't think he's put together that Lawrence's wife hired me. Because he's not very bright." Hannah laughed a little, then composed herself. "But I was able to get something out of him anyway. This Lawrence guy was involved with Manticore, all right. Crossley says he left of his own volition and they haven't heard from him since. I'm guessing you don't find that all that likely."

Concern rattled Hannah's typically collected composure. "Forget unlikely, it's impossible. But there's another thing: I ran those names through the computer like you asked, Thomas Lawrence and Warren Hyde. There's no record of either of them being involved with Manticore. And our—that is to say, their—records are meticulous. From what I can tell," she added.

I thought that over. "So Crossley is lying, either to me or through his records. Hardly a surprise there."

"But why not just deny any connection to this Lawrence? Wouldn't that have been the better lie?"

"I don't think so," I said. "Crossley surprised me by summoning me to the meeting, but I returned the favor by springing that name on him. He couldn't pretend the name meant nothing to him, not after how he reacted to it. An involuntary reaction."

"Then his lies are in conflict now."

"Right. Either Lawrence was never there or he departed of his own free will, but not both. And nothing on Hyde?"

"Nothing. You think they ran him off too?"

"I'm not sure," I admitted. "He's connected to Lawrence, and to Manticore through Lawrence, I suppose, but I don't know if he was ever part of the Cooperative."

"If he was, they deleted any record of his existence too."

A thought occurred to me, one that should have come to me much sooner. "What about your sister?" I asked. "Do they have records of Caroline?"

"They do," Hannah said. "Nothing to indicate anything suspicious happened, but of course they wouldn't include that part. You know, I still find myself looking for her in all the faces I pass. Like one day she will just show up again. I guess that's silly."

"No it's not," I said, genuinely sympathetic. "Interesting that they disappeared Lawrence and not Caroline though, don't you think?"

"It suggests some difference between them," she acknowledged. "But what it is, I'm not sure." She looked at her watch, then back to me. "But I should get going. You're handing two friends over to Manticore Monday then?"

"I'd feel better about it if you didn't make it sound so perfidious," I said, "but yes. They can handle themselves." At least I hoped they could

"Crossley will be back on you about the third name soon," she said, a hint of warning in her tone. "He might have been too surprised to react in the moment, like you said, but that won't last. He'll be keeping a closer eye on you now too, you can count on that."

"Then it will be mutual," I said. "May the best man win." She didn't look all that confident in me, but I pretended not to notice that.

"I guess we've done all we can until Monday then?"

"Not quite," I said. "Tonight I'm going to the Silver Rabbit, purported refuge of the scoundrel Warren Hyde. I have a contact down there who thinks a friend of his by the name of Curly will show up tonight."

"Interesting," Hannah said, processing. "Can I come?"

I wasn't prepared for that. Not that it was a bad idea necessarily, but it was an idea I hadn't had the chance to properly examine. I tried to buy myself some time to examine the angles. "To what end?"

"You think Hyde has something to do with Lawrence's disappearance, right?"

"Well, his wife does, maybe."

"Right. So maybe he knows something about Caroline. It's only a chance, but I'm not going to let it pass me by."

I realized then her question had been merely a formality. In actuality she had been telling me she was going to go to the Rabbit, and she was magnanimous enough to pretend to care if she had my blessing. Which meant there was no point in my fighting it.

"Of course," I said. "Do you want to meet there or try our luck separately?"

"Separately. Initially anyway. If we decide to work tandem after that, that's an easy transition."

"Makes sense," I agreed. "I figure I'll go for around nine."

"I'll be there," Hannah said.

I stepped off the bus under a dimming velvet sky. Nine o'clock was still an hour off, but I wanted to get there ahead of Hannah. Not that I didn't trust her, but if there was any advantage to be gained with that extra sixty minutes, I was going to take it. The air was brittle and cold again, and I pulled my hood up over my head, feeling like some Antarctic explorer. The world seemed to have lost track of autumn and sped straight from summer's end to the early days of winter.

I found the same bouncer from before manning the door. "How's the action?" I asked, figuring we were old friends by now.

He didn't see it that way and gave me a look that said he would just as soon smack me upside the head if he thought there was a chance he could get away with it. "ID, boss," he said mechanically.

"Aw come on, you remember me, don't you? A week

ago, I about ran into the door. You remember."

He stared at me coldly. His figure was not an especially imposing one, but his unfeeling eyes and a couple conspicuous scars attested to the fact that he had seen his share of scraps, and my guess was he had won most of them. I produced my ID again and presented it to him without further argument. He looked it over thoroughly with his blacklight, handed it back to me, and waved me through the door. All of this was done without a trace of human feeling threatening to break through the veil.

The unseasonal temperature seemed to have taken its toll on the Rabbit's client base too, because the place was largely deserted when I stepped up to the bar. Bruce and Janie were working as before. Bruce gave me a quick, dismissive glance, but Janie waved and came over to talk.

"Well, hello, Stranger."

"Eddie," I said. "Remember?"

She shrugged. "Not really. But Eddie, ok."

"Any sign of Curly?"

"Not that I've seen. Feel free to look for yourself though," Janie said, gesturing with her hand.

A quick glance around the place was all I needed to confirm that Curly was nowhere to be seen. "Well," I said, "I guess it's still early."

A couple drinks helped pass the time and by nine o'clock business was starting to pick up. I kept an eye on the door but didn't see any sign of Curly or Hannah. All the waiting lately had made me good at it, so I had no problem waiting a little more. I tried conversing with a few of the regulars but that didn't take. It was about twenty after nine when Hannah came walking in. She was dressed down for a change, with her hair pulled back in a tight ponytail, to the point I almost didn't recognize her at first. All the better to blend in with the Rabbit crowd, I figured.

I didn't pay her any attention, like we agreed, and held down my station near the pool table just as I had been doing. The players had asked me to join in a couple times, not such a bad group of guys really, but I politely declined each time. Not that I liked billiards any less than the next man, but I wanted to be free to disengage in case Curly or the man in the blurry picture showed up after all. Hannah and I made eye contact, enough to acknowledge each other, but otherwise stayed apart. She set up shop at the bar and seemed to be questioning Bruce. No surprise, she looked to be doing a lot better with him than I ever had.

Eventually she must have decided she had enough, because she left the bar and came over near where I was standing. "Buy you a drink?"

"Strict teetotaler," I said.

"I'll bet." She grabbed my arm and pulled me aside, where we wouldn't be overheard. "No Curly?"

"Haven't seen Larry or Moe either."

She ignored the joke. "Well, our bartender friend over there seems to know him pretty well."

"Bruce said that? I could never get him to give me the time of day."

"Clearly you don't have my skills," she said with a smile.

"Clearly."

I looked over to where Bruce was, and he seemed to be taking notice of the two of us together. "We need to get outside, separately. Meet me in five." I set my drink on a nearby table and made for the men's room. It was empty so I killed some time in there, waiting for the heat on us to die down. Where was Curly anyway? Janie had made it sound like his appearance was a near certainty, and here we had come away empty. Except maybe not quite, depending on what Hannah was able to ascertain from my old pal Brucie.

When enough time had passed, I went back through the bar and walked out into the night's chill. Hannah was waiting just beyond the light that shone out from the Rabbit, a solitary black silhouette in the deep indigo. I stepped out past the reach of the light, trying to will my eyes to adjust to the darkness. I opened my mouth to speak, but the words never got out. First came the sound of a footfall, somewhere behind me, swiftly followed by a sudden and savage strike to the back of my head. The rest was darkness.

That darkness was still there when I came to, my head throbbing painfully in rhythm with my heartbeat. My shoulders were sore too, and as my senses slowly returned, I realized two strong arms were shaking me with all the delicateness of a paint mixer.

"Easy!" I cried out, my voice creaking through my lips.

"He's up!" someone called out. I recognized that voice, but my head was still clearing, and I couldn't yet place it. "Come on," it said, and I felt my neck wrench upward until I was sitting up.

"Bruce," I said, finally starting to feel whole again.

"If you're going to fight, keep it off our property," Bruce scolded. "No, he's fine," he said to someone back towards the bar's entrance. "I'm sending him on his way now."

I reached up to my head and felt a substantial cut running alongside my left eye. A flash of pain fired through me as my fingers made contact with the wound. I looked down and saw a trail of blood across a rock sticking out of the dying grass. "What happened, Bruce? I stepped outside and next thing I know—"

"What do I know? I was bartending. More importantly,

what do I care?" he said, yanking me up to my feet. I stood unsteadily and saw Janie hurrying over to us.

"You're going to hurt him, Brucie," she said and hit him in the arm to no physical effect.

"Somebody already beat me to it," Bruce said with a laugh. "Hey Janie, if you're out here, who's running the bar?"

"You go run the damn bar," Janie said defiantly. "I'm checking on my friend."

Bruce laughed again. "Some friend. You can take it from here, but I want this guy off the property. I told you before he was trouble."

"Yeah, yeah. Now get back in there before those knuckleheads steal all our booze." When he left, she continued. "Jeez, Eddie, what happened out here? I hear all this commotion and somebody runs in from outside saying a guy just got knocked out. Your poor eye!" She touched up by the cut and I pulled away instinctively, wincing as I did it.

"I guess you've answered your own question," I said, rubbing at my neck and head. "You didn't see a woman around here, did you?"

"I only just got out here myself. But no, I don't see any other women around. Do you?" I didn't. She draped my arm over her shoulder and led me back towards the light of the Rabbit.

"I was meeting a friend, but she was in the dark. I went over to talk to her, and next thing I know, it all goes black. And now," I looked around to be sure, "now she's nowhere to be seen. What do you make of that?"

The glow of the lights showed lines of worry on Janie's face. "I don't know, Eddie. You think she set you up? Who would want to hurt you?"

"No," I said, "starting with your first question. The second one's going to require a longer answer."

"So tell me." She sat down on a step and motioned for me to join her. "I had a break coming up anyway."

I didn't much feel like getting into the complexities of the Manticore case with a near-stranger, and I was pretty sure Janie's break wasn't long enough for that even if I did. But I appreciated her interest, and I thought she deserved as much of an answer as I could handle.

"Suppose I've rubbed some people the wrong way lately," I said. "I'm sure your friend Bruce could tell you all about that. But no, I don't believe it was a setup."

"No? Seems like a heck of a coincidence if it wasn't."

"I don't think she lured me into the dark so someone could knock me out, if that's what you mean. One, she didn't have a motive and two, I don't see what that would accomplish even if she did."

"Knocking you out, you mean."

"Right."

"Unless," Janie said, "that wasn't the plan."

I didn't know if it was post-concussion haziness or just my standard issue confusion, but she lost me with that and I told her so. "I don't follow."

"I said there was a commotion, remember? And someone came into the bar saying you had been knocked out. Maybe that person was a witness and got in the way of whatever your attacker had planned." I didn't like where that thinking led us, but that didn't mean she was wrong.

"That still leaves us with the question of motive."

"You never said why you trusted her in the first place. Is this a long-time friend, or a close relationship?"

"Neither," I admitted. I could tell how Janie wanted to respond by the revelatory look on her face, but she managed to keep from vocalizing the thought. For the first time in a while, I recalled Hannah's line back at the coffee shop about her powerful friends, and how reticent she had been to elaborate on that. "But that doesn't mean it was a set up," I insisted.

Janie shrugged, working the gum in her mouth. "Doesn't mean it wasn't either. You're not one of those schmucks who believes every word a pretty face says, are you?"

"Pretty much." She shook her head disapprovingly. "Does that apply to you too, Janie?"

"Aw." She smiled. "Aren't you the charmer."

"No, I don't trust anybody as a rule," I said.

"Smart. Listen, I've gotta get back to work, but you need to get that cut looked at. You good to make it home safely?"

"Yeah," I said, though my head was still hammering. "Thanks Janie, again. I guess I owe you another one."

"I'll put it on your tab," she said and gave me a quick kiss on the cheek. "Take care of yourself, Stranger." She opened the door to the Rabbit. As the dull roar of the people inside poured out into the night, she turned to give me one last look and some parting wisdom. "It's a jungle out there."

There was no bus when I got to the stop, so I walked the whole seven or eight miles home in the dark, feeling stubborn, low, and mean. My soon-to-be scar throbbed all the while. Janie was right about getting it looked at, but I wasn't willing to commit the time a hospital visit would require, to say nothing of the bill. I made it back home safely, just as promised, but a whole lot worse for wear too. I dragged myself to bed and slept soundly, with my exhausted body winning out over my troubled mind.

12

A Lifeline

It was late in the day when I awoke. My head still hurt, but in a smaller area than it had the night before, and the pain was a little duller. Got to take your victories where you can find them. I cleaned the cut the way I should've done the night before, then stumbled into a chair by the window and gazed outside. The gray landscape looked even uglier than usual.

What I really wanted to do was get Hannah's side of the story on last night, but all I had was her work number and she wouldn't be at Manticore on a Sunday. She could have gotten my home number from my paperwork if she really wanted to, but she hadn't made any effort to reach out to me either. Unless, and this was a concerning thought, she hadn't been able to for some reason. What had my attacker done with her after I was out? Maybe I wasn't the primary target at all, but just an obstacle in the way of getting to Hannah. Or maybe Janie was right that I had been too trusting of the blonde with the pretty smile. No way of knowing, but the idle speculation wasn't doing me any good. I needed to take some kind of action.

I couldn't see any way forward on the Hannah angle, not until Monday. Tony and Leonard's interviews were still a day off too. That left Veronica Lawrence. By then I had some news worth reporting, or at least that's what I convinced myself of. I walked over to the phone, but when I reached out for it, it was off the hook. I ran my finger along the phone, which laid ever so slightly crookedly in its place on the hook. It wasn't off by much, but it was enough.

"Maybe that explains not hearing from Hannah," I said to myself, or maybe that was wishful thinking. I pushed it back into place and gave the receiver a second to engage. When the dial tone returned, I punched in Veronica's digits.

"Mrs. Lawrence," I said, "I have news on your husband."

"Yes, yes." Her voice was curt. "Very good. What is it you have then?"

"I've been doing some snooping around Manticore," I said.

"Perhaps my question was unclear," she broke in. "What is it you have on my husband?"

I had lost my cordiality somewhere in the unpleasantness of the previous night's events, regardless of how well she was paying me. "Did you know he was involved with Manticore?" I asked, none too diplomatically.

"Manticore, of course. I'm the one who sent you there."

"You did," I agreed. "But you didn't tell me Thomas was a member of the Cooperative, or how deep he was in. You didn't tell me that they have gone to great lengths to make it look like he never worked there at all."

"Worked there? Oh, I don't know about all that. He did... Well, he did jobs for them, I suppose. Let's call them commissions. It's not like he was an employee or something."

"Commissions?" I thought back to what little she had told me about Thomas. "Like painting houses?"

"That's right. But you said you had news. Who's behind the disappearance then? Is it that Crossley, or Raymond? What did you find on Hyde?"

"Too many questions," I said. "I can't even remember them all, let alone answer them. Who disappeared him, I have no idea. No proof, anyway. But yes, Crossley certainly seems connected somehow. Hyde, who knows. I'll say it again: I need you to tell me everything you know. Anything less only delays us, which is death—pardon the expression—for missing person cases."

Veronica let the silence hang between us, then spoke. "I'll come by today," she said, "at three o'clock. I have something to show you."

"I'll be here," I said. "See you then."

I spent the joining hours icing my head, wondering about what Veronica had to show me and why she wasn't willing to mention it over the phone. I came up with a whole lot of nothing in the way of theories. But, like always, eventually I didn't have to wonder anymore because time sorted it out for me. Just before three o'clock there was a knock on my door and I beckoned Mrs. Lawrence inside.

"I owe you an apology," was the first thing she said.

"Oh?"

"I realize I have been, at times, rather difficult to work with. And, at times, ungenerous towards you in particular. For that I am sorry. But I confess this predicament has been a terrible imposition upon my well-being. My primary goal, of course, is the safe return of my husband. But secondly, and this is of nearly-equal importance, is to not draw attention to the fact that I am doing so. Forgive me if this next part is indelicate, but you must have wondered why a woman of means such as myself came to you in the first place. This 'business' you've got here," (I could tell she didn't think my operation quite merited the word business) "well, it's not anybody's idea of the top outfit in town, is it?"

"I imagine not," I said. "But we all have to start somewhere."

"You see, in my case, your lack of acclaim was an asset. I can't be sure how far our enemy's reach extends. You seemed like you would be, if you'll forgive me again, hardly worth their trouble. And here," she took a deep breath, "I'd like to say a few words about the Manticore Cooperative."

"Please." The dull ache in my head hadn't subsided, but for the moment my attention on it did.

She reached into her coat and pulled out a large envelope, placing it on the table between us. "This is what Thomas was doing for the Cooperative. I will show you shortly. But I want you to understand, Thomas is a good man, and he entered into this mess with the noblest intentions."

In my experience, very few people thought of themselves as anything other than good, but I was content to play along. "I understand. Go on."

"I said before that money was not an issue when it came to this case. Thomas and I have both done well in the corporate world. Of course, I'm sure you discovered as much when you did your research on us."

I hadn't, but I also didn't see any reason to divulge an unflattering truth. "Of course."

"That's where he first heard about Manticore. If I could

only go back and prevent the infection at its source... But there's no good in that line of thinking, is there? A trusted employee of his was a convert, and you know how fervent new adherents of any religion are."

"A religion, you say?"

"Oh, I suppose they wouldn't call themselves that. Not in those terms then, fine. 'Lifestyle enhancement' or whatever buzzwords they're using these days to entrap new members. Their disciples," she insisted, "are every bit as devoted as those of any church you'll find."

"And Thomas was among them," I surmised.

"Like Paul after the road to Damascus. He tried to get me to join the flock—or pride, shall we say—but I have my own faith. One that precedes Patrick Raymond and his foolish adventures in Africa."

"You heard that story too, huh?" I was almost starting to warm up to her.

"Some of it I recall, yes. Have you ever known someone to be brilliant in one area of their life and a complete disaster in another? Because that was Thomas, with business and with Manticore. And I'll grant you, the exercises did him some good in the beginning, the mind training as he called it. But it wasn't long before they started to pressure him for financial contributions. In time, even our healthy personal reserves started to dwindle. I believe Thomas would have paid them all the way to the poorhouse if I hadn't put a stop to it."

"And I'll bet the altruists down at Manticore didn't much appreciate that," I said. "One thing that's bothering me, though. When you first brought me the case, you said Thomas was a house painter. None of this 'successful businessman' talk."

"That may have been just a little bit of subterfuge,"

Veronica said coyly. "I didn't want to lay all my cards on the table right away, you understand. But it was true when I said he paints houses. Not the houses people live in, but cityscapes, landscapes, that sort of thing."

"He's an artist?"

She nodded. "Of remarkable talent."

"If you stretched the truth in that original story any more, it would have snapped in two," I bristled. "But ok, less coveralls and scaffolding, more palette and canvas."

"I kept thinking, or hoping, he would show back up, but with each passing hour, the situation seems more and more dire. If you are not what you seem, if somehow this undertaking is itself the latest trick of some Manticore machination, that is a chance I must take. As you've said, there is no point in hiding the truth now. Thomas always was a masterful painter. Which is not to say his pieces made money. Profit and merit don't often have much to do with each other in the art world."

"So I've heard." She was sure taking her time with it, but I felt she was getting somewhere. Hopefully soon.

"Manticore never cared about that—the verve of human emotion behind the work, I mean. What they cared about was his uncanny ability with the brush. He was as good as a photograph." Here she reached into the envelope and pulled out five pictures, passing them to me. They were photographs of paintings that looked to be hanging in museums.

"Cityscapes and landscapes, just like you said. These are Thomas's?"

Veronica laughed. "You don't know much about art, do you?"

"No," I admitted.

She fingered the photographs one at a time, naming them

as she went. "This one is Wyeth, these two Monet, this one Constable, and finally we have Pissarro."

"Ah. Well, now that I see them in the light here..." That lie wasn't even worth finishing. "I have heard of Monet," I averred. Context made it obvious the other three must have been esteemed painters as well.

"Now," Veronica said, reaching for another envelope, "these are Thomas's." She spread the new photos out next to the original five. It became immediately clear to me how Thomas made all that money, even if the art world didn't care one whit about his original compositions.

"They're nearly identical," I said.

"Better than nearly. Look closer. You'll see they are perfectly identical. Do you have any idea what such a skill is worth?"

"It must be a rare talent, no question. Never got too excited over paintings myself—the bare walls in this office will attest to that—but I can appreciate that there's a market for them. So when you put a stop to Thomas handing over your personal funds, he thought selling these paintings would be a suitable replacement for getting Manticore their money."

"You're close. I'm sure I'm asking this question too late, but our conversation is confidential, right?"

"Strictly. I'm like a doctor, or a priest. Doctor-priest. Who would want a fake, though?"

"Oh, I don't know. People who care more about impressing their friends and rivals than any real bond to the original art? What's so important about originality anyway? Look at the photos here, no one would ever know the difference. His work was immaculate."

I looked at them again, more closely this time. "You're absolutely right," I said. "If you mixed up these photos and handed them back to me, I would never be able to tell, that's for sure." She seemed satisfied with that answer.

"But," I continued and her face dropped a little, "I don't think you're going to find many art collectors who would be so understanding if they found out their big investment wasn't the brushstrokes of good old Claude Monet at all— just Tommy Lawrence, one-time corporate star turned cult stooge." That came out crueler than I had meant it to. "Just thinking out loud," I said, "and it may be nothing. But what if Manticore is telling the truth, for once? Here you and I are thinking they had him bumped off, but why would they do that if he was bringing them money? Swindled art collector with a temper, maybe that's who we're after."

I could see this idea hadn't crossed Veronica's mind up to that point. As she wrestled with the possible new reality, I studied the photos she had provided some more. They really were unbelievable likenesses. Finally, I asked, "What do you think?"

"I don't think so, no. Do you remember that folder I gave you when we first met, with the three names?"

"Of course. It's right here in my desk drawer."

"I didn't put that together myself," Veronica said. "Thomas did. He said if anything suspicious ever happened to him, one of those three men would be responsible. I thought it was paranoia at the time, but now it seems he was right to be prepared."

"Which is why you were so sure then, and why you're so sure now. I don't think it proves anything, but it sure tilts the odds heavily in that direction. When did he give you the folder?"

"Maybe a month ago. And then nothing happened, so I thought we were ok. But I guess a part of me must have believed him, because I held on to that folder. Now I'm glad I did."

"Was Thomas happy at Manticore?"

"Very much so. Like I said, he was a total adherent. Whether they were happy with him, I don't know. They always seemed impossible to satisfy, which made Thomas work all the harder to please them. It was a major source of conflict in our marriage."

"I imagine it would be. That explains Crossley and Raymond's presence in the file, but there's no record of Warren Hyde ever being part of Manticore. Why include him?"

"I don't know," she said. "I didn't make the list. But if Thomas put him in there, there was a reason for it. I trust the significant sum I'm paying you is enough to find out why."

"Yes, I've made some progress on that front."

"On finding Hyde or on running up my bill?"

"Both, actually, but I assume you're more interested in the Hyde part."

"As you say," Veronica said. "What have you got?"

"You mentioned—that is, Thomas mentioned—a bar, The Silver Rabbit, in Hyde's file. That's about all he mentioned, in fact. I've spent some time there, spoken with a friend of his, got in good with one of the bartenders. It's been productive, although I don't really have anything to show for it just yet. I went to try again last night and I got knocked out for my troubles." I pointed to the red line above my eye. "By whom, I don't know."

"My goodness," Veronica said in a voice that made it clear she was not accustomed to associates of hers getting knocked unconscious outside of seamy bars. "I saw the cut but didn't want to call attention to it. You're all right now?"

"For a given definition of all right, yeah." Veronica and I were both putting more of our cards on the table, but I still wasn't going to mention Hannah. Her secret wasn't mine to tell. "The point is, apparently somebody didn't like me asking questions. Which makes me want to ask those questions all the more."

"We don't have the time to be patient. You said it yourself."

"That's right. I'm back at Manticore tomorrow. Crossley's having me bring a couple people in for indoctrination sessions, or interviews, as he calls them. I've clued them in ahead of time, they won't be joining up, but it should keep him off my back for a while. I've tried to see if anyone else at Manticore knows about Thomas, but they circle the wagons with the best of them over there." Then I made a promise I wasn't sure I could keep. "I will find Hyde, though. He will unlock a lot of these mysteries."

"It sounds like you have a plan forward. That is all I can ask. But please, do hurry. Another week and I fear I will need to go to the police after all, no matter what illegalities Thomas caught himself up in." She stood up and headed for the door. "Be in touch."

The rest of the day was full of nervous energy. I had been running so constantly from one lead to the next lately, I wasn't used to sitting around with nothing to do. But that was all I could do as far as the case was concerned, so I didn't have much choice in the matter. Instead I caught the bus down to the lake and tried to run off my nerves along one of the winding bike paths. That didn't accomplish much aside from reminding me how lousy I was at running, but I kept at it, and if nothing else, it had the benefit of redirecting my attention for a while.

When I got back home I was physically spent, but my

mind was still a live wire. I wrestled with Melville some more before giving that up too. After a cup of tea I went to bed early, the sky outside my window just beginning to darken. That wasn't the end though, and I spent several hours tossing about in bed, trying to find a position that would bring about sleep. I never did get comfortable, but sleep came all the same. Sure enough, when I awoke it was Monday; time for Tony and Leonard's big debut down at the Manticore offices.

13

What Do You Need?

Hannah's eyes flashed when she saw me enter the lobby. "Eddie, I'm so glad to see you!" she said.

"I was looking forward to this myself," I said. "For different reasons maybe." I had a list of questions for her as long as my arm, but I didn't get the chance to ask any of them, because at that moment Crossley poked his head out of the hallway and made his way towards us.

I had to think fast. Hannah had followed my cipher once before, and I hoped she could do it again. "Did you see that sunset on Saturday night?" I asked.

"Some of it," she said. "Didn't catch as much as I would have liked to." I took that to mean she had picked it up, but Crossley was upon us before we could take it any further.

"What's so special about a sunset?" he said. "You've seen one, you've seen them all. And if you miss one, there's always plenty more where that came from."

"Until there's not," I said, but my meaning was lost on

him.

"Follow me, Eddie," he said. "Your recruits are waiting in the interview room."

"Wait, what?" That hadn't been the plan as I understood it. "You want me to interview them?"

"Of course not," he said as I followed him down the hall. "That's my job."

"So what do I do?"

"You don't *do* anything, Eddie. You must have had your recruiter sitting in on your initial meeting, didn't you?"

"I was a walk up," I said. "Open interviews."

"Well, that explains that. You're here to be a bridge from the familiar to the novel. We want to ease them into this new opportunity, right? You just sit there and make them feel more comfortable, because they know you and trust you. Think you can handle that?"

"I am an excellent sitter," I promised.

He stopped outside of the door to the conference room and looked at me, trying to figure out if that was compliance or insolence. It was the second one, but he didn't seem to notice, so he nodded at me and we stepped inside.

Directly in front of us, a row of Manticore employees sat at a long table. I recognized their faces from my first interview with Crossley and company, except this time I would be sitting on their side of the table. Across from us, on his own, I saw Tony fidgeting with the complimentary bottle of water they had placed in front of him. He had dressed nicely, or Tony's idea of nice anyway, and I appreciated the effort. We made eye contact and he gave me a subtle smile. For a moment I panicked, thinking he might go so far as to wink at me, but discretion prevailed.

"No Dennis?" I whispered to Crossley. Dennis Markley, that is, the pseudonym I had given Leonard.

"He's next," he whispered back. "One at a time."

All the other Manticore employees had notepads and pens in front of them, and I wished I had something of my own to make me feel more official, but then I remembered what Crossley had said about my job being just to sit there. I resigned myself to my role as a spectator and settled in for the show.

Crossley opened the interview much the same way he had started mine. *Might as well be reading off a script*, I thought, though he had apparently memorized his lines some time ago. He moved through them flawlessly, first introducing his colleagues, then launching into his patter about the manticore. That was exactly what I had prepared Tony for, of course, and he did an excellent job pretending to be powerfully impressed with the whole pitch.

"Strength, fearlessness, intelligence," he repeated back to Crossley. "That sounds like my kind of operation."

"That's who we are here," Crossley said. "That's what we're bringing to the table. So, my next question is what do we stand to gain by bringing you aboard? Convince me." Tony and I had practiced that too, as much of it as I could remember.

"I'm a guy who can get you things, for one," Tony said. My eyes widened involuntarily.; that was not the answer we had rehearsed at all. I slipped back under my camouflage of false calm before anyone noticed.

"Oh yeah?" Crossley asked with evident interest. "Like what?"

"Anything," Tony said. "What do you need?"

Tony's gone rogue, I realized with a dropping feeling in my stomach. *He's trying to get something out of Crossley, probably to help me with my case.* And while my friend was well-intentioned and cagey, he could also be reckless. The risk hardly seemed worth it, but I had no way of pulling him back without breaking my cover. I set my jaw and stared hard at Tony, trying to signal him with my eyes. He never even looked my way, so I could only sit back, a powerless observer.

"We don't *need* anything," one of Crossley's underlings to my left said, offended at the very suggestion that they could. "We are the ones who can offer—"

"Not so fast," Crossley said, cutting the speaker off with a raise of his hand. I recognized the routine playing it out much the way it did in my initial interview. The interchangeable subordinates rough up the prospective client while Crossley swoops in to protect them like an avenging angel. "Bill's simply answering the question we asked him, and it sounds like he might have a pretty good answer. Go on," he indicated to Tony.

"Like I was saying," he resumed, "what do you need? I mean, I don't know what it is you guys do here, but if I did, I could hook you up, hey?"

Billy Shakes, as he had insisted on calling himself, was being as subtle as a six a.m. jackhammer. Each ensuing line increased the chance of drawing suspicions on himself and, by extension, me. I had no choice but to break in before he gave up the whole racket.

"Mr. Shakes," I said, slipping into the Manticore jargon, "what we do here is offer revolutionary lifestyle solutions. A higher consciousness, Mr. Shakes."

Crossley put a hand on my wrist and squeezed hard at the pressure point. "My colleague speaks out of turn. I apologize," he said. "You may not know it yet Bill, but you are poised to join the most elite group of thinkers on the planet. Forget the life you knew before. That was less than a shadow of your true existence. We are, each of us, unlimited possibility. But I ask you, how many ever achieve their true potential? One in ten, one in a hundred?"

Tony looked at me then, not Crossley. Our eye contact was brief, less than a second, but it was enough to get my point across. Tony backed off the investigatory path and followed where Crossley led him, never allowing himself to get pinned to any binding or intractable commitments. Eventually, Crossley finished regaling him with the wonders of Manticore and Tony was free to go. He left the room with a flurry of praises for Crossley's operation and empty, unenforceable assurances to return to the facility in the future.

It was all I could do not to let out an audible sigh of relief when he was finally gone. Crossley stepped out of the room for the moment, walking Tony to the lobby as he had done with me, presumably. I took the opportunity to chat up my fellow panelists.

"What did you think of that guy?" I asked the table. "Pretty good pull, wouldn't you say?"

I received silence in return until finally one of the older women said, "Quite so, Eddie."

Something about her dry tone annoyed me more than it probably should have, and I didn't mind letting her know about it. "It's Mr. London, actually. And I would appreciate it if—"

"You are Eddie," another broke in curtly, "because we are of a higher level than you."

The table laughed pompously and one of the men said, "Don't tell me you haven't picked up on that yet?" I hadn't.

"Is that why everyone is so hung up on formalities around here? Another one of your goofy little power plays? Well, that's just great." The sound of footsteps approaching the door echoed in the hallway. "That must be Crossley," I said, taking no small pleasure in omitting the honorific.

The braintrust around the table went different shades of indignant at that, but before anyone could offer a defense of their boss's honor, the man himself came through the door, with Old Leonard trailing gingerly behind him. I had to reach my hand up over my mouth to cover my smile at seeing Lenny in such an incongruous place such as this. Hopefully he would stick to the plan better than Tony did.

Crossley led the interview as he always did, and Leonard was as good as I had hoped, lithely answering the questions just as we had practiced, and sometimes better. Like a fencer whose reflexes granted him impregnable defenses. Crossley did most of the talking, and went through his Manticore monologue verbatim, just as he had done with me, and with Tony, and with who knows how many dozen others. Still, some of his usual vivacity seemed to be lacking this time. The script went on unchanged like that, right up until it didn't.

"Strength, fearlessness, intelligence. That's who we are here," Crossley said. "That's what we're bringing to the table. So my next question is what do we stand to gain by bringing you aboard?" Then, "No offense," he added in an addendum that was meant only to bring offense.

My face didn't betray it, but the unexpected deviation doubled my attention. That was the first time I had heard Crossley break from the verbatim. Leonard handled it gracefully, calmly offering the wisdom gained from his extensive life experiences, but Crossley was unmoved.

"So, what you're saying is you're old," he summarized. "That hardly sounds like an asset, Dennis."

"Not much fun getting old. But it sure beats the alternative I always say," Leonard chuckled.

Crossley went on talking as though he didn't even hear him. "For all I know, we'll pour all these resources into you—

our time and money—and next thing I know, you'll up and die on us."

Old Lenny didn't let that ruffle him either. "We're none of us promised tomorrow."

"Some less so than others, I might say." Crossley let out an annoyed sigh. "We're done here. I'd thank you for your time, but you've wasted mine." He gestured towards the door. "You can find your way out."

If those insults were bait for a reaction, the fishing came up empty. "That I can," Leonard said genially. "I thank you, folks." He exited to the hallway, closing the door gently behind him.

"What an absolute waste of time," Crossley spat, turning to me. "You're going to have to do a lot better than that, Eddie."

"You seemed to like the first guy all right."

"First guy, sure. Second guy, the fossil? Useless."

I noticed, not for the first time, the stark dichotomy between how Crossley treated people he thought could do him some good, and those who couldn't. The useless, in his preferred nomenclature. The more I learned about this guy, the less I cared for him. But, I had to remind myself, that didn't necessarily mean he was responsible for whatever had happened to Thomas Lawrence. More work remained to say one way or the other on that front.

"What's next?" I asked Crossley.

"I want you to follow up with this Billy Shakes," Crossley said. "There's some potential there, maybe. I can't tell yet."

"Will do." I got up to leave.

"Have a seat," Crossley said. "We need to talk about starting your mind training."

I did as he asked. "Do we?"

"Session One will be with Mr. Desereau." Crossley

smiled then, for what reason, I didn't know. "Report to Room 104 directly after lunch. He will be expecting you at one o'clock sharp. Good day."

I waited for Crossley and the others to leave, but they didn't. When they all turned their eyes to me, I got the idea. "Oh, right." I smiled sheepishly and waved goodbye, glad to extract myself. The interviews had gone well, all things considered, even if Tony nearly blew it by trying to get too clever. Leonard had made out especially well, and from what I could tell, he was now truly free and clear. Billy Shakes, not so much.

As soon as I was out, I went straight for Hannah's desk. She was on the phone, just like the first time I saw her, but this time my mood was a lot different than that initial encounter. I leaned over the desk and pressed down on the button that would hang up on the call. She looked up at me, alarmed.

"Bad connection," I said. I shot a quick look around the lobby and confirmed we were alone, though for how long I didn't know. Had to make this quick. "What the hell happened Saturday night?" I asked quietly enough that only she would hear.

Hannah's answer came through nearly-clenched teeth. "They hit you," she said, "or he did. I don't know why, I had rather hoped you would. And then, I'm sorry, I kind of panicked and took off. I'm sorry," she said again.

I leaned closer. Who did?"

"I don't know. Some guy."

"Super helpful," I said bitterly.

"He was short. Like, unusually so. But big. You know, built."

"Just my luck that the man who wants to take a swing at

me is a big guy.”

“Does that description ring any bells?”

I tapped my knuckles on her desk, thinking. “Maybe. Let me get back to you on that.”

“He came up from behind, like maybe he had been hiding out in the night waiting for you. He slugged you, I screamed, and people started gathering.”

“Hmm,” I said, noncommittally.

“It all happened so fast, Eddie. I should have stuck around, I’m sorry,” (third time) “but I didn’t want to have to explain what I was doing down there, like if I was a witness, and... I just feel so bad.”

That last part made three-and-a-half apologies. Whether that amounted to a sincere expression of regret or the manifestation of a guilty conscience on overdrive, I wasn’t quite sure. For now, I favored the former.

“Well, nothing to be done for it now,” I said, fingering the knot on my head. “I have my first mind training session after lunch, with a Mr. Deserau. You know him?”

“I don’t think so. My sessions are with Mrs. Amesh.”

I thought about how Hannah had gone through the mind training sessions too. I wished I had asked her for more details on what to expect back when we were able to speak freely, at the coffee shop or the Rabbit. I didn’t even know if the training would be one-on-one or in a group. But the opportunity was gone now and I didn’t dare risk being so forthright in the Manticore lobby.

“I should get back to work,” Hannah said, derailing my train of thought.

“Right.”

“But Eddie, I’m glad you’re ok.”

“Right.”

14

Walls

Lunchtime was fast-approaching but I didn't have much of an appetite. Instead, I bided my time in the bullpen, not really doing anything productive but managing a passable enough job at faking it. When twelve-fifty came around I made my way downstairs to Room 104 where Mr. Deserau would be waiting for me. It was a couple minutes to one when I knocked on the door.

There was no answer from within. I tried the door handle and found it turned easily, obviously unlocked. Quick glances to my left and right revealed the hallway was empty, so I gently pushed the door open. It swung noiselessly on its hinges and clicked softly into place when I closed it behind me. The primary lights were off and the room was mostly dark, with a couple rows of emergency lights granting some subtle illumination. I was happy to leave it that way. A large cherry desk sat opposite the entrance and there were six smaller tables with their two chairs each, all facing the front of the room. On either side of the desk were tall gray filing cabinets holding six drawers each.

The large digital clock on the wall read 1:00 now, but still no sign of this Deserau. Turned out he hadn't been waiting for me after all, just the reverse. There wasn't much of interest in the room just yet, except those filing cabinets had piqued my interest for sure. I listened for any noise from outside the door, but it was silent as a grave. What was in those cabinets anyway? Ten to one they were locked, and I probably didn't have much time before Deserau showed up, but I thought it worth checking to see if I could get anything out of them anyway.

I moved swiftly towards the cabinet on the left and gave its top drawer a tug. They weren't locked after all, at least not that one. It slid open without resistance and I was awarded with a view of dozens of folders packed tightly together. I threw another nervous glance over my shoulder and rifled through the files, scanning the names on their labels as I went. Connor Ashley... Lee Bostwick... Harrison Carter... Maria DeSantos...

None of the names trigged any recognition for me. The last names started at A and ended at D. The other drawers must have accounted for the rest of the alphabet plus whatever else was in there. I made a quick mental rundown of the subjects that were of interest to me: Thomas Lawrence, Warren Hyde, Samantha Jones, Patrick Raymond, Hannah... Something. None of them fell within the purview of the drawer's alphabetical range. Jake Crossley sure did, though. I flipped towards the back of the C section, but before I could go any further the sound of a door opening behind me stopped me cold.

There was no sense in pretending I hadn't been snooping around. My only hope was to come up with a passable cover story, and quickly. I turned around to face whoever had just come in, doing my best to make the movement look casual. Standing in the doorway with every hair in place was the man I took to be Deserau. He wore a navy blue sweater vest over a white button up shirt and well-pressed khaki pants. He was what my grandma would have called a clean-cut kid, despite clearly being on the far side of forty.

"What are you doing?" he demanded. I leaned back on the cabinet drawer, pushing it shut as though I couldn't have been less interested in its contents.

"It's about time," I said. Before he could respond, I went on with exaggerated annoyance. "Fifteen minutes I've been waiting for you."

Deserau found himself unexpectedly on the defensive. "Well, it's only a couple minutes after and I—"

"And you are late. So yes, I got bored and started looking around for some reading material to pass the time. Who wouldn't? I've got half a mind to go to Mr. Crossley about this. That wouldn't reflect very well on the guy who was supposed to be watching over me though, would it?"

I had him there and he knew it. There was no way to get me in trouble without throwing himself overboard too. Falling back on mutually assured destruction wasn't exactly ideal, but it would have to do under the circumstances.

Deserau stared at me with something just short of contempt. But it was a passing phase and soon his demeanor was replaced with that slick salesmanship I had seen so many times before in these Manticore folks. A second later it was as if our initial acrimony had never happened at all.

"Allow me to introduce myself," he said, a big smile plastered across his face. "I am Mr. Deserau. It's a pleasure to meet you, Eddie. Welcome to your first mind training session. You must be excited!"

"So excited."

"Let's get you set up with the equipment here." His tone carried enough excitement for the both of us. Deserau directed me to sit at one of the tables, then retreated behind the desk and pulled a chunky briefcase out of one of the drawers. He laid it on the table in front of me and looked at me expectantly. Then he took a seat across from me and looked at me with a smile. "Ready?"

I nodded. "What have you got in there?"

He clicked open the case and reached inside. "First," he said, and handed me something that almost looked like a pair of sunglasses. Except when I placed them on my face (without bothering to wait for further instructions), the lenses were far darker; I couldn't see a thing. Either side of each lens, and above and below them, was wrapped in a hard black plastic that further blocked any light from getting inside. With the glasses on I was blind a bat, as they say. Apparently, a blindfold would have been too on the nose.

My ears still worked just fine though, and I heard Deserau say, "Ok, I see you've got the glasses figured out. Give me a finger."

There was one finger I would have been more than happy to give him, but I didn't think that was the one he meant. "Which one?"

"The right index will do," he said, and I did as he asked. I felt a pinching sensation on the tip of my finger, like a very wide clothespin clamping down.

"Lie detector?" I guessed.

Deserau laughed. "A lie detector—polygraph, that is—is as far removed from this machine as a paper boat is from the Titanic."

I sat with that a moment. "Your machine is the Titanic in this analogy?"

"Yes. The finest—"

"The ship that plowed into an iceberg and sank to the bottom of the ocean, killing hundreds? That's your machine?"

I still couldn't see a thing with the blinders on but it was easy enough to picture Deserau's flustered face from his shaky response. "Well, no, of course not."

"So you're the paper boat. Gosh," I said, "that seems even worse." Silence from beyond the blackness.

Finally he said, "I'm going to ask you a series of questions, then put you through a series of exercises." There he went again, pressing forward, pretending the awkwardness between us had never happened. "What is your greatest desire?"

At the moment it was getting this training session over with, but I was disciplined enough to avoid saying that. I thought of the Thomas Lawrence case, and how maybe it could serve as my ticket from an unknown rookie private eye with no reputation or esteem to a guy with a half-decent name in this town.

"Success," I told him. On my finger the pincher spasmed and a soft beeping sound answered it, presumably coming from the machine it was connected to.

"That's too vague. Tell me what that looks like. In details, Eddie."

Success was returning Thomas Lawrence safely to his wife. Nothing else much mattered, really, at least professionally speaking. If I wanted to go full altruism with it, however, I would pursue the same for Hannah and Caroline. Unraveling the mystery of Manticore might not have been strictly required to achieve either of the previous two goals, but I'd be lying if I said it wasn't a personal priority. Meanwhile, Deserau was still waiting on an answer.

"I want to save the planet," I said. The finger clip seized and the machine did its beeping again, as they would continue to do after each of my responses.

"Be more specific."

"I want to reach people, the ones who don't know about Mr. Raymond and about Manticore. I want them to have the same access to the training I will receive. Training that will unlock my full potential. Complete and total consciousness."

"Your personal idea of success is to be a successful recruiter for the Cooperative here?" It was hard to gauge his tone without the benefit of a facial expression to go along with it. I couldn't place whether it was guarded skepticism or unbridled enthusiasm.

I decided to lean into the flattery. "I don't know what brought me to Manticore, Mr. Deserau. I suppose it's what some people call fate, or God, or even just pure luck. But I would rule out that last one, personally. I feel, and maybe you feel too, that I was sent here for some great end, to do the work as it were. We mustn't let opportunities like this slip through our fingers. Wouldn't you agree?"

"Oh, most certainly," Deserau said. "Most certainly, Eddie." I got the feeling my Gospel of Manticore was a hit with this true believer. If I wasn't careful I might find myself caught up in the enthusiasm along with him.

"I think that's enough of that for now," he continued. "I'd like to try some visualization exercises with you. Would that be all right?"

"Fire away." Matching his enthusiasm turned out to be a bridge too far, but I saw I could at least earn some more points for put-on adulation.

"I want you to think of a place," Deserau started, "a place from your past. Perhaps even your distant past." I was torn between resisting whatever this mind game was trying to accomplish and earnestly giving it the old college try. Before I could decide, he sprang his next question on me. "Ok, where is it?"

There was no time for thinking, only free association. "A coffee shop," I said, then immediately regretted saying. Apparently, Hannah had been on my mind, but I didn't much want Deserau knowing that.

"That will do just fine," he said, like that was the answer he had been hoping for all along. "When was the first time you visited this coffee shop?"

I was getting good at lying, and that window between the questions was all the time I needed. "Many years ago. Fifteen?"

"And the most recent time?"

"Maybe three years ago."

"Very good. I want you to compare these two experiences and identify something that changed between them."

"I don't follow."

"Identify something that changed between these two experiences," he said more slowly.

Well, that was just restating what he said before in the reverse order. "The speed of the words wasn't the issue," I said but took a shot at his meaning anyway. "Like someone who died between my first and last visit?"

"Sufficient, but hardly necessary." Deserau clicked his pen and I heard him scrawling onto a piece of paper. "Interesting your mind went there though, isn't it?"

"If you say so. The walls were pale yellow the first time." "Hmm?"

"And pale green the last time. That's what changed."

That answer didn't impress him half as much as the previous one had. "That's hardly a... Well, in the strictest sense, sure, I suppose that qualifies as a change."

"Can hardly say it's the same," I agreed.

More writing sounds from where he sat. "The point, Eddie, is we never experience the same place twice, do we? Something has always changed in that passage of time, no matter how brief. Why, it could be as simple as the color of the walls, as you so astutely pointed out."

I nodded and waited for him to go on.

"Well, that concludes our lesson for today. I sure thank you for coming by." Deserau packed up his pen and paper and helped me remove the training apparatus. He then pointed me towards the door.

"That's it? *That's* the lesson?"

"For now," Deserau said cheerfully. "Your first step into a larger world, I assure you. Check out with Hannah at reception and she'll get you all set up for the next session."

I sat there dumbstruck, but I could see Deserau wasn't going to leave me in the room by myself, especially not after my near-tryst with the filing cabinets and all the personal information therein. For the moment I was beaten. I shrugged and got up, making my way towards the exit.

"When's the next one?" I asked as he gently pushed me back out into the hallway.

"Check out with Hannah at reception and she'll get you all set up for the next session," he said again, no less robotically cheerful than the first time.

"What was that all about?" I asked Hannah when I got to the lobby.

"Just finished your first lesson, huh?"

"Sure," I said, "if that's what passes for a lesson around here."

"I'm trying to remember... Something about change,

right?"

"Yeah. A total revelation." I tried to hide the sarcasm in my voice in case anyone was listening in, but I didn't do a very good job of it. "Deserau told me you'd get me all set up for the next one, whatever that means."

"That would be the schedule."

She pulled out a folder only a little thinner than the New York City phone book and flipped to September on a calendar. I leaned over the desk none-too-surreptitiously and tried to get a look at the names that filled the boxes. Again, none I recognized.

"Looks like we're booking into October. Do you prefer to stick with Mr. Deserau?"

"Candidly, does it matter?"

Hannah wasn't the woman I'd bonded with at the coffee shop anymore, not in that moment. She was back to pretending to be a Manticore lackey. Probably smart, given the circumstances. I followed her lead.

"Actually," I said before she could answer my question, "Mr. Deserau was top-notch. It would be my pleasure to resume my training with him."

She smiled warmly. "Wonderful, Eddie. I've got you down for the fourteenth. That will be one o'clock again in Room 104."

"Exemplary." I spun off in the direction of the main entrance.

"They didn't have anything more on your agenda this afternoon, Eddie?" she asked as I walked away. "Are you done for the day?"

I answered her second question first: "I am." The first question I ignored altogether. As I stepped out onto the sidewalk I half-heard Hannah say something about settling my bill. Her voice was buried in the sounds of the street; partially at first, then submerged past the point of existing.

15

A Deadline

The air had a pre-storm feeling to it as I circumscribed the city blocks towards the bus stop. Everything seemed colored in a light-gray hue and heavy with moisture. I put it at maybe fifty degrees, like the temperature didn't have enough courage in its convictions to lean either hot or cold. Sure enough, the skies opened up just as I got to the bus stop. The clouds that had been gray were now black, and heavy raindrops poured down on the city.

I scampered under the small metal roof that served as shelter for the waiting passengers. Probably not the best place to be if the rain turned to lightning, but at least I was dry(ish) for the time being. The wet streets shone in the headlights of the passing cars and it wasn't long before the driving rain turned low points in the ground into little puddles. There was still no sign of any bus so I sat on the intentionally-uncomfortable bench and watched traffic splash water up over the curbs.

I'd had all I could stand of Manticore for the moment. Inevitably, I'd have to return, as soon as the next day even, but for now I had no problem just staying away and embracing my rancor for the place. I still trusted Hannah, mostly, but I didn't mind leaving her behind for a while either. I guess the frustration at my lack of results was getting the better of me and, truth be told, I wasn't handling it very well. Stymied though I was, surely there existed some way forward.

Tony and Leonard both merited following up with. Tony first, since Manticore didn't seem to be done with him yet if it was up to them. As for Leonard, I hadn't even had the foresight to arrange a way for us to meet post-interview, an absolute rookie mistake on my part. And while I could have granted myself some measure of grace on that count, rookie though I was, my better nature wouldn't allow it. Instead, I sat there and brooded, feeling some mix of guilty and sorry for myself.

Well, when had that ever accomplished anything? The obvious next step was to get in touch with Tony and debrief. Plus, I still owed him some guff for his unauthorized deviation from the plan we had agreed to. It wasn't often I had a chance to give the big man grief, so I wanted to take advantage of the opportunity while I had cause to.

By the time I got off the bus, the rain had lightened to a half-hearted drizzle. I went right for the phone when I got home, and dialed Tony's work number. "Tony, let's recap. Is now a good time to come by?" He said it was, so that sent me right back out the door I had just come in.

My bus pass sure was getting a workout lately, even more so than usual. I disembarked near the docks and made my way to Tony's trailer, rapping three times on its metal door. The weather had turned cold again and my knocks sounded brittle in the chilly, damp air. I heard Tony stomping around inside and he soon threw the door open and welcomed me in.

"Come on in, get out the cold, you knucklehead!"

"You say that like this weather is my fault, Tony. Way above my pay grade, I assure you."

"Pay grade," he laughed. "You and your jokes. Sit down, we can have that talk you wanted."

I sat on an ancient and not especially comfortable couch, sinking deep into its resistanceless red cushions. Papers were stacked haphazardly throughout the trailer; I could see bits of words and numbers, but nothing that made any bit of sense to me.

"What is it you do down here, anyway?" I asked him.

"Ah, better not to say," Tony said, pulling up a chair across from me. "Never you mind about that. No, no, never you mind."

"All right then," I said casually. That answer was no more or less than what I expected but it was a worth shot anyway. "So, about Manticore..."

Tony smiled under his big bushy mustache. "I did a good job for you, hey Eddie? I told you I wasn't going to let those schmucks push me around, hey? Remember how I told you?"

"Right. Well, the thing about that Tony, we were going to get you in and out of there without any commitments, remember? To not even make an impression, just to be a name to get them off my back."

"Billy Shakes. We gave them a name all right." He laughed at his own cleverness.

"We did. But then you started talking about how you could get them things. What the hell was that, Tony? Not at all like we practiced."

"Not what we practiced, no. Better than what we practiced. Didn't you notice? Because I told that guy I could get him stuff. And then I said, 'What do you need?' That could be valuable information for you, Eddie."

"Tony, you don't have to keep calling me that."

"No, no, it's good for me. Good practice in case I see you back at the Manticore."

"You're not going to see me back at Manticore! The whole point of this was to get you in and out of there without them ever seeing you again. It would have worked if you followed our plan, just the way it worked for the other guy. You know, the one who actually listened to me."

Tony slumped down in his chair, moping like a puppy that had just been scolded for an accident in the house. "I was just trying to help you with your case," the big man said apologetically.

"Well, now you've got me feeling bad for yelling at you besides." I sighed, feeling weary. "But they think you're interested. And they really liked you, which means they'll be following up with you. And you insisted on giving them your real contact information, so they'll actually be able to find you. And they will come for you. And then what?"

A comprehension came into Tony's eyes, like he was realizing all this for the first time. "Hmm," he said.

"Exactly. Because that's not very reassuring, is it?"

We sat with that for a while, each of us thinking through the angles. Rain pinged off the trailer's metal roof, an encore performance from the earlier storm. Finally, Tony spoke.

"Ah, let them come," he said, recovering. "If they try to play the tough guy with me, they'll see what happens, hey?"

"Maybe. The way I see it, Tony, we've got two ways forward from here. We can still get you out of it, it just occurred to me how. Or we go deeper, like your original thinking, and use you to see what we can figure out about these guys. I guess you bashing all their heads in would be the third way forward. Although, I have to say, I don't see how that would help me with my case."

"Probably not," Tony conceded on the last point. "How can you get me out? I'm not scared," he added quickly, "you know that. I'm just wondering."

"Of course. Well, as I said, they were interested in bringing you into their special little club. But this other guy I brought in, Old Leonard, they got him out of there as quickly as they could."

"The real bum's rush, hey?"

"That's right. And do you know why?" Tony's shrug showed he didn't. "Because he was, in their estimation, useless. See, they only want people who can benefit them—I think they're mainly after money, though free labor seems to be a plus too. Well, one look at Leonard and anyone can see he doesn't have money, and what work could he do for Manticore in his frail condition? They couldn't very well get any labor out of him. If anything, he would have been a drain on their resources."

"So, we make me up to look really old?" Tony asked without any particular conviction. "And then they say, 'Hey, we don't want this guy, he's too old.'"

"Well, no, Tony, I don't think that would work at all. Because they've already met you. They know you're not really old."

"Ah."

"But there are other ways to convince them you're not worth their time or effort. You go back looking shabby, demonstrate that you don't have any particular skills, fumble a bunch of simple tasks. It seems easily done, doesn't it? And then they decide they don't want you, rather than you needing to convince them to let you walk."

Tony nodded, running a thumb and forefinger over his mustache. "I like it," he said. "A good plan."

"Or," and I hoped I wouldn't regret saying this next part, "we double down. Use you as another avenue for getting information out of this place."

"There would be more compensation in it for me that way, I suppose."

"Always quick to seize on the money angle. I'd have to run it by my client, I don't know if she's willing to double her expenses. But if so, then yes, I suppose there would be."

Tony thought that over. "Well, I'm pretty busy these days. You'd really have to make it worth my while."

I tried to throw my arms up in an expression of disbelief, but my awkward position sunken into the couch wouldn't allow it. Instead, I had to let my words do the talking as it were. "Hell Tony, you're trying to play hardball on the bill with me here? It's not even my money to spend."

"Exactly, not your money. That should make spending it easier."

I had to admit there was a certain logic in that. "Ok, but remember, I have to run it by the client. It's her call."

"You let me know," Tony said. "Now we say goodbye because I have to get back to work."

"Back to work doing whatever it is you do around here."

"That's right." Tony reached out his hand and pulled me up from the couch with a sharp tug. "You let me know," he said. "So long, Eddie Paris."

"London," I said, exasperated.

"Just testing," he said with a smile, patting my back as he ushered me out the door.

*　　*　　*

When I got home I called Veronica. She wasn't due to get another update just yet, not per our strict agreement, but this seemed worth ignoring the rule for. I let her know right off not to expect too much.

"So, I haven't found your husband," I said. "Let's start with that."

"No." She wasn't shy about laying on the mock disbelief. "You could positively knock me over with a feather right now."

"I'm calling to see if you're willing to authorize a second... well, an associate of mine on the expense account. It won't be cheap, but I think it will be worth it."

"I wasn't aware you had a partner," she said none-too-warmly. "Strictly a solo operation, as I understood it."

"Not a partner, no. Well, sort of. You see, Manticore asked me to come up with a couple names, because I'm a recruiter for them now—"

"Frankly—may I be frank?" She didn't wait for me to respond but just kept going, rather frankly indeed. "Frankly, you're already overpaid. Grossly, I might even say. Because by my count it's been ten days, and I don't know any more about Thomas's disappearance than I did when I came to you that first day. I won't even bother to ask what the bill is up to now. And it's not the money, you understand. It's the principle."

"Well, hold on now," I said, but that was as far as I got with it.

"In fact, I was just thinking—even before this request, but especially after it—that we might both be better off ending this hiring arrangement right here and now. I will pay you whatever I currently owe of course, but I hope you would agree that this arrangement has been of no benefit whatsoever to me."

"I don't—"

"And now," she laughed incredulously, "and now you want more money? Double the money! Have you absolutely lost your mind?" I had to move the receiver away from my ear but I could still hear her just fine.

"Point taken."

"I'd like you to total your expenses and send me the bill," she said, more calmly. The indifference made me feel even worse than the hysterics had. "I see now that I took the wrong approach in coming to you. A foolish idea has led me to a foolish end, as I should have known it would. Perhaps a second, competent, private investigator might yet save my husband. I can only hope you haven't wasted too much time already."

I sat in stunned silence. All the work I had put in, the hope that this case would be the break I needed to launch something of a career for myself, it was all disappearing through the unseen phone lines. This called for something dramatic on my part, and I didn't have any time to spare. I started speaking before I even knew what I was saying.

"If you fire me now, you will never find your husband."

Her turn to sit in silence. "What did you say? What does that mean?"

"I know where he is," I said, digging the hole deeper. "I can't be more specific than that right now. This is a very delicate situation to say the least."

More silence. "I don't believe you," she said, but I could tell she hadn't actually made up her mind on the subject.

"I found Warren Hyde." The lies were really piling up now, like I couldn't stop once I had started. "All you gave me was the Silver Rabbit, and I still found him. It seems he and Thomas worked together pretty closely, didn't they?" I didn't know that for sure, but it seemed a reasonable gamble.

"Perhaps they did." I didn't have her all the way back on my side yet, but I was getting there.

"I'm not going to lie to you," I continued, feeling more than a little guilty about my choice of words, "Thomas is still in danger; pulling me off the case now will increase that danger tenfold. I told you about the progress I've been making at Manticore. You think that comes easy, or cheap?" I repeated what had become my extemporaneous thesis: "If you take me off this case, you're signing your husband's death warrant. You will carry that guilt with you until the end of your days," I added gravely. Not a half-bad pitch, considering I had not expected to need to make it.

"You will get him out, return him safely?"

"I can't promise that. I'm not an oracle, Mrs. Lawrence. I can promise you I've been making progress" (hey, that part was actually true), "and I will continue working towards his safe return with everything I have" (that too).

"I need," her voice was on the edge of pleading, "some kind of timeline. You have to give me something beyond this vague, evidence-less promise of hope."

Again my words were ahead of my brain. "One week. I will reunite you with your husband in one week, or," in an unneeded tacked on shot of bravado, "die trying."

"One week," she agreed. "That gets us to October third."

I counted the seven days on my fingers, tracking the date. "Indeed. And Mrs. Lawrence, about my associate?"

"Don't push your luck." She hung up before I could even go back to the 'until the end of your days' well. But given what little proof I'd been able to provide her with, that compromise was more than fair on her part.

I hung up myself and collapsed into a nearby chair. Funny how some conversations can drain you more than purely physical exertion could ever dream of. I reflected: The good news was I hadn't lost my job. But then I didn't know losing my job was even a possibility before I made the call, so that seemed like a small victory indeed. The bad news was I had *nearly* lost my job, Veronica had rejected my request to put Tony on the payroll, and (worst of all), I had talked myself into a deadline of seven days. Oh, and I now had a whole bunch of new lies to keep track of to go along with the several I already told Manticore.

Darkest before the dawn, so they say. Except by that time the literal sun was setting outside, too. An hour later it had plunged below the horizon, leaving the city bathed in the blackness of night. I was still sulking in my chair, so I hadn't turned on a light and couldn't see much of anything in the house. It was just as well; there wasn't a whole lot worth seeing. I really was overdue to do something about those bare walls. Instead, I went to bed and slept haggardly.

I dreamed—or is it dreamt? I *had a dream* that I was in a basement, already strange material for a lifelong Californian. This dream basement had no doors or windows (in my dream logic I still somehow knew I was underground) to go along with a ceiling that was just low enough to force me to hunch over uncomfortably. It was a most disconcerting feeling, one that tripled when the basement started to fill with water from some unseen source. The water level rose, not rapidly, but steadily. Soon it was up to my shoulders, then over my mouth. As my nose fell below the water line, I woke up.

It didn't take old Sigmund Freud to interpret that one. I was feeling boxed in, with no way out of it. And the life-taking water was rising.

16

Doors and Windows

Luckily for me, I hadn't turned off my alarm before falling asleep, because I surely would have if I had thought of it. But I didn't, so it rang out as enthusiastically as ever the next morning. As tempting as it was to silence it (maybe by tossing it out the nearest window) and go right back to sleep, I just couldn't go out like that. I forced myself up, threw on a pair of shorts and made my way to the window to look out on the streets in the dark gray half-light of early morning.

The streets were dead, everyone apparently still snugly tucked into their beds. My eyelids felt heavy, so I ran them through a few blinks to kickstart them to alertness. It didn't much work, but time would do that job well enough if I could summon the patience to let it. Time was good for almost any job in that way.

I must have stood like that, almost hypnotized, for the better part of five minutes. Finally, there was a sign of life below. Slowly, but with evident determination, an early morning jogger appeared near the bottom of the hill, working her way up. I couldn't make out her face particularly well in the dimness, but I could see enough to know she had been at it for a while. She wore baggy gray sweatpants and a baggy gray hooded sweatshirt so formless they seemed to flow together, like running in a giant sleeping bag.

She hadn't been moving very fast in the first place and the hill's incline cut even that meager speed in half. But she kept at it. I kept watching, another thirty seconds maybe, and while she never did hit a higher gear, neither did her resolve waver in the slightest. The hill's will wasn't breaking—and it never would—but, for that morning at least, its challenge couldn't conquer the woman running. I was struck with an almost overwhelming sense of admiration, so much so that I nearly called out to her to say so. I didn't do that though; I just watched. A minute later she crested the hill and vanished below my sightline.

And then it was like that was all I needed to attack my predicament with a newfound tenacity. Extra mental psyching up was no longer needed. I showered, put on a respectable set of clothes, and went right out the door. I was off for the bus stop with a veritable spring in my step, and soon burst through the doors of Manticore.

Hannah was working the phones, looking almost as tired as I had felt the night before. "Eddie?" She was evidently surprised to see me. "Why are you here so early?"

"Call it something in the air," I said. "What's on my agenda today? More recruiting, I'll bet."

The lobby was empty, being that early, so she lowered her voice and spoke in the more confidential tone I'd recognized from our coffee shop rendezvouses. "What's up with you lately? You've been blowing me off every chance you get."

"Was I?" I asked, though of course I knew I had been. I suppose the truth was the attack that night outside the Rabbit still didn't sit too well with me. Maybe her connection to it had been purely coincidental, but then again, maybe not. I didn't have long to decide if I was going to give her that honest answer or not.

My lies were already piling up as it was. Not for the first time, I decided to trust her with the truth.

"You ask me to meet you out there in the darkness and when I do, somebody knocks me out from behind. And then, when I come to, you're nowhere to be found." The empty lobby still afforded me the benefit of candor. "Fact is, that strikes me rather odd."

"Eddie, I'm—"

"Sorry, I know. We've covered that. But that makes me wonder what it is you have to be sorry for. Because if you had no role in it, there'd be no need for apologies, right?"

"A role in it?" Her eyes went cold on me. "I'm sorry that you got hit! Or at least I was. I'm not apologizing for my role in it—whatever that implies—because I didn't *have* a role in it." I leaned on the desk and let the silence linger. "After everything I told you, you're going to throw these suspicions at me."

"Well, hell," I said, "you're telling me you wouldn't have suspicions if you were me? Awfully big coincidence, Hannah."

"I don't know anything about who attacked you or why." We held each other's eyes. There was nothing romantic in it, but, again, I felt I should trust her. "Believe me or don't, Eddie. I don't care."

Talk about your no-win situations. If Hannah was lying and I trusted her, I was the world's biggest sucker. If she was telling the truth and I didn't trust her, its biggest heel. I went where my instincts led me.

"I'm sorry," I said. "For my role in acting like an idiot. Everything's piling up around me. I'd like to tell you more, to tell you everything. Meet me for lunch?"

My apology softened her a little, but only a little. "You can't today. I have you scheduled for your second mind training session with Mr. Deserau at noon."

"So quick? Yesterday you said you were scheduling into October."

She shrugged. "Change of plans. It's not like I decide these things. I tell people to go where and when they tell me to tell them to go."

"It's a little early in the morning for me to follow that sentence," I said, hoping for a smile from her I didn't get. "Noon with Deserau, got it. And Hannah," I added, doubling down on my sucker bet, "I'm sorry."

She nodded. "Talk to you later." She returned to her work and I set off in the direction of the bullpen.

I spent the morning cold-calling people from a list Samantha provided, trying to sell them on the wonders of Manticore. Maybe my heart wasn't in it, or maybe I was just a lousy pitchman, but either way I came up empty. It was just as well, as I didn't need to add coordinating extra interviews to my to-do list that was already bursting at its ragged seams. A few minutes before noon I made my way back down to Room 104.

I figured the old 'sneak in a little early and see what I could see' routine was worth another shot, but this time when I tried it, Deserau was already seated at his desk waiting for me.

"Eddie, early again," he said, sounding not all that

unhappy about it.

"Imagine that." I forced myself to dial up my enthusiasm. "What will I be learning about today?" I asked with childlike fervor.

Deserau returned my energy. "Today we will be discussing memory."

"Ah," I said, letting my artificial sense of awe hang in the air. "Memory."

"Wonderful. Have a seat. Last time we spoke of," he glanced at his notes, "a coffee shop. With green, then yellow, walls."

"Yellow then green."

"Hmm?" He rechecked the notebook. "Ah, right. Yellow, then green. Good memory."

"Maybe you were thinking of bananas," I offered.

Deserau laughed a little and then continued. "The yellow walls you put at fifteen years ago, and the green walls five."

"Three years on the green."

"Isn't that what I... Oh, how silly of me. I have it here, yes. Three years on the green."

One slip-up I could overlook, but two in such quick succession was no coincidence. He was testing my recall. For what purpose, I didn't know.

"In either case, a significant amount of time. A lot of life lived since both, I would hope."

"I should say so," I agreed.

"Here's where the fun begins." I couldn't read the smile that followed. He was going for roguish, I think, but only got as far as slightly insolent. "You said that the walls were green, then yellow—yellow, then green—and as I recall, you were quite certain about both. Fair statement?"

I nodded. "More than fair."

"That is to say, you were sure the walls were yellow fifteen years ago, and equally certain they were green three years ago."

"Right."

"What I would like you to do now, and you'll notice I didn't ask this at the time, is to tell me where this coffee shop is. Or was, at any rate."

I was annoyed at myself all over again for the coffee shop answer. For starters, I hated coffee, which Manticore knew since I told Crossley as much. As far as places I would've been a repeat visitor to, coffee shops would've been somewhere between art museums and voluntary root canals at your less-prestigious schools of dentistry. Secondly, I had maybe inadvertently left a clue as to the link between Hannah and me that had nothing to do with Manticore. And three (not that I needed a three), it was an especially hard thing for me to lie about, given such a dearth of experiences. There were times I could think all right on my feet, but answering that way sure hadn't been one of them.

As to the second point, it was evident I couldn't answer the only coffee shop I really knew, which is where Hannah and I held our treasonous get-togethers. No, I needed to add another lie to the pile that was forever climbing and forever teetering, and then hold up that pile while riding a unicycle with one eye closed. I picked somewhere far from California, nothing he could trace.

"It's in Nebraska," I said. Even that felt too close to Kansas, but you could hardly get more non-descript than Nebraska. "At least it was last I checked."

"What's it called?"

Now I was supposed to name a Nebraskan coffee shop off the top of my head? Deserau was talking laps around me and the worst part was I didn't even think he meant to. Luckily, my reply came more as a reaction than considered response, like a quick-handed tennis player returning serve.

"Irma's," I said without hesitation. No idea where that came from, but if there wasn't a coffee shop somewhere in Nebraska called Irma's, I'd eat my hat. Deserau looked satisfied with that answer as well and didn't press me any further on it.

"Irma's. I like that." He added the name to the log he had running in his notebook." Now follow me on this next part..."

"Sure."

"I want you to imagine we're sitting in Irma's, back fifteen years ago. Can you do that?"

"I think I can handle that, yes." I didn't know where he was going with this, but he had me intrigued.

"Now Eddie, how certain are you—and I want you to really think here—how certain are you that the walls would've been that pale yellow you mentioned?"

It was all I could do not to break out laughing at the absurdity of the thought exercise. Here Deserau was asking me to envision a hypothetical time travel scenario in which the two of us were transported back to a coffee shop in Nebraska that didn't actually exist owned by a dreamed-up person from somewhere deep in my subconscious called Irma. And then, if that wasn't enough, I had to testify as to my certainty regarding the would-be colors of the all-too-fictional walls in the all-too-fictional coffee house.

To say I was unprepared to handle this particular conundrum would be an understatement. On the other hand, it's not like refusal was an option.

"I'm certain," I said. "Yellow walls."

"On a scale of one to a hundred percent, in terms of certainty?"

"A hundred. Well," I caught myself, "I can't really say a

hundred, can I? Let's call it ninety-eight percent."

"That's interesting." The pen was going again. "You said a hundred then backed off it."

"Well, I can't very well be certain, right? It's been fifteen years. Pretty sure, though. Ninety percent."

"And you're how sure the walls were green three years ago?"

If the question made this little sense, I didn't know what kind of hope my answer had at being any kind of coherent. "Ninety-eight percent." What difference did it make?

"Would it surprise you if I could prove to you they were white, both times?"

Would it ever. I was doing my best to play along with whatever this so-called training was supposed to be, but I could hardly play my part when I didn't even know where this was supposed to be leading. "Certainly," I said.

Deserau put the pen down and folded his hands like some deeply-contemplative monk. "Sometimes what we think is a window is actually a door. Other times, what we think is a door," he paused, "is merely a window."

I had never had that experience in my life, either one, but that wasn't going to stop the flattery train. I furrowed my brow and nodded, as though what he said was entirely profound. "That's so true."

"You must learn to let go of what you think you know. Only then will your mind be open enough to receive the universal truths that Mr. Raymond discovered so long ago."

It felt like we were heading towards an ending every bit as anticlimactic and unsatisfying as the previous lesson's. I did what I could to forestall the curtain's descent.

"How long ago?"

"Hmm?" Deserau's head picked up.

"How long ago was it that Mr. Raymond discovered the

universal truths? I would love to hear more about him."

Deserau smiled as broadly as he had since I met him, and that was saying something. I don't think anything could have delighted him more than an open invitation to talk about the otherworldly wisdom of Patrick Raymond.

"I don't know that I could put a year on it," Deserau said, but obviously the nebulousness of that didn't cause him any concern. "He came to the United States from England, you know."

"From near Blackpool, wasn't it?"

"Just outside Blackpool, yes, very good." That smile just kept growing, and I could see how straightforward (and easy) it was going to be to get in my mind trainer's good graces. "He had a very difficult time coming up. His father had been a sailor, see—"

I jumped in to save myself from hearing the same origin story over again. "What I'm wondering is, how did Mr. Raymond go from a penniless young man—brilliant though he was—to the head of an empire such as this. Financially speaking, I mean."

"Excellent question," Deserau said, nodding enthusiastically. "And of course the cash flow is one of the pillars of Manticore's success. Not to its own end, you understand."

"Certainly not."

"But the extended reach it provides us with allows us to affect so many more people."

"To change so many more lives," I added.

"Exactly! So, where was I? Oh right, the money. Well, it's all very circular I suppose, in that mutually beneficial type of way. Because Mr. Raymond—through Manticore—uses all that money to help people."

"But," he was missing my point, either intentionally or

out of ignorance, "where does the money come from?"

"Well, from our clients, of course. You take me, for example. Before I did this, before I found my true calling you might say, I was the head of a lucrative business myself."

"Oh?" I hadn't thought much of who Manticore people were before they became Manticore people."

"Just as importantly, I got out at the right time, but that's another story."

"What was your business?" I asked, genuinely curious.

"It was a rather funny thing, really," Deserau said. "I made my fortune in protestactors."

I wasn't sure I heard him right. "Come again with that last word?"

"Protestactors," Deserau said. "A portmanteau of protestors and actors."

"Protestactors," I tried it on myself. "Doesn't quite roll off the tongue, does it?"

"Oh, you get used to it. I got to the point where it was the unadorned originals that sounded odd to my ear."

"If you say so," I conceded. "So, what's a protestactor?"

"Well, Eddie, the secret to being successful in business is to find yourself an unmet need. That's your market, see?"

That hardly seemed like a secret. "I get that, sure."

"In my case, the foresight was this: Think of how many people have causes."

"I think we all have causes, Mr. Deserau."

"Political causes, I mean. People who have some strategic end they are after, but are perhaps unable to form compelling arguments in their favor. You know, to convince the decision-makers, or people in general, to come to their side. That would be a resource worth selling, don't you think? And therefore, a resource worth buying. We supplied these folks with a group to help influence the court of public opinion."

That still didn't make a whole lot of sense. "People to act as protestors?"

"In a sense, yes. Our employees provided a face to act in accordance with the objectives of our clients. Influencers, you might say."

"Could hardly call them influprotestactors, though."

Deserau laughed politely. "As luck would have it, I sold off the business at its peak and walked away with a most considerable sum of money. Not a month later the whole operation had gone belly up."

"You don't say. And so suddenly. What happened?"

"Rather obvious in retrospect," Deserau said, looking positively forlorn. "Our protestactors decided they wanted to protest for better working conditions for themselves, more pay, that sort of thing. And then—here is where the obvious part comes in—they had become so well-versed at influencing others, they were positively unstoppable. No demand was outside of their capabilities. Such clever slogans, and you just wouldn't believe the effectiveness of their picket signs. The new owners, poor souls, soon lost whatever power they had and were forced to shutter the entire business."

"Protestactors, huh?" I fell into silence, trying to figure out if the story was a parable, a bad joke, or the fever dream of a lunatic. A lot of Manticore stories fell somewhere between the three, it seemed. I endeavored to take this one at face value, though. It was easier than parsing through any alternatives.

I tried to summarize. "So everyone who belongs to Manticore pays for the privilege of belonging to Manticore, is that it?"

"That's one of the benefits, sure. But think, have you ever been on the forefront of a revolution?"

"How did you get to be a..." I didn't know what his job title was exactly, but I took a stab at it. "Well, whatever it is you are here. A mind trainer, I guess they said."

"It was no short process, I can assure you. Earned every bit of the way."

"Naturally."

"But if you want to go all the way back..."

"I do," I insisted.

"Well, I suppose I came into the fold much like yourself. It started with a curiosity, right? The deeper I got into the material, the more fascinated I became. I was more than happy to pay what they asked for the mind training. I know it's slow in the beginning, but you'll see what I mean once you've stuck with it for a while." Seemed awfully presumptuous of him to take it as a given that I would stick with it at all, but that sure seemed to be the way these Manticore people operated.

"Then what happened?"

Deserau's eyes went kind of far away. When he spoke he said, "Then everything else that had seemed so important before—the money, the status symbols, the silly things we chase through life—well they all just subsided, Eddie. Turned gray sort of like, you might say. And I cared for them no longer."

"Manticore replaced them."

"Replaced them, yes, but... what's a better word? Ameliorated them. Like removing a blindfold to see the sunrise."

"At which point you threw full in."

"That I did, as others had before me. Mr. Raymond led the way, as you know, and Mr. Crossley has carried that torch forward, bright and burning. But Manticore is remarkable people all the way down, I promise you."

Now we were getting somewhere. The people beyond the two darlings Raymond and Crossley. Somewhere on that list was Thomas Lawrence, but I was going to have to finesse it out of Deserau. Bring it up without seeming like I was bringing it up.

"Such as?"

"Oh, I've met so many in my time," he said, an answer that could hardly have been any more vague. "Politicians for one. Did you know—" He stopped himself, then leaned in and continued confidentially. "Between you and me Eddie, and this isn't confirmed, but I've heard it said enough to know that—" He caught himself again. "Let's just say a certain Senator Vastillo is very well-acquainted with Manticore, indeed." He touched the side of his nose and gave me a knowing wink. It probably wasn't meant to look ridiculous, but that sure was the way it ended up.

"Never had much use for politicians myself," I said with obvious disinterest. I could tell the Vastillo name drop was supposed to impress me, so I wanted to see what else he would play to that end. "My father used to say one true artist is worth ten of their lot, and I've always felt he was underselling it."

Deserau didn't wait long to return that volley. "We have artists too, Eddie. Wonderful artists."

"Like who?"

"Well, there's Miss Togo for one. Now, she's a fashion designer of high acclaim."

"Fashion designer? Like, she makes shirts or something?" I saturated my voice in disappointment. "Well, that's kind of like an artist, in a sense. I guess."

"Other artists too," he insisted. "Let's see, what is his name, the painter..."

It took everything I had not to jump all over that, but I

didn't want to appear overeager. "Painters," I said casually. "They're artists, yes."

"Yes, yes. One of our members is a wonderful painter. Just wonderful, Eddie. You should see his work."

"Just the one?"

"As far as I know," Deserau admitted.

"Hmm." I sighed then, like one painter was ok, but not something that was going to increase Manticore's esteem in my eyes.

"What was his name, something with an L? I don't recall. But Eddie, I don't mean someone who paints for a hobby on the side. This guy is good. I mean, a real professional."

"He actually makes money from his work then?" I put on a show of brightening up a little.

Deserau seized on that. "Oh my, yes! The money he has brought into Manticore—well, I really shouldn't say anything about that. I just want to be sure you know that we're talking about a major, major talent in the art world."

"Not so major that you remember his name, though."

"I don't know what difference the name makes," he said, and it was a fair point. I didn't want to press the issue too far. Then he said, "I can find out for you, though."

"Don't bother," I said, as though it made no difference to me. In truth, there was no need for Deserau to exert himself. A highly successful painter working for Manticore whose name started with an L. I was comfortably certain this painter was the man I was after.

"So, he's a painter and he contributes to Manticore," I went on. "How fascinating. I'd love to meet him," I added, almost as an afterthought.

An odd look crept quickly over Deserau's face, vanishing as quickly as it had come. I couldn't quite read it. Concern, I thought, but for what reason I couldn't tell. "That's certainly possible," he said, glossing over the contradiction. "You know, we usually schedule these training sessions weeks apart—gives the mind a chance to fully digest the lesson." *Gives Manticore a chance to rack up their membership dues too,* I thought. "But given your enthusiastic interest, I'd like to get you in here for the next one as soon as possible, Eddie. Same time tomorrow?"

That was an unexpected turn but welcome all the same. I needed things to move as fast as they could. "That sounds just fine, Mr. Deserau."

"Excellent, excellent," he said with a big smile. "But for now I see I've taken up too much of your time. I will see you tomorrow then. And remember what I said about the doors and windows."

I promised to do just that, bid him goodbye, and closed the door behind me on my way out. So Deserau knew Thomas Lawrence too, or knew of him anyway. That was something, but it wasn't much. All he had really done was confirm what I already knew. Or at least what I thought I knew. *Doors and windows,* I thought with some amusement. I had played the Lawrence card too clumsily with Crossley before; maybe Deserau was the better approach to unraveling the mystery of the vanished house painter. Meanwhile, Veronica's seven-day deadline blazed in the forefront of my mind, like bright neon through smoke.

I stopped by the lobby, but Hannah wasn't working the front desk. In her place was the young man I'd seen there before. Not like I knew their schedules, anyway. He and I had never gotten acquainted and I didn't much feel like starting now. Besides, as far as I could tell, no one at Manticore knew where I was supposed to be after the mind training, so I took the opportunity to skip out while the skipping was good. To what end I wasn't really sure, but I did know I would be able to think a whole lot more clearly back at my place rather than the soulless black fortress the Cooperative called home.

Except the thinking in my office didn't turn out to be all that productive either. I laid Veronica's dossiers out in front of me again, ran through them in my mind. I tried to suss out connections I may have missed before, or leads not yet explored. Basically, I came up with a whole lot of nothing, slowly. Evening was falling when my phone rang. I grabbed at it eagerly, hoping to hear from someone connected to the case.

If it wasn't the person I least expected, he was at least in the top five.

"This is Curly, from the Silver Rabbit. You remember me?"

"Curly," I said, "of course. How are you?"

"I hear you've been visiting the Rabbit."

"Oh? Who told you that?"

"Never you mind, pal," Curly said almost amiably. "Too many questions, that's your problem."

"Or too few answers."

"But," he paused, then decided to go on, "that doesn't mean you deserved it either."

"Deserved what?" I asked, though I suspected I already knew.

"They didn't need to... Well, listen, you've got Bruce all wrong. And for what it's worth, I think he's got you wrong too."

"I'm listening."

"Friends protect their friends, right?"

"Good ones do."

"Well, that's all that was, that unpleasantness. I thought you deserved to know."

"Me catching a haymaker in the back of the head, you mean."

"Bruce was looking out for me is all. He was out of line, but he meant well. I straightened him out. Won't happen again."

"How do you know all this, Curly? I didn't see you anywhere around the bar."

"That's right you didn't see me. Doesn't mean I didn't see you."

His meaning was clear enough. "It's like that, huh?"

"It's like that."

"So it was Bruce that hit me?" I thought over the facts as he had presented them. "No Curly, I don't think it was. At least that doesn't track with the information a friend gave me. Which means one of you is lying."

"Not lying at all," Curly said. "Wasn't Bruce that done it."

"You just said—"

"What I said was Bruce was looking out for me. What I didn't say was that he was the one who hit you."

A short guy, Hannah had said, unusually short. I knew one man from the Rabbit who matched that description. "The bouncer then. Bruce had him send me a message, quit asking around about customers?"

"I'm not saying as to that one way or the other," Curly said. "I just wanted you to know you don't need to worry anymore. In case it was weighing on your mind."

"Not especially," I said, a lie without any particular motivation.

Curly dismissed that with a snort. "Right. Then that concludes our business here."

"Hold it," I broke in before he could lower the receiver. "What about Warren Hyde? Did you pass along my message?"

There was silence from the other end and I feared I would be hearing the dial tone momentarily. Instead Curly responded, although not entirely on-topic.

"The thing about Bruce is he don't like snoops..." he paused, searching for the right verb, "snooping around his establishment. Bad for business, to say nothing of the soul. Doesn't mean you deserved what you got, but as far as I'm concerned, his reasoning was straight-forward enough."

"Well, Curly, respectfully, if you get me in touch with Warren Hyde, this particular snoop might not have to darken the door of that particular establishment ever again."

"Hmm," Curly said, drawing out the sound. "I'll call you back."

"When can I expect—" I started, but my counterpart was already gone. Moments later the dial tone buzzed in my ear, sounding as dead as I had ever heard it. "—an answer," I finished into the void.

So, I had one mystery solved, that of who knocked me out at the Silver Rabbit. The far larger one remained: What happened to Thomas Lawrence, and where was he now? It was as good a time as any for a drink, and since I was apparently newly welcome at the Rabbit, I thought I'd head down for a couple. The fresh air would do me good and I might even stumble upon some connection to Curly or Warren Hyde. Supposing, of course, that the two men were not actually one and the same.

17

El Silencio

I went through my usual ID routine with the little bouncer who packed a big punch. He didn't show any signs of giving away our recent history together, so I played it ignorant myself. Stepping through the door I saw Bruce at the bar, but not Janie. Story of my life.

I settled onto an open stool and held up a hand like I was waving down a drink. Bruce met my eyes but ignored me, bound off on some other task, so I resolved to wait him out. Eventually he grew impatient with my patience and resigned to engage with me.

"Janie's not here if that's who you're looking for."

"Not at all," I said.

"Come to ask more questions about that Warren Hyde character then, I'll bet. Well, that's not going to get you anywhere either. Best go on your way back to wherever it is you came from."

"I'm done with that Warren Hyde stuff too."

"Then what the hell are you here for?" Bruce's people skills hadn't lost a step since I had last seen him.

"Must be the ambience." I passed him a bill. "Seven and seven. Keep the change."

I didn't think he much felt like getting me a drink, but then he didn't much feel like letting Mr. Jackson get away either. In the end, his financial sense won out and he grabbed the money.

Bruce returned with the drink and slid it across the bar to me. "You're not afraid of getting yourself knocked out again tonight, coming back around here?" He didn't quite manage to suppress his smirk, but I could appreciate the fact that he had tried to.

I shook my head. "I'd sure like to avoid it if I could, don't get me wrong. But afraid? No."

Bruce nodded, an answer he could respect. "You ever find out who did it?"

I shook my head again. "Don't suppose it much matters now. Best to leave it behind us."

"Could be." He pointed at my drink. "You're getting low," he said, although I wasn't. "Next one's on the house."

When he returned with a second drink I took a chance. "I guess this means Curly vouched for me."

Bruce looked me in the eye. "Don't know what you're talking about," he said, but his eyes didn't lie half as well as his mouth. Curly had vouched for me all right, and now he knew that I knew as much.

My point made, I pivoted subjects. "Janie working today?"

"She'll be in later tonight," Bruce said, glad to get off the subject of Curly. "Seems she's taken something of a liking to you. For what reason, I can't imagine."

The addendum was somewhere between a brazen insult

and a gentle rib between friends, but unless my ears deceived me, I thought it closer to the latter. I laughed good-naturedly, though the cut over my eye flared up in pain when I did. There was something to be said for forgiving, but not for forgetting. Two drinks turned into three, the third one also free of charge. Whether this was a result of Bruce's generosity or his guilty conscience, I wasn't sure. But we passed the time cordially and a little over an hour after I arrived, Janie came through the door.

"Stranger!" She bounded over to me with a big smile. "It's nice to see you. Oh, your cut though, it looks awful." She ran her finger along my left side, feeling at the bump that was transitioning to a dull white from its original scarlet. "I'm sorry, that came out wrong."

"No problem. I'm getting used to looking like something that just stumbled out of Dr. Frankenstein's lab."

"Adds some character to your face, that's all," she said by way of recovery.

Bruce rolled his eyes at us, but in a conciliatory kind of way, and departed to the other side of the bar.

"Still looking for your friend?"

"Warren Hyde, yeah. Well, no. That is, yes, but that's not why I came."

"Well, that was clear as mud. You haven't found him then?"

"No," I said. "But soon it won't matter."

"How's that?"

I debated how to answer her question. I had let Hannah in on the details of my case a while back at the coffee shop and that hadn't accomplished much. Not yet, anyway. I wasn't sure what good it would do spilling my story to Janie. Which made what came out of my mouth next all the more surprising, even to me.

"I have seven days," I said, and the dam broke from there. "No, it's six now. If I don't solve the case I'm on—the one I think Warren Hyde might be the key to, or some major part of at least—I'm cut off. No more money, no more chances, no more anything. To say nothing of losing the opportunity to make a name for myself. How often do you think something like that comes around in my business? This is the one shot, Janie. Fail this and my future as a private investigator is going to be limited to hunting down poodles who snuck out the doggie door for their owners who are a hundred times richer than I'll ever be. The poodles will probably be more financially stable too. It's no kind of life, Janie. Six days."

"You need to find Warren Hyde in six days? Maybe I can help. I mean, I don't know where he is, but—"

"No, not Warren. A man by the name of Thomas Lawrence. A house painter." I left out the unabridged intricacies of his painting career.

"And you think Warren knows where this Thomas Lawrence is?"

"Not really," I said, "especially with the luck I've had lately. But he's connected, and I think he would at least have some information I could use. Which right now would be a life preserver in the tempest." My next question I asked hoping against hope. "Do you know Warren Hyde, Janie?"

She shook her head. "I had never heard of him before you showed up. Sorry, Eddie."

I swirled what little liquid was left in my glass. "How about Curly?"

"Well, I at least know who you mean there. But do I *know* him? I wouldn't say that, no. Haven't seen him around here for quite a while, in fact."

"Unusual?"

"I'd say so. Any connection, you think? To your case?"

"Seems like a big coincidence if not, but what do I know?" My glass was empty now.

"Janie," Bruce called from the other side of the bar, "you planning on doing any work tonight?"

"Sure thing, Brucie," she called back. "Good luck, Eddie. I hope you crack your case, I really do." She grabbed a pen and scribbled on a napkin, sliding it across the bar to me. "Give me a call if I can help at all, ok?"

I tore off a blank section of the napkin and gave her my number back. "I appreciate that, Janie. And you give me a call if Curly shows up again, ok? Or, somehow, Warren Hyde."

"You got it." She kissed two of her fingers and placed them gently up next to my cut. "Take care of yourself, Eddie."

"Someone's got to," I agreed. I walked out of the Silver Rabbit and into the black of the night.

The next morning I returned to Manticore with all the reluctance of a cat to bathwater. My head still hurt, partly from the previous night's whiskey and partly from the scar on my face that was starting to feel like the mark of Cain. When I came in through the doors I saw Hannah working the front desk, and that felt like a small grace. She was on the phone, but I hung around to see if we might pass a word or two.

I stood there with my head throbbing as her conversation wore on. Eventually she said, "One moment, please" into the phone and turned her attention to me. "Lunch?"

"Sure," I said, and she returned to her call.

I wandered a bit before making my way over to the

bullpen. Samantha was still there, stalking up and down the rows like a jungle cat. The building seemed pretty dead otherwise, but then it was still early. I tried to slide into one of the desks unseen, but nimble as I was, I was no match for Manticore's sentinel in a pencil skirt.

"Eddie," she snapped just as I sat down in my chair, "I need to speak with you." I gave her a head raise in acknowledgement, put on a brave face, and walked over to where she was pacing.

"What can I do for you, Miss Jones?"

"How did your meeting go with Mr. Crossley? The three names you gave him."

"Oh, just fine. We've got this guy, Billy Shakes. 'Looks very promising,' Mr. Crossley said. Could be a real asset to the Cooperative here."

My answer didn't have much of an effect on her disposition one way or the other. "And what of the other two?"

"Well, there was..." Put on the spot like that, I couldn't recall what name I had used for Leonard. I didn't even want to hazard a guess. "There was another gentleman, an older gentleman. Mr. Crossley seemed less optimistic about him."

"How old?"

"Hmm..." I truly didn't know. "In his seventies, I suppose."

"And you thought this soon-to-be octogenarian would be a valuable addition to our team." She said that like it was on par with thinking the moon was made of cheese.

"Worth a shot," I said. "That's what the interviews are for, right?"

She ignored my question. "What of the third name?"

"Long story short, that one didn't work out either. But I found a promising lead in my first week. I feel that's gotta be worth something."

Her eyes remained indifferent. "Well, you're still here. But we'll need another three names by this time next week. And, so you know, one out of three is a lousy conversion rate. This isn't Major League Baseball, Eddie."

"Guess I'd better get on it then." I departed our conversation before she could change her mind and took up my place at one of the bullpen desks. It was an unproductive morning at best. Sure, I made a few calls, but without any verve, and hours later I still had nothing to show for it. I mostly just sat around trying to ignore the pounding in my head and waiting for noon to come around so I could make my return to the coffee shop.

I used our walk to apologize for my overly-contentious attitude during our last couple conversations, and Hannah said she could have handled things better too. We congratulated each other on our magnanimity and resealed the working partnership with a handshake that turned into a hug. It lifted my spirits to have the ugliness behind us, hopefully for good.

"Any updates?" Hannah asked after we had settled into our usual spots.

I still hadn't decided how much I should trust her. Janie's implied warning that Hannah, too, could be just one more part of the Manticore subterfuge had not left my mind. But if I didn't solve the case for Veronica in about five days, I would be sunk anyway. In the end, I decided there was little risk in telling Hannah all I knew. Hopefully she was on the level, and hopefully she would have some insights to share with me too.

"So, here's what I know. Thomas Lawrence is a painter,

immensely talented though not particularly renowned. Furthermore, he is a fanatical Manticore adherent, to the extent that he was willing to nearly bankrupt himself and his wife to give his money over to the Cooperative. Lawrence recently went missing, and his wife is looking for him, which is how yours truly got involved in this whole circus. We can assume, I hope, that Lawrence's sizable donations have dried up as well, although which came first—his disappearance or the money getting cut off—I'm not sure."

"I follow."

"I also know that Lawrence has a close associate by the name of Warren Hyde, although the exact nature of their relationship remains unclear. As with Lawrence, I haven't been able to track down Hyde, but I met a man who knows him. This man calls himself Curly, and his real name is unknown to me. It is my suspicion, and you'll note we have left the shores of facts and are drifting into the open water of suspicions here, is that Curly could be Warren Hyde."

"What makes you say that?" Hannah asked.

"Well, you'll remember Mrs. Lawrence gave me a photo of Hyde at our first meeting. It's awfully low-resolution and I can't say for sure, but there seems to me a resemblance between that photo and this Curly from the Silver Rabbit. The man in the photo is mostly clean-shaven with wild, you might even say curly, hair. The man from the Rabbit is bald with a goatee. If a fellow were to disguise himself, that would be precisely the smart way to go about it, don't you think?"

Hannah's eyes were warm and thoughtful. "If that's the case, why is Hyde in disguise?"

"To prevent being found, I assume."

"By whom? And if so, why not just leave town?"

"These were my questions exactly. Because there is something keeping him here."

"Something like what?"

"It must be related to Thomas Lawrence, right? As for who he's hiding out from, who do you think?"

"Manticore."

"They seem like the most likely suspect of the players, don't they?"

Hannah took a small sip of her coffee, more like a formality than anything else. "So maybe it's like Caroline. Maybe this Thomas Lawrence decided he had enough of Manticore, except they weren't so eager to let him go."

"I don't think so," I said. "The way his wife talks, Lawrence would have died before he turned his back on that screwy cult."

"Maybe he did," Hannah said delicately. "Maybe he's already dead, Eddie."

"The thought's crossed my mind," I agreed. "More than once. Meanwhile, Mrs. Lawrence has given me till Monday to solve this thing. If I don't, I'm fired, and there goes my shot at my big break. If that happens, I doubt I'll ever find out what happened here."

"That leaves you five days?"

"Five including today. There's one more thing." I went on to tell her about Deserau, how much more information he was willing to offer up than Crossley, with the exception of the filing cabinet he had been so protective of me snooping through.

"Deserau is pretty far up the ladder," Hannah said. "It's good that he's taken a liking to you. We can use that."

"I like that word, 'we.' I feel like I've been working this thing on an island lately. How can you help?"

She thought my question over. "I don't have anything much to share, Eddie."

"That's a shame," I said, about as charitable a rejoinder

as I could manage.

"But wait. You said Deserau really didn't want you going through the membership files in the cabinets, right? I'll bet those have information beyond what I have access to. The full truths instead of the sanitized versions."

"That was my impression, yes."

"What if I can help you get into those files?"

"That would be huge," I said. "But I don't see how. I lucked into an unlocked room the first time and Deserau went apoplectic when he saw I had opened the cabinet. He won't make that mistake again. In fact, I'll bet the cabinets themselves are locked up now too."

"There's a clock in Room 104, right? What time is your training session?"

"There is, yeah. We start at one o'clock. In fact," I took a quick look at my watch, "you and I need to be getting back."

We tossed our cups into the garbage and headed for the door together. "Get Deserau to open the cabinets at exactly fifteen minutes after one," Hannah said. "I have an idea for how I can get you a couple minutes alone in the room."

"I don't know how I'm supposed to get into the cabinets, but I'll figure something out, sure. All I need to look at is Lawrence's file, a couple minutes should be plenty."

"Two files," Hannah said as we walked through the city streets back towards Manticore. "Lawrence's and Caroline's."

"Two files, ok." I was more than a little curious to see what Caroline's file said myself. "But I'll need to know her last name. That's how the files are alphabetized."

My accomplice was silent for a while, and I let the sounds of the wind and traffic soundtrack our walk without further prompting.

Finally, she said, "Her last name, that is, our last name, is Natal." She added, "I sure hope I can trust you, Eddie."

I knocked on the door and found Mr. Deserau waiting for me when I went in. He wore his usual navy blue sweater vest to go along with a finely-pressed shirt and slacks, plus the omnipresent smile that must have been doing a number on his facial muscles over time. For my part, I had at least upgraded to a button up shirt, wrinkled though it may have been, and jeans that didn't have any holes in them anyway.

"Come on in, Eddie, great to see you, great to see you." He spoke at a rapid fire clip, hyper-caffeinated and overly-chipper to my aching head. I did my best to match his enthusiasm, as that had proved to be the most effective way of extracting information from this particular cog in the Manticore machine.

"Great to be here," I returned. "Always a great day to be at Manticore, hey Mr. Deserau?"

His smile got even bigger. "'Always a great day to be at Manticore.' I love it, Eddie! I should touch base with marketing on that. I think you've really got something there!"

"What are we learning about today?" I asked as though there could be no greater aspiration in the world.

"The power," Deserau said, "of..." He abandoned his sentence and stared at me, a vacuous look I wasn't sure how to take.

I stayed quiet, trying to mirror his expression. I looked at him and he looked at me and mostly we just went on like that for quite some time. I couldn't tell whether this was a test or a battle of wills or what, but after anywhere from five to ten minutes I was invested enough that losing didn't feel like an option.

"...silence," Deserau finally finished.

"The Spanish call it el silencio." That was an odd thing for me to say, but I thought this particular mind game might have warped my sense of normalcy, temporarily at least. I stole a glance at the clock. Twelve minutes after one.

"We discussed a painter last time," I said, "another shining exemplar of Manticore's excellence. Were you speaking of Trevor Lartas by chance?"

"Lartas." Deserau stumbled over the word. "No, no. Close to that, though. You know, I meant to look that up for you, I really did."

Thirteen minutes after one by the clock. "Can you look it up now?"

"I have the information back in my office. I'd be glad to get it for you this afternoon if you'd really like, although I don't—"

"Hmm," I cut him off, as I didn't like where that sentence was probably leading. I wanted to shout at him about the cabinets that were right there in the room with us, but looking overeager would only raise his suspicions, and I couldn't have that either. Instead I relied on the power of silence, fixing my eyes on the cabinets and letting Deserau make the connection himself. He met my eyes, then turned to see where I was looking. The clock read fourteen minutes after one.

"Ah, what am I saying, my office? Do me a favor Eddie, turn around, will you?" I did as he asked and heard the turning of a key, followed by one of the cabinet's drawers sliding open. "I could swear it started with an L." I heard him flipping through folders. "What was the name, what was the name..."

I was still turned around when I heard Hannah throw the door open. "Mr. Deserau, come quick," she pleaded, "there's an intruder in the lobby!"

I spun back around, counting on the unexpected chaos to spare me the reprimand. Deserau's head swung between the open files and Hannah's put-on panic. He decided the cabinet took higher priority and pushed it closed with his hand. But Hannah was on him then, grabbing him by the opposite arm and pulling him towards the open door before he could turn his attention to the key.

"Hurry, I think he's dangerous!"

"Eddie," Deserau ordered, "stay exactly where you are, I will be back as soon as I can." With that he rushed out the door after Hannah.

I wasted no time in getting up to close the door behind them. Hannah's intruder idea was a good one, and she sold it beautifully. She had promised me a couple minutes to myself, but I had a hard time seeing how she was going to get a non-existent trespasser to last that long. Oh well, that part wasn't my problem. I soon had the cabinet drawer open and pulled Thomas Lawrence's file up out of the pile.

The folder's contents were a single page. Much of it I already knew from what Veronica had provided me, the biographical details. Beyond that, there were some key dates and dollar amounts next to them. Donations, I gathered. The numbers were sure bigger than any I was used to seeing. Most significantly, written across the top in neat red letters, it said, "Severed Compound." I knew those words (both of them, even) but not what they meant in conjunction with each other. I felt my clock ticking down, so I replaced Lawrence's file and flipped back to the N's.

"Natal, Caroline." Her file was one page as well, and the first thing I noticed was the same red designation across the top. "Severed Compound." I scanned the rest as quickly as I could and saw she had a list of donations too, her numbers far more modest than Lawrence's. It seemed I heard footsteps from the hall, and my visions of Deserau bursting back into the room grew stronger with each passing second. I saw nothing else to be gleaned from Caroline's file, so I replaced it and pushed the door shut, hurrying back over to my seat.

I made it by maybe two seconds. A breath later Deserau was back. "False alarm," he said, rushing back into the room. "I'm sorry Eddie, but I think that's enough excitement for today. Let's get you back in here soon though, ok? Remember, the power of..."

"Silence," I said, forgoing the ten-minute staredown this time.

Hannah smiled at me when I came back through the lobby, subtly though, not in a way that anyone would've suspected anything was afoot. She really had a beautiful smile, and it seemed to me more beautiful as of late.

"Dinner?" I asked quietly as I passed her desk.

"Where?"

"Call me when you get off," I said. "I trust you won't have any trouble finding the number."

18

SevCom

We decided to meet at some vaguely-Italian family friendly restaurant a good distance from Manticore. I wasn't aware what the recommended attire was so I shot squarely for the middle and went with a black polo over a nice pair of jeans. Can't ever go too wrong with a black polo over a nice pair of jeans.

"Eddie," Hannah said, waving me down as I stepped into the restaurant. She looked nice in a silvery blouse-ish thing that I'm sure had some fancier name I was never going to bother to learn. It felt strange having her call me by the fake name, as I did the same to her. I considered broaching the subject, but on the other hand, what difference did it really make? I had been thinking of her as Hannah long enough that pivoting to anything else was going to feel like a wanting sobriquet. A rose by any other name...

"Been here long?" I asked, but there was no future in that line.

"How did it go with the files?"

"Right to business then, ok."

A waiter poked his nose into our conversation in that polite sort of way they do and asked if we were ready to order. We said we were and requested a couple forgettable pasta type dishes.

"I found both the files," I started. "Didn't have time to go over them with the depth I would've liked. Thank you for getting me any time at all, by the way. I wouldn't have thought of that."

She smiled. "Don't mention it. Kind of fun actually."

"I take it there was no intruder?"

"No. Took us a while to verify that, though."

"An awfully convenient inconvenience."

"The files," she prompted again.

"Right. So, there was one similarity that jumped out at me. Have you heard the phrase Severed Compound?"

"Severed Compound," she repeated. I could read nothing in her tone that showed any sign of recognition. "I don't think so."

"Well, it sure seemed important. Big red letters across Caroline's sheet. Thomas Lawrence's too."

"Was it on any of the others?"

"I don't know," I admitted. "Didn't have the time to check any others." Didn't have the foresight to think of checking our names against a control either, if I was being honest. But I wasn't, about that part anyway, so I kept my mouth shut.

"Severed," she said, dwelling on each syllable. "That's such an out of place word, isn't it?"

"Practically archaic."

"Sever... Sev..." A light went on in her eyes and she reached across the table and grabbed my hand, hard.

"SevCom!"

I stared at her blankly.

"I manage Crossley's schedule, remember? Every Thursday at five o'clock, Crossley goes to SevCom. I never knew what it was, I don't know what a lot of that stuff is, but Severed Compound! It has to be, right?"

"Sure seems like it."

"So, Caroline and Thomas are being held at this SevCom?" Hannah's excitement at the would-be revelation had her as animated as I had ever seen her.

I wasn't as positive. "Well, maybe. All we know for sure is their paperwork said Severed Compound on it."

"But that's what that has to mean, right?" Only then she let go of my hand. "Why else would it say that?"

"You're probably right," I assured her. "This whole situation just has me especially careful about jumping to conclusions. Things too often being not what they appear and all. But your explanation is the most likely one, and that has to count for something."

The waiter returned with our food and set the plates onto the table. "Careful, they're hot," he said with a friendly flair. "Enjoy!"

Neither of us paid much attention to whatever the pasta was, both deciding our latest conversation topic was far more interesting. I spoke first. "Any idea what it is, this SevCom?"

"A separate Manticore site, it must be. Severed, like separated. And then the compound, I don't know. Sounds like a nicer word for prison, doesn't it?"

"It does. When Crossley goes to these weekly meetings, can I assume he has to travel somewhere?"

Hannah started in on her dish in a perfunctory sort of way and I followed suit. "Yes, he leaves the office and," she paused, stopping to think, "goes somewhere by car, I guess.

Definitely off site though, yes." Her green eyes shone with the bright light again. "Are you thinking what I'm thinking?"

"I've never understood that question," I admitted. "I can only give you a yes or no if I know what you're thinking, which I don't. And you can only interpret that yes or no if you know what I'm thinking, which you don't. Unless we both already know what the other is thinking, in which case there's no need for the question at all." My head was starting to hurt again.

"You think too much, Eddie. Or maybe not enough," she added and smiled again. "What I'm thinking is this: We should follow him. Follow Crossley to SevCom. Today is Wednesday, which means they'll be meeting tomorrow. We can leave straight from work. Do you have a car?"

"I've never needed one." I thought on it. "I can get one, though."

"If you say so."

I nodded. "Seems like a solid plan, so far. Have you thought about what we'll do when we get there?"

"Well, then we follow him inside, and we get our people out of there. I can save my sister and you can bring your guy back home to his wife. Happily ever after."

I pushed a meatball around my plate aimlessly. "I don't think so, Hannah. I think that would be walking right into the lion's jaws. A lion with dragon wings, even."

"Then what do you propose?"

"To make tomorrow night a recon mission. All we need to do for now is find out where the place is. Maybe your FBI friends could help us from there."

"I never said I had FBI friends, Eddie."

"Well, not in those words as such, no. Anyway, I'd rather revisit this compound when we know Crossley is otherwise occupied."

"I've waited so long," she said, hesitant to accept putting off her sisterly reunion any further than she had to. "And now we're so close."

"That's right we're close. Just need to wait a little longer. I've got this deadline hanging over my head too, remember. But going in tomorrow isn't the smart play."

"The day after then?"

"Seems that would be fine," I agreed. "Just fine."

The next day I woke up early, though not by design. The excitement of the day ahead must have revved up my internal clock because I was out of bed by six. Manticore was expecting me to come in at my usual eight a.m. start, but I knew I'd go stir-crazy if I had to suffer through that routine until five in the afternoon. One benefit of Veronica Lawrence's looming deadline was that I didn't have to keep up the Manticore charade much longer.

I sleepwalked through the morning, then handed Samantha another story about an off-site recruiting appointment around lunchtime. The severe look I got in return told me she probably didn't buy it, but she also wasn't willing to stand in the way of Crossley's recruitment drives, even the likely-fictional ones. A couple more days and the Cooperative nightmare would be behind me. Whether or not a career as a private eye would be there to take its place was still an open question.

There were a few potential diversions located within walking distance of the Manticore building. My destination was the art museum. There was the professional angle, given how Thomas Lawrence had made his money lately, but I had to admit a newfound personal interest as well. For the first time in my life, I wanted to go look at some paintings.

*　　*　　*

The museum itself was impressive enough, architecturally-speaking. Its ceilings were high, with a circular balcony on the second floor overlooking the main entrance. Skylights throughout saturated the place in pleasant, natural lighting and, sparsely populated with visitors as it was, the overall atmosphere made for somewhere I wouldn't mind spending several hours. A sort of reverse Manticore, in that respect.

I wandered along, none of the art ever quite catching my eye. Sculptures in one room, inscrutable modern pieces in another. Finally, I found a room full of paintings, many of them dating back a hundred years or more. Others were far newer, and of course many in between, but I was happy to take them all in. Lots of portraits of people who were long dead but, because of those paintings, not forgotten. There was a certain nobility in that, I thought. Others were of battlefields or nature, all intricately drawn and colored. They made my sketches look frightfully amateurish.

I paused in front of a lake and mountain scene, the turquoise water and varying shades of green trees giving way to purple-gray mountains. The first hints of an orange sun peaked out just over the tops of those mountains. I moved closer, picking out the individual brushstrokes that formed the sunrise, and noticed shades of yellow and green in the haze as well. I leaned in even closer when a voice cried out with some urgency behind me.

"Sir! Excuse me sir, you must not touch the paintings!"

I froze where I was and realized I had leaned in awfully close without fully realizing it. My nose was practically on the canvas.

"Sorry," I said, taking a step backwards. "This is really something, isn't it?"

"Quite so." The newcomer was an older woman, well-dressed in a black-and-white checkered jacket with a stylish hat and scarf to match. "Do you know her work?"

"Just this one. She's done others?"

"Yes. Quite a lot, yes. If you're drawn to nature scenes," she said, leading me to another painting, "I imagine these would be to your liking as well." She showed me a couple others in a similar vein, but none hit me quite like that first one.

"Very nice," I said.

"But of course art need not limit itself to nature or portraiture," she said, bringing me into another room. "Now you take this work, for example: *O Verdant Life, Unchanging.*" She pointed towards a square canvas, roughly four feet to a side, that had been painted solid green. "This is the work of a young up and coming artist from Salinas. Currently on loan from a collector who recently purchased it for three-hundred thousand dollars."

"Three-hundred thousand, huh?" The number sounded even more unbelievable the second time around. "For its... greenness, I guess?"

She laughed demurely. "Think of what the artist is expressing with that greenness, as you put it. About life, about love, and yes, even about death." I didn't know what the artist was expressing at all, and I had a feeling she didn't either, but I was trying to keep it respectful.

"Heck, I could've painted that," I said, not all that respectfully.

"Ah, but you didn't."

"If I do, will you buy it for three-hundred thousand dollars, or will this collector? My big square can be blue. *O Marine Ocean, Limitless.*"

"You're welcome to try." Her tone told me my ocean idea was dead in the water.

"Now this," I said, moving towards a painting of a village overlooking a wide blue bay, "this seems like it took some talent."

"Mm-hmm, you have a good eye. This is a Cézanne."

I had never heard the name in my life. "*The* Cézanne?"

She nodded vigorously. "One of our most valuable pieces. Currently on loan from the Metropolitan Museum of Art in New York."

I studied the blue water and the beige houses. This one had mountains too, but no sunrise. "I like that first one better," I announced. "This is good too though," I added so as to not give offense.

I thanked the woman for her time and insight, then did some more wandering. Before I knew it, it was time to head back to Manticore and get a start on trailing Crossley on his weekly trip to SevCom. Everything depended on this mission going well. That went for Thomas, Veronica, Hannah, Caroline, and, not least of all, me. These were high stakes indeed.

I made it to the Manticore lobby by quarter to five. Not that I expected Crossley to stray from the precision of his weekly schedule, because he didn't strike me as that type of guy. Rather, I could see myself botching the timing and showing up a couple minutes late if I tried to make it for five o'clock sharp. Because I was exactly that type of guy. I sat in one of the fancy black chairs, swirling my foot in lazy circles in front of me. Hannah went through her usual duties without paying me any mind.

A dark green Dodge Dart that had seen better days was parked outside the Manticore headquarters, a few cars back from the entrance. At least it had been there last I checked.

The urge to get up and make sure it was still there hit me, but I trusted that if Tony said it would be there for five, it would be there. He had jumped at the idea of pulling another one over on Manticore, but that didn't mean he wasn't savvy enough to secure some cash for his troubles too. An exemplary use of Veronica Lawrence's money as far as I was concerned.

Crossley came walking briskly through the lobby a couple minutes before five. He waved to Hannah but passed me without taking notice, his eyes trained on the exit. I followed him outside, leaving a safe distance between us. Hannah trailed me the same way. Had anyone suspected anything, the three of us exiting in succession might have raised an alarm, but only if they had suspicions in the first place.

Crossley got into the backseat of a pristine black Mercedes sedan. I made my way back to where Tony was waiting and hopped in the passenger seat.

"Eddie London," he said and winked at me for no one's benefit other than maybe his own.

"And his righteous companion Billy Shakes," I said, laughing a little in spite of myself. "Thanks again for this, Tony."

"Billy," he said. "You're getting sloppy."

"Oh, I don't know. That implies there once existed a time when I wasn't sloppy."

Hannah came up to my passenger side and leaned her head into the car. "Ready?" she asked.

"All set," I said. "Not sure how long this'll take, Billy, but we'll return the car here when we're done. I'll give you a call when you can pick it back up."

"She's all yours," Tony said, and handed me the keys.

"Not me," I shook my head. "She'll be driving."

"What?" the other two exclaimed in unison.

"I've never done this before."

"Tailed a car?" Hannah asked.

"Driven a car."

There was a half-second where I could feel both of them looking at me, trying to ascertain whether I was joking. I wasn't.

"What?" they both said again, even louder than the first time.

"Don't give me that look," I said, suddenly defending myself against a two-front war. "When did I ever say I knew how to drive?"

They were talking over each other then, Hannah saying that following Crossley was my idea and Tony asking why the hell I would ask to borrow his car if I couldn't even drive the damn thing.

"Hannah can drive," I said, hoping that would assuage both their protests at once. "Now hurry up, Crossley's car is pulling out."

"I've never met this person in my life," Tony said. "I'm not handing my car over to some lady."

Hannah leaned further into the car. "Excuse me?"

"She could be a total nut job!"

"Tony—Billy, that's idiotic. She's a government agent."

"About that—" Hannah said.

"We don't have time for this." Crossley's ride was beginning to blend into the passing traffic. "He won't go back to SevCom again until next week, by which time we'll have missed Veronica's deadline." The black car was now on the edge of disappearing. "Hannah, get in here. Tony, give her the damn keys!"

But he didn't do that. Instead, he shoved a key into the ignition and turned the engine over himself. "Hop in the back, lady. I'll catch that car." With no time left to argue,

Hannah did as he said.

The wheels spun like cyclones and the Dart jolted forward gracelessly, sending Hannah and me jostling back into our seats. The black Mercedes already had a headstart on us and I could barely track it as it glided through the vehicles ahead. Tony's lead foot was up to the challenge. A minute later Crossley's ride was comfortably in view. Hannah and I had our seatbelts secured by then, though Tony was content to weave through the rush hour traffic without one.

"My price just doubled, by the way." He slugged me in the shoulder and laughed happily.

"I guess I'm not in much of a position to negotiate," I said as Tony spotted an opening in the left lane and slammed down on the accelerator. "Let's make sure it's worth it. How are you holding up?" I asked our backseat companion.

"Wishing I'd stocked up on Dramamine," she answered.

"Not much longer I hope," I said, but a hope is all it was. For all any of us knew, SevCom could have been another hour out, maybe more. As I said that, Tony hammered the gas again and jumped in front of the Mercedes.

"What are you doing, Billy?" I had alternated enough between calling him Tony and Billy by then, Hannah could hardly have missed the contradiction. I decided to stick with Billy and hope for the best. "If he turns off the freeway behind us, we'll lose him."

"Use your brain, Eddie. We're between Bay City and Vaquero. Where's he going to go in the next three miles? I'll fall back by the time we get anywhere he might turn off."

"Makes sense," Hannah agreed. "It'll seem less like we're following them if we're sometimes ahead of them."

"Ok, ok. Just remember, this is the only shot I have at this thing before my deadline is up."

"You worry too much," Tony said. "You should listen to this lady." He caught himself. "This woman, I mean." I stole a glance at Hannah in the mirror and she seemed satisfied with Tony's attempt at what was going to have to pass as chivalry.

"She works for the FBI or something, you know."

"You said that," Hannah said, "not me."

"Well, the CIA then, or some government…" The doubt in her face made me trail off.

"That may have been a cover story," she admitted. "Back before I was sure I could trust you. The truth is Eddie, I'm just me. No secretive operation, no government backing, just me."

"Huh." My surprise lingered a little, but I banished it. "Well, I'd say that's more than enough."

"How charming." She smiled. "Besides, I think we're in good shape. Your friend here seems to know what he's doing."

"Not my first rodeo," Tony beamed. "Not by a long shot." No sooner had he said it then he fell back and let the Mercedes pass us by two lanes to our right. At least I could be reasonably confident Crossley hadn't picked up on our following him yet.

"What's the plan when we find this place?"

"Billy, is it?" Hannah's question was rhetorical and sly. "Today's strictly recon. Eddie doesn't want to try to force our way in as long as Crossley is there. Which is smart."

"Nah, I say we bust in there," Tony said. "They won't see that coming, hey?"

"We're just finding the place tonight," I told him, "scope it out a bit if we can. Then, when we know its location and defenses, we can figure out the best approach and come back tomorrow to get Thomas and Caroline out of there."

"I guess you'll be needing a driver again then." Tony looked at me and smiled.

"We'll see. Keep your eyes on the road."

I tried to figure out how long we had been driving for. I guessed it was better than an hour, and my watch agreed. Night was still a ways off, but darkness was threatening, some combination of encroaching dusk and storm clouds. Tony switched on the headlights, which made the grayness feel even darker. If the black Mercedes carried on like this much longer, I feared we would have to contend with it slipping away and fading into the cloak of a rainy night.

"Well, they did say this compound was severed from the headquarters." Hannah had apparently read my mind. "Can't be much longer though now, right?"

"There he goes." It seemed Tony's declaration was out of his mouth even before Crossley's car signaled a right turn and drifted towards an exit. The darkening sky and the mundanity of the tail job had apparently conspired to overtake our driver, even briefly, and we were badly out of position to follow. "Ah, damn. Hang on," Tony said, still unbelted in the driver's seat.

We didn't have the chance to before he peeled the tires and spun the steering wheel to the right in one smooth motion. The green Dart jerked into the lane immediately to our right and then into another lane past that. There was a bit of daylight between the other cars but it left a vanishingly small room for error. I reflexively tightened my muscles and braced for impact. All I got was the scream of horns and a screech of brakes as we glided through the lanes without meeting any resistance.

"Easy, Tony!"

"Well, that was inconspicuous," Hannah said from the backseat.

Up ahead, the Mercedes was already progressing past the off-ramp and receding into the distance. "They're far enough ahead of us that I doubt they noticed that." Whether that was meant to reassure Hannah or myself, I wasn't sure. Call it a little of both.

"You two worry too much," Tony said, deciding Hannah apparently was now guilty of the same fault he had accused me of earlier in the trip. He switched on the windshield wipers as fat drops of rain started to smack against the windshield. "They didn't see nothing."

By all appearances he was right. We fell in behind our target, still keeping a healthy distance between us, and they seemed none the wiser as to our presence or intent. We followed like that for a number of blocks as our surroundings steadily turned increasingly rural.

"Where the heck are we?" Hannah asked.

"Looks like farmland," I wagered, surveying the fields of long, tall grasses.

"Lots of farmland out this way," Tony confirmed. "Don't have to worry about running into traffic out here, hey?"

"A lot harder to blend into the crowd though too." That tradeoff hardly seemed worth it. "Don't get too close, Billy."

"What, you want me to lose them?"

We had gone from an urban freeway to suburban streets to what was rapidly approaching single track dirt roads. "Look around you," I said. "How do you think they're going to react to a car following them down a road like this?"

"Gunshots," Hannah said gravely.

"Well, that's just great." I was equal parts frustrated and disappointed, with maybe a slight edge to frustrated. "This was supposed to be the simple part of the plan." We all stayed quiet a while and listened to the sound of the wheels and the rain hitting the roof of the car. "Maybe this rain will make our job easier."

"How do you figure?" Hannah asked.

"They won't spot us if we're following the tracks instead of the car. We can stay out of sight, see which path has fresh track marks."

"In the dark like this?" Tony laughed. "You watch too many movies."

"I still don't like the idea of following them too closely."

We passed a Dead End sign and one that read No Exit a short time later.

"No forks in the road yet," Hannah observed. "If those signs are right, there won't be one coming up either."

"Well, that's something." The tall grasses gave way to trees. I watched them pass by at moderate speed, as Tony had slowed down to match the terrain change. Ahead I spotted a small clearing on the right side of the road.

"Crossley ever spend the night at SevCom?" I asked Hannah.

"No. Or if he does, he's always back in the office first thing in the morning the next day."

"With how long we've been driving, that seems like a safe no," I said. "Pull over, Billy."

"You don't want me to do that. We'll lose them."

"On a dead end road?" Hannah said.

"If you want to get paid for tonight, you'll pull over," I repeated. "Up here on the right, reverse in, and kill the lights."

Tony stopped the car and shot me a sideways look. It took a beat but eventually he made the connection. "Ah, I see, Eddie. I see."

He did as I asked and tucked the car away off the sight line of the road. The rain picked up and started hammering the Dart. Tony shut off the engine and the three of us sat without talking.

"They'll have to come back out this way." I knew by then my compatriots had already figured out my plan, but it felt good to verbalize it anyway. "And when they do, we'll head back the way they came. When we're good and unexpected."

Hannah spoke up from the back. "Are you sure about this?"

I wasn't sure at all. "Sure I'm sure," I said.

The night was young, as they say, and we sat in the cramped discomfort of the car, mostly silent, on into the lengthening hours. We couldn't step outside our claustrophobia-inducing quarters for even a brief respite, because the downpour didn't once flinch. Hannah made the best of her backseat apartment and stretched out across the bench seats, while Tony looked right at home in the driver's seat. Which left just me, shifting uncomfortably against the leather seat for what couldn't have been less than four hours. I tried striking up a conversation every now and again (mostly mundanities about the weather), but the other two weren't in a conversing mood.

Finally, after such a long time that I couldn't swear it wasn't some kind of mirage, headlights appeared far off to my right. I could see them only faintly through the rain, but as they got closer, there could be no mistake. That was Crossley's car all right, and it splashed past us on its way back towards civilization.

"The perfect hiding spot," I announced proudly. Tony reached for his keys but I held off his hand. "Not yet. Let them pass out of the range of hearing."

"You kidding me, Eddie? They ain't going to hear anything through this rain," Tony protested.

"He's right." Hannah rose back up to a seated position. "We've come too far to mess it up now."

Tony didn't like it but consented to the will of democracy. "One more minute will be plenty of time."

"Plenty," I agreed.

When the minute was up he gunned the engine and tore off in the direction of the compound. I thought of telling him to slow down, especially as we were still running with the headlights off, but on a deeper level, I shared his impatience. The way ahead seemed pretty straightforward as far as dirt paths went. It was maybe another ten minutes before the trees cleared and we came upon a sizable wood cabin.

"Voila." Tony stopped the car just short of what I could almost call the driveway, killing the engine. The building was two stories high, with eight windows we could see, and those windows were every bit as black as the clouded night sky above us. The rain was slowing a bit now but still had some fight left in it. It occurred to me that probably none of us had the slightest idea what to do next.

19

Meet with Triumph and Disaster

Hannah echoed my thinking. "Now what?"

Tony reached over to open his car door. "Now we go sneak around and see what we can find out."

"Wait," I said. "Look there, through the darkness, coming around the corner of the house." I wasn't sure what I had seen myself, but something was moving around out there. "See it?"

"I don't see nothing," Tony said, though that might have been due to a lack of trying.

"No," Hannah said, "Eddie is right. Something moving slowly. Two things."

There were two of them all right, both pacing on four legs. They looked small as seen from a distance, but I had the feeling they would be plenty big up close. "Guard dogs," I realized. "Dobermans, I think."

Tony pulled his hand away from the door. "You didn't say nothing about no guard dogs, Eddie."

"Well, how the hell was I supposed to know? It's my first time here too. You ever think of that?"

"Stop arguing," Hannah said from behind us. "That's not going to solve anything."

"You're right. Sorry, Billy."

"You think they'll attack?" Tony asked.

"I don't know. You want to risk it and find out?"

"Either way, there goes your stealth operation," Hannah said.

"Drive right up to their door, Billy."

"Won't that alert the dogs?" Hannah asked.

"That's what I'm after. If the dogs wake up whoever's inside there, that will draw them out to see who we are and what we're doing here."

"And what do we say we're doing here?"

"We're lost travelers," Tony suggested. "Our car broke down and we need somewhere to spend the night. They invite us inside, and boom, you're in."

"Or," I countered, "we don't drive up in a working car and then claim our car broke down. They're not likely to buy the lost travelers story either. Not in a place as remote as this."

Even in the dim glow of moonlight I could see Tony's hurt at having his plan discarded so casually, but this was no time to get careless trying to salvage somebody's wounded pride. "It's best if I do this alone."

"Don't forget, this is my fight too," Hannah said. "But what do you have in mind?"

I laid out my plan as it came to me and my companions eventually agreed it was probably our best play given the circumstances. They both needed some convincing, for different reasons, but in the end I won them over.

"You two going to fit back there?" I asked after Tony relocated himself to the backseat.

"Tight squeeze," Hannah said charitably. "We'll make do. But hurry."

Under other circumstances it would've been a funny image, the little blonde woman and the burly mustachioed man contorted together like pretzels, both ducking low to stay out of sight. But under the grim circumstances we found ourselves in—well, yes actually, it was still pretty funny.

I turned the key and heard the engine fire up. "Where are the lights on this thing, Billy?"

"On your left." I fumbled around with my left hand. "No, push in the—" Tony tried to peek his head above the seat to look at what I was doing and I heard Hannah cry out with discomfort.

"Oops, sorry about that," Tony said.

"I'm fine. Hurry though, will you?"

"What are you twisting over there? Your left, Eddie. No, that's the—don't touch that!"

We went on like that for longer than I'd care to admit, but eventually I got the headlights going and Tony settled back down into his nest.

"Ok, now this I've seen before." I grabbed the shifter and yanked on it.

Tony wailed from the backseat. "The brake, Eddie! Press on the brake, you dummy!"

"Left pedal," Hannah added helpfully.

"I know where the brake is," I insisted. Fifty-fifty chance anyway.

"Yeah? Like you knew where the headlights were?"

"Don't make me turn this car around," I said, the absolute emptiest of threats.

"Press down on the brake, shift into Drive, then release the brake," Hannah said with more patience than I really had any right to.

"What about the gas pedal?"

"You," Tony said, "do not get to touch the gas pedal. Ever."

I shrugged. "And reverse the steps to park, I suppose. Easy." In fact it wasn't easy at all, but luckily I didn't have far to go. I crept the car up the driveway, all the way to the house. By the time I stopped for good, the dogs got sight of us and paired running circles around the car with deranged barking. Whoever was inside the house sure wasn't going to sleep through that.

"Step one, check. Now we wait."

"Any lights on in the windows?" Tony's voice came through muffled, like his mouth was too close to one of the car seats.

"Give it time."

The line was hardly out of my mouth before the place lit up like a pinball machine, one window after another shining to life. I focused my eyes on the front door through what remained of the drizzle. Sure enough, it opened a minute later and I saw the figure of a man cutting a dark silhouette against the light that poured out behind him.

"Stay down," I reminded my passengers, and rolled down my window. "Hello there!" I yelled towards the house, leaning the top half of my body out the window. "I'm going to need you to call off those dogs."

"And just who the hell do you think you are to show up to my place in the middle of the night and give me orders?" the voice came back. Here was a man who clearly had no intention of calling off any dogs.

I said the only thing that would change his mind. "Mr.

Raymond sent me." He didn't say anything back to that, and I couldn't read his face as he stood in the backlight, but the shift in temperature couldn't have been more obvious. "Now," I repeated, "I'm going to need you to call off those dogs."

The man put his fingers to his mouth and let out a shrill whistle. The dogs froze in their circling and scrambled for the house. He side-stepped them as they came up the stairs and they sped inside through the doorway.

The grounds safe again, I stepped out of the car and shut the door behind me.

"Not sure I heard you right," the man said as I made my way towards the front door.

"Yes you are. That's why you called off the dogs."

"Well, I..." He had no follow-up and instead just extended his hand as I came up the stairs to the front porch.

"It's all right," I said. "Good that you were cautious. But set those cautions aside now. I don't want them getting in the way of what I've been sent here to do."

"No sir, Mr. ..." he left the space for me to fill in my name but I declined, taking the conversation forward on my terms. He was determined though and tried it from another angle. "Begging your pardon, you are..."

"I am Mr. Raymond's envoy." We stepped into the house together and I got my first clear look at the man's face. He was perhaps forty-five years old, with a face like an eagle, and as conservatively put together as the rest of the Manticore lot. There was something incongruous about his business-like face and the rumpled blue and white striped pajama getup he wore.

He was trying to keep it together, but the unsure eyes gave it away. They always did. "I trust that will be enough," I said without feeling the need to inject any invectiveness; the words carried that weight themselves.

"Yes, yes, no, of course." I took this man and his bundle of contradictions to be the head of SevCom, but I had him out of his element now. His was the face of someone who wasn't used to groveling this way. More used to having that particular shoe on the other foot maybe.

"I would have thought my position in the Cooperative merited an introduction on your end," I added with more than a little affected self-satisfaction.

"Surely you know who I—" A raised eyebrow from me was enough to cut his protestation short. "That is to say, my name is Charles. Kallen, he added."

He closed the door behind us and the Dobermans regarded me warily from under a table in the room ahead. The cabin was more impressive on the inside than it had been as seen from outside. Impressive in its construction, anyway. The decor, if one could call it that, less so.

The walls were littered with banal motivational slogans, arcane-looking charts, and even oversized iconography of the great Patrick Raymond. The picture was of the same photo as the one in Veronica's dossier, perhaps suggesting where Thomas obtained it in the first place. I ran my gaze over what I could see of the other seemingly empty rooms from the entryway, nodding as though it was just what I had expected to find.

"I'm sorry about the dogs, sir. It's just that we don't get many visitors out this way. Well," he corrected himself, "that is to say we don't get any visitors. But then I guess you knew that. Sorry."

I looked at him again. The angels of my better nature wanted me to put my arm around the guy and tell him to take a deep breath, but that would have been in direct contradiction of my objective. It sure was amazing what name dropping this Mr. Raymond could do among the Manticore crew, though.

The problem with impromptu plans like this was that one could never think too far ahead. I didn't have the slightest idea of what I should do now that I had fast-talked my way into SevCom, into a position of some illusionary authority, no less. I decided to stay silent and let the man's evident discomfort do the work for me.

"Is there—"

"I'll ask the questions," I said before he could finish. My footing was too advantageous now to yield any of it back. I let the curtain of silence fall between us again.

"Well, sir, you will be glad to know—that is, Mr. Raymond will be glad to know—"

"Don't presume to tell me or Mr. Raymond how we're going to feel about anything."

"No. I mean, yes, sir. I'm sorry... sir."

I nodded. "Let's have it then."

"I..."

"Out with it, man!" I raised my voice for the first time, just a bit, but it was more than enough.

"Begging your pardon sir, what is it you're asking for?"

"A sitrep, Charles. You know, where we stand at the present moment. A lay of the land, if you will."

"Yes, certainly. Well, as I just told Mr. Crossley—"

"Crossley nothing." I really shouldn't have been cutting him off as often as I was, but in my defense, it was pretty fun. I resolved forthwith to let the man finish a sentence or two. But not that one. "This report goes straight to Mr. Raymond himself. Spare no details."

Charles looked like he could double over with sickness at any moment. Luckily for both of us, he kept it together. "The students are upstairs," he said. "Sleeping. That is, they had been. Probably not anymore."

"Probably not, Charles," I said agreeably. "You're quite right there, I believe." I didn't know what students meant in that context, but I took a shot that was vague enough that I figured to be on safe ground. "How goes their education?"

"We—that is, they—are making progress, sir. Some more than others, but we have been working hard."

"For their benefit, no doubt." Apparently SevCom was a reeducation center of sorts. "Much pushback?"

"You know how it is, sir. We wouldn't be doing our jobs if there wasn't. But we'll whip them into shape yet." How literal said whipping was was anyone's guess.

"I don't doubt it." There was only one thing left to do. "Well, let's go see them then."

Charles balked again. "As we have said, sir, this would be the time they are sleeping."

"As we have also said," I corrected, "they can hardly be expected to be sleeping any longer, what with all the commotion."

"Quite right, sir," Charles conceded. "Quite right." He still hadn't moved towards the stairs but it wasn't so large a building, and finding them was no trouble. I set off in that direction.

"Transparency, Charles. That's the word Mr. Raymond kept coming back to. A quick hello with the students and then we'll get them right back to Dreamland, hey?"

"Excuse me, sir. Begging your pardon of course, I was informed that I would have sovereignty over the running of SevCom."

"You were misinformed." I found the stairs and started my march up them, Charles scrambling to keep pace behind me.

The stairs opened to a wide room that covered the

entirety of the second floor. Two rows of beds stretched off into the darkness, maybe ten to a row. In the beds I saw bodies, but none that had acknowledged our presence. There was an eerie quiet to the place, and the darkness wasn't helping ease any of that eeriness. I broke the silence with a great gusto, like annihilating fine glassware with a baseball bat.

"On your feet!" I cried out in my best impression of an overworked drill sergeant. I heard bodies rummaging around in the dark and the shapes on the beds rearranged themselves almost synchronously. A couple heads popped up, and soon several of this place's tenants were sitting up on their elbows or rubbing their eyes to see what all the fuss was about.

"Up, up! You heard the man!" That was me again, and I don't know why I started in with the third person like that, but it felt right. Sure enough, the people all got to their feet and moved robotically out towards the edge of their beds.

Charles was alongside me now, and his protests hadn't lost any of their vigor. "This is highly irregular, sir. I must say, highly irregular!"

"Nonetheless." I carried on. "Get us some lights, Charles. Can hardly see a thing up here."

"I—"

"Now."

I wasn't sure how much longer this fake authority act was going to hold out for. Maybe Charles had backup somewhere, or maybe I would stumble into a slip-up of my own that would give up the game. I had a tendency to do that, slip up, when I talked for long enough. It was just a matter of time, honestly.

The overhead lights came on and I got my first good look at the so-called students, though prisoners was probably the more accurate term. There were more than ten but less than twenty, a roughly equal mix of women and men of all ages.

I had long since committed Thomas's visage to memory, and I called it up now as I scanned the faces of the SevCom detainees. Finding a potential match turned out to be harder than I thought though, with the faces all looking as worn out and beaten down as they did. Each of the men standing before me was a far cry from the glamour shot Veronica had provided me with. I moved towards a man who looked to be about Thomas's age for a closer view.

"Name."

He gave me an uncertain look. The surprise of my visit and the natural grogginess of recovering from sleep had combined to make even that simple request intractable to him.

"Your name, man. Out with it. Keep up. The questions get harder from here."

"Miles Harris. Sorry, sir. Mr. Kallen," he added, unbidden, "has done an excellent job with us, sir. An excellent job."

Upon closer inspection, this surely wasn't the man I was searching for. I threw another perfunctory question or two at him just to keep up appearances, but I was anxious to keep things moving and proceeded down the line.

Another three interviews passed that way. I pretended to take an interest in each of the people before me, but one after the other revealed themselves to be nothing more than strangers to me. I could tell Charles didn't much like my accounting for them this way, but for the moment he was willing to let me proceed. The fourth person wasn't Thomas Lawrence either, but was perhaps an even better find.

Her hair was a brownish shade of blonde and she kept her eyes on the floor until I approached and asked for her name as I had done with the others. She looked up at me with green eyes that I felt I had almost seen before. I shouldn't have even needed her name to make the connection, but the truth is I did.

"Caroline Natal." Her voice was just above a whisper, and though she was younger than a lot of the others, she looked every bit as drained by whatever Manticore had set up there.

It's a good thing I wasn't chewing gum, because if I had been, I probably would've swallowed it. I couldn't give anything away to Charles though, who was becoming increasingly disagreeable with my whole operation here.

"Where are you from, Caroline?" I asked, looking to make a near-sure thing sure.

"Originally?" Her face had the look of someone slaving through the motions for no sake of her own. "Kansas, sir."

That was all I needed to hear. I set to work on a plan to get her out of there, but again, it couldn't look like that's what I was doing. Instead I passed by her just as casually as I had the rest.

Another seven or eight interviews passed without uncovering anything worthwhile. Charles's "Is this entirely necessary?"s had turned into "This is most irregular, sir"s and then "I'm afraid I must protest"s.

"Can it, Charlie," I said, careful not to underplay or overplay my hand. "I'm almost done here. Don't forget, I'll be reporting your cooperation, or lack thereof, directly to Mr. Raymond. That's Mr. Raymond himself," I added, unnecessarily. "Directly."

That bought me a little more time, but the card was obviously wearing thin. That's the problem with only having one card to play. Finally, on the third to last person, I saw him. Thomas Lawrence. Again I forced myself through the routine.

"Name."

"Thomas Lawrence," he answered proudly. Lawrence stood with his hands clasped behind his back, at parade rest as I've heard it called. Unlike everyone else I had spoken to, there was a resilient quality to his voice. He was either a tougher customer than he had looked in the photo or else just a glutton for punishment. I passed him by just as I had Caroline and finished up with the last two in line.

"Very good then, very good," Charles said. "We thank you for coming and please give my best to Mr. Raymond." Speaking to his charges then, he said, "Back to bed with you. Morning comes early and we have another full day ahead of us." If that wasn't a barely-concealed threat, I was the King of England.

"Not so fast, Charles. I'm not done here at all," I said. His face froze up again and I thought he might take a swing at me, but he repressed acting out whatever he was feeling inside. "Nearly so," I added by way of appeasement.

"With respect sir, I don't see what could be left to do here. We have no other students, as I'm sure you know."

"I'm sure you're sure I'm sure, Charles. The fact is, I'll be taking two students back with me."

Everything Charles had been fighting so hard to keep bottled up came exploding out at once. "Taking students out of SevCom? And without my approval? Absolutely not, sir. Highly irregular!"

"Take it up with Mr. Raymond," I said. I pointed at Caroline. "You first."

Her eyes widened in surprise. She looked from me to Charles and back to me again, unsure of what to say or do next, if anything. As for me, I could practically see the sands falling through the hourglass as I felt my time running out. "Quickly now," I said.

"She will be doing no such thing. I decide when these students are to leave. Not once in the history of—"

"First time for everything." Caroline still hadn't moved, and as much as she probably hated SevCom, I hadn't yet offered her any indication that leaving with me would be any better. The next words out of my mouth were going to be important. "We understand she is a talented pilot. Although," I met her eyes and hoped she would read my intentions, "perhaps not as talented as her sister."

"A pilot?" Charles about hit the roof. "What on earth are you talking about?"

"I'm ready," Caroline said. "I will go."

"You'll do no such thing-"

"Secondly," I was back to cutting Charles off again, "I'll be taking this Thomas fellow."

"I suppose he's a pilot too."

"A painter, Charles. Sometimes I wonder if you pay any attention at all." Thomas and I made eye contact. "We have a project calling for just his talents. 'The Marriage of Heaven and Hell.'" I didn't even know where that last part came from, some clumsy attempt at reminding him of his wife, but it sounded suitably impressive.

Caroline was at my side now, but Thomas hadn't moved. He hadn't even relaxed his military stance. "I'm afraid I can't do that, sir," he said.

Now it was me who was too flustered to speak. My idea, even with all its improvisatory planning and haphazard execution, was on the absolute doorstep of success. Caroline rescued and reunited with Hannah, Thomas rescued and reunited with Veronica, a massive win and payday for yours truly; it was all right there. Except it wasn't, because Lawrence wouldn't get in the car that would take him to freedom. Defeat from the jaws of victory.

"This is not a request, Thomas. Straight from—"

"Mr. Raymond, right? I thought you might say that. But the fact is, sir, I'm not ready. My reeducation, it's not complete. Maybe Caroline's is, as you said. But I still... It's not complete."

"I understand you have a wife," I tried, "who would like to see you again."

This time it was Charles who jumped in. "You heard the man, it's not complete."

"'It's not complete, sir'," I corrected him.

Thomas's inexplicable defiance had emboldened the captain of SevCom and I could feel my control of the situation loosening with each new exchange.

"I rather like your idea," Charles said.

"Which was that?"

"To take it up with Mr. Raymond. I think those were your words. Yes, I believe I'll do just that. A phone call to headquarters would suffice, don't you think?" The man was literally threatening to call my bluff.

"You do that," I said. "We're leaving." I took Caroline's hand and led her down the stairs, Charles following closely behind us.

"Let's make that call first." His tone told me what was left of the window dressing on my undercover operation was quickly falling away in torn shreds. Time to jet. I hoped we might catch a break and find the Dart outside ready to take off.

It wasn't. As we came to the foot of the staircase, the front door flew open, and there was Tony.

"Where are you, Eddie?" he yelled from the entry. "What are they doing with you in here?"

Then several things happened at once.

The guard dogs went berserk at the sight of a new

intruder. Caroline gripped tighter on my hand and I hurried her down the last couple stairs, both of us almost losing our balance completely but managing to remain just upright. Tony stormed towards us, hollering at the dogs, which only made them bark all the louder.

He was probably seconds away from catching a serious bite or several, but instead Caroline and I ran past him towards the exit, which seemed to confuse the massive Dobermans for just long enough. Charles was a step behind us, yelling at us to stop, but that was never going to happen. As he came within arm's length of Tony, Manticore's own Billy Shakes reared back and unleashed a furious right cross that caught Charles square in the jaw. The man collapsed in a graceless heap, which snapped the dogs out of their indecision, sending them leaping at Tony.

I grabbed Tony by the collar and pulled him with everything I had, falling backwards through the doorway and into the night. Meanwhile, Caroline swung the door shut with perfect timing that allowed Tony out but blocked the dogs from getting at him. The maneuver could hardly have gone any better if we had practiced it for years. The three of us spilled out together into a pile, each of us trying to keep the other two upright while tumbling.

"Hurry," Caroline said, "that won't hold them for long."

Hannah saw the commotion on the porch and started up the Dart. Tony got to it first and tossed Caroline and I into its open backseat. He climbed into the passenger seat and told Hannah to floor it. She swung the wheel sharply and got us onto the same path we had come in on, this time heading away from the compound.

"Woo!" Tony exclaimed. "You see the look on that guy's face?"

"Before or after the clobbering?" I laughed. "Good

timing, Billy."

Caroline spoke up from her place next to me. "Hannah? Is it really you?"

"Yes. You're safe now, Caroline. Thank god, you're safe."

"I don't know about that just yet," I said. "Caroline, does SevCom have any vehicles? Are they coming after us?"

In the dark I felt her shake her head. "With that punch your friend here threw, I don't think SevCom is going anywhere any time soon."

"That dunce is the whole operation?"

"Well, he has the backing of Manticore. But as far as staff actually being stationed out there, yes. Mr. Kallen is all there is."

That didn't make much sense. "And he keeps all fifteen or so prisoners under control by himself?"

"They do that for him themselves. We're all there as punishment because we've disappointed Manticore, which usually means Mr. Crossley, somehow. You'd think that would breed resentment, but it's usually just the opposite. Those people are in far too deep. If the Cooperative says they deserve something, then they feel they deserve it. They've imprisoned themselves in the dogma."

"But not you," Hannah said.

"Not me, no. I wanted to leave Manticore, and had almost said as much to you. Which is why they never would have let me go. You saved my life, Hannah."

"I think these two deserve some credit too." She punched Tony in the shoulder and he responded in mock agony before letting out a big laugh. The dirt trail we had been driving on alone opened up to a wider path, which soon turned into asphalt. I'm sure it was just my imagination, but even the car seemed to feel it was more comfortable to be back on familiar terrain. Not long after we reached the freeway. I felt we had truly made it.

"All downhill from here," I said proudly. "Or uphill? Which is the good one?"

"All downhill from here," Tony said. "Nice and easy."

"No," Hannah said, "going downhill is bad. You want to be uphill."

Tony called her crazy again and I said they both sounded wrong to me. We debated the finer points of the uphill versus downhill issue for a while, never quite arriving at a conclusion. At one point Caroline suggested "all level ground from here" but that didn't satisfy anyone either.

"All good from here," I finally summarized, and the group decided we could live with that.

Caroline and I filled the others in on what happened inside the compound before Tony burst through the door. From there, the sisters talked most of the ride back to the city, catching up on the time since they had last been in contact. Hannah was her real name after all, though she had needed to invent a fake last name when she signed up with Manticore, lest they make the connection to her sister. I was happy to hear that somehow; she looked like a Hannah and I didn't know that I could get used to calling her Patty or whatever else.

Caroline didn't have much specific to say about what went on at SevCom, but I heard enough to get a pretty good image of people being broken down for offenses big and small, imagined or otherwise. Crossley visited once a week to make sure everything was still running smoothly, but other than that, Charles ruled over his fiefdom of isolation as brutally as he saw fit.

For my part I was eventually able to break her of the "Mr. Kallen" nonsense. He became "Charles" and then, when we decided that was too good for him, "Charlie," and later "Chuck." Even that seemed overly dignified; by the end of the trip I think we settled on "C-Bone."

We dropped the girls off at Hannah's place and Tony reclaimed his station in the driver's seat. "You did an ok job behind the wheel there," he said, an apology of sorts for originally writing her off as "some lady" who couldn't be trusted with the Dart. Hannah's smile told me she recognized it as the same. We said our goodbyes and then it was just Tony and me driving back towards my house.

"I guess that about wraps it up then, hey?" Tony said.

"How do you figure?"

"Well, heck. That lady hired you to find her husband, right? And you found him."

That much was true. "I'm not sure if she'd see it that way, Tony. There was a moment back there I was sure I would walk out with both Caroline and Thomas. Save Hannah's sister, save Veronica's husband, and close my first big case all at once. Three birds with one stone, Tony."

"Would have been a tight squeeze on the drive home with three in the backseat."

"You always keep the big picture in mind, don't you?" I smiled. "You think I should pitch it that way to the wife? I did what she hired me to do, strictly speaking."

Tony agreed emphatically. "That's right you did. Beat her little deadline with days to spare, too. Heck, you did more than that. You offered that guy a free ride out of there. All he had to do was walk out the door just like that Caroline girl did. Wasn't your fault he was too stupid to do it."

I nodded and watched the road go by quietly. "Can't save people from themselves, can you?"

"Can't save people from themselves," Tony echoed. "You sure can't."

Neither of us said much after that. I just sat with that thought until Tony dropped me off.

"I can't thank you enough," I said. "We would have been sunk without you."

"Sunk and buried on the bottom of the ocean, I think! You call up that rich lady and you get paid what you deserve. And then..."

"You needn't finish the thought, my friend. And then Billy Shakes gets paid what he deserves. And then some."

I closed the door while Tony was trying to figure out if that last part was a compliment or a gentle ribbing. A little of each, I liked to think.

20

The Prestige

The next day I could finally call Veronica Lawrence with some unquestionable, above reproach, downright verifiable news. I slept in, felt I deserved it after last night's heroics, and even took the time to write out what had happened at SevCom so the facts wouldn't get slippery as I recited them. I hadn't made up my mind yet on if I should present the case as closed, as Tony suggested. True, I found her husband, but even I thought the ending unsatisfying, and I didn't have near the emotional stake in it that she did.

"I have news," I began. I told her the story of SevCom, minus the Hannah and Caroline angle. That part was nobody's business but their own. "He refused to come," I reiterated, "even after I dropped your name as subtly as I could manage." Veronica had let my story unwind without interrupting, and now there was more silence on her end of the line.

Eventually she said, "Yes, that sounds all too believable,

I'm afraid. I tried to convince myself—and I guess I almost succeeded—that they did something to him against his will, that he would return to me if he could. But it's not like that, is it?"

"There may have been a time he was conflicted between his love for you and his loyalty to Manticore; he put together those files, after all." I tried to hit the right note of empathy. "But there was no conflict last night."

"They control his mind now. I suppose they have for some time." Her voice broke a little with the last line. "Bastards."

I didn't know what to say to that, so I didn't say anything. Tony's voice was in the back of my head, telling me to ask about the money, but I repressed his lobbying in absentia. It didn't seem like the right time was all, except there were some things in life that needed doing, even if a right time never presented itself. I sat wrestling with that paradox (and losing) when Veronica did the hard part for me. Maybe Tony had somehow worked his way into her conscience too.

"And yet, the fact remains that you accomplished the job I hired you for. I admit I had more than my fair share of doubts almost every step of the way, but you did it, didn't you? You found my husband."

"I did." My voice sure didn't sound like I had accomplished anything worthwhile, though. For Hannah and Caroline, yes. For Veronica and Thomas, no. "Although I can't imagine this was the ending you were hoping for when you came into my office that day."

"That's true. Hardly your fault though, is it?"

"I suppose not."

"I will come by tomorrow with a check for the full payment. I trust that will give you enough time to total up your bill. Thank you," she added, sounding positively despondent.

I hung up and did as she asked, accounting for my rate and expenses, plus all of Tony's considerations. By the end it added up to a significant figure, but nothing Mrs. Lawrence couldn't cover.

It should have been the happiest day of my short career. I had solved the case that could have been dead-ended a dozen different times, saved Caroline from the cult and reunited her with Hannah, and made what to this point was the most money I had ever seen in my life. And yet. I was less than inspired by what was apparently going to have to pass as a resolution. In a word, dissatisfied.

I hung around the house for hours, doing not much of anything at all as the day died away around me. That evening the phone rang. It was Janie.

"Eddie, your friend is here."

"Warren Hyde?" At last?

"No, not him. Curly. Sounds like he's in a jocular mood tonight. Thought you might want to come down."

"Definitely. Thanks, Janie. See you soon."

I consulted my trusty dictionary on the word 'jocular' and went on down to the bus stop once again. Veronica Lawrence had come to me on a sultry day at the tail end of summer. That day had been full of possibilities, both for what directions the case might take me in and where my career was bound. The ensuing days had clarified both avenues. The original great unknown, Thomas's whereabouts, lay slain. My big payday was assured, and I hoped it would give my burgeoning resume a boost as well.

The days since then had been a narrowing. The potential paths to finding Thomas had dwindled, until there was only one, which he waited at the end of. The days themselves were shrinking too, the sun rising later and setting earlier. The light that remained between them was grayer and chilled, the bright summer sun existing only in our collective memory now. The cold, dead moon afforded no warmth, and the brisk autumn winds cut through me. I gathered my jacket around me and set off towards the Silver Rabbit.

The short, stocky bouncer and I were on head nod terms by now, and I stepped smoothly into the bar without needing to show him my ID or struggle with the door. The music had been loud even from the street, and it was louder still now that I was inside. Curly's bald head stuck out and I saw he was sitting at the bar talking with Janie. He looked every bit as jovial as Janie had said. I picked up 'jovial' while I was looking for 'jocular.' At this rate, I'd be a wordsmith in no time.

"Trying out a new hairstyle?" I sat on a neighboring stool and slapped him on the back.

It took him a moment but eventually the joke clicked, and Curly about fell over backwards with unrestrained laughter.

"Not his first drink of the night I'd wager," I said to Janie.

She leaned in close to me and whispered in my ear. "He's been talking a lot, Eddie. Telling stories. Might be in the mood to give you something you can use."

"You're a star, Janie. Thank you." I looked back to Curly. "How goes it, old timer?"

He pointed to the scar above my eye from when the bouncer knocked me out. "That's new," he said, playing dumb. "How'd you manage that one?"

"It's nothing. Just something a friend gave me."

"If that's how your friends treat you, I'd hate to think about what your enemies would do," Curly said darkly.

"You know, there was a time not so long ago that I didn't think I had any enemies."

"That's changed lately, huh pal?"

"Seems so."

"I remember you, you know that?" Curly said, as if just now seeing me. "I remember you and your questions."

"Oh? What were my questions?"

"That's right, you and your questions. Your questions are even questions about questions."

I wasn't all that interested in getting lost in the labyrinth of wherever this conversation was headed. "How about we get to the point?"

"Always with the questions." Curly was laughing again.

"I saw Thomas Lawrence," I said. He wasn't laughing after that.

Curly eyed me suspiciously. "You what?"

"Spoke with him, too."

"Where?" He leaned forward on his barstool and almost fell over again. "Where is he?"

"Now who's got the questions?"

"Still you." Apparently Janie had been eavesdropping on our conversation, not that I could blame her.

I ignored her teasing and soldiered on. "I'll tell you what I learned about your friend, if that's what he is. After you tell me what I want to know."

"Sure, sure. What do I care?" Curly said. "Sure, sure, sure. Ask your questions, Question Man."

"What's your connection to Lawrence? To Manticore?"

"One at a time, I think," Janie advised.

She was right. "Your connection to Lawrence then."

"We were what I guess a fella like you might call

coworkers," Curly said.

"You're a painter?" I didn't take him as the type, but then I hadn't taken Thomas Lawrence as the type either.

Curly laughed. "Fingerpaints maybe. No, I'm not a damn painter."

"But Lawrence is."

"That he was." He leaned in closer. "You don't have the first idea what he painted though, do you?"

"You're wrong there, Curly. Janie, give us a minute, will you?"

"Sure thing." She walked towards the other end of the bar and out of earshot.

"He painted fakes," I told Curly. "Perfect replicas, to the point that no one could ever tell the difference from the originals."

"You're wrong there, Eddie." He laughed a little to himself.

I gave him a confused look. "But that information comes directly from—"

"The last part. You're wrong about the last part. He painted fakes, well done, yes. But you really think they don't have ways to tell the difference? Even if every stroke was actually perfect, impossible by the way, they can test the chemicals in the paint. Old paint is different than new paint. Don't you know that?"

I didn't. "Well, how was I supposed to know that?" I thought for a minute. "So why go through all the trouble if people were still able to tell them apart?"

Curly put away what was left of his drink. "They can only tell them apart if they're trying to tell them apart."

I had two and two but couldn't see how they were supposed to make four. "But why wouldn't they try to tell them apart?"

"Because," he winked, "they didn't have any reason to think the paintings had been switched."

Switched? "I thought he sold them to be passed off as authentics and gave the proceeds to Manticore."

Curly shook his head. "That doesn't make much sense, pal. People aren't going to drop that kind of dough without knowing they're real. Use your damn head."

I tried to do just that. "The only way he could make that kind of money was by selling the original paintings."

Curly nodded. "Getting closer, pal."

"But the paintings he painted were not the originals."

"So..."

I thought back to the exhibition at the art museum. "So the paintings he sold were not the paintings he painted."

"Hence the switch."

I thought I had it, almost. "So he paints a copy of a famous artwork and switches it out for the real one, presumably from a museum. Then he sells the real one through some shady underground channel. The museum, having no reason to suspect any kind of switch has been made, never learns that the piece they think is a Caesar" (as soon as I said it I knew I'd bungled the name, but it was too late to turn back), "is actually a Lawrence."

Curly called for Janie and ordered another drink. "Not bad. One mistake, though. Tommy didn't do any breaking and entering, or stealing, or switching, or any of that. Not with the modern security systems the museums have in place these days, no way. You forget, that's asking a lot of one person, with the artistic talent on top of it. Let alone fencing them afterwards. Nobody's that good at two things, never mind all three."

That sounded fair. "So someone else broke into the museums and switched out the paintings, is that right? A thief as talented in his discipline as Thomas was with a brush. Then Manticore had someone dedicated to the fencing part too." A name shot up through my memory. "Warren Hyde."

Curly nodded in a non-committal sort of way. "Maybe." Janie slid a drink across the bar to Curly and left us alone again. He took a big swig from his glass. "I got paid and that's all that mattered to me."

So, the two men were different people after all. "What happened to Hyde?"

Curly shrugged. "Beats me. Gone away somewhere, I guess. Maybe for good."

"I suppose it hardly matters now," I said. A desultory nod indicated his agreement.

So Lawrence painted the forgeries while Hyde fenced the originals. That left only one role in the trio left Curly could have played. "You were the thief."

"Best in the world." He backed off that a second later. "Well, best west of the Mississippi at least, I promise you that. You don't want no amateur, would get himself caught in half a second. It takes, it takes the best is what it takes."

"Why admit it to me?"

Curly laughed again. "Well, hell, what are you going to do about it? And how would you ever prove it? There's no trail left now and if they ever bring me up on charges, I'll deny it all. But," he grabbed my shoulder, "that doesn't matter either, because you're not going to do it."

I thought for a moment, but I guess my mind was already made up. "It's not exactly my highest priority, no. For now anyway. I'll admit though, it disappoints me to hear you were involved in that Manticore racket. There's no honor in that."

"Honor. That and a nickel will get you..." He stumbled, forgetting how the saying ended. "It was money I was after, not honor."

"In that, you're not so unique."

"Now, that said," he continued, "I had every reason to want to quit. It didn't have anything to do with honor pal, I promise you that. But Tommy was getting greedy. More likely it was those Manticore ghouls who were putting him up to it, but he kept pushing past the point we should have pushed it, if you follow my meaning."

"A smart thief knows when to get out of the game."

"There you've said it, yes. There you've said it. Except Tommy didn't see it that way, wouldn't take no for an answer is more like it."

"Sounds like you two were at an impasse. What happened next?"

"Well, I had to make him take no for an answer."

That didn't jive with the hard-headed Manticore adherent I had seen the night before. The Thomas Lawrence I knew wouldn't give up his commitment to the Cooperative for anything.

"Last night I told him his wife was looking for him, offered him a chance to walk away, and you know what he did?"

"I'll bet he told you to get lost."

"In so many words, yeah. Which gets me to wondering what you did to make him take no for an answer."

"Use your damn head, would you? I swear you don't use your damn stupid head. How do you stop a painter from painting?"

It sounded like the setup to a bad joke. "Take away his paints?"

Curly looked at me like I could hardly be more obtuse, then took another drink. "Set your hands on the bar for me there. Palms down, good, just like that." With a quickness that surprised me, he brought his glass down upon my left hand as hard as he could. I pulled away instinctively, the pain radiating up my arm.

"What the hell did you do that for?" I demanded.

"Now imagine," Curly leaned in, "imagine that was a hammer hitting your hands. Maybe seven or eight times I bring my hammer down on your precious little painter hands. You tell me how much painting you're going to do after that." He leaned back, satisfied that he had made his point.

I shook my hand trying to get some blood going to it. It didn't feel like anything that was going to amount to long-term damage, but it sure hurt a lot in the short-term.

"You broke his hands?"

"Broke them good. Hey, it's not like I wanted to. You said it yourself, he wasn't going to stop unless I made him stop. So I made him stop." His voice took on a sleepier tone. "Did it for his own good, that's all."

I sat in silence, grappling with this new bit of information and seeing where it fit in with the others I had amassed. After a few breaths Curly's eyes shot back to alertness, or as close to alertness as they were going to get in his current state.

"But hold on now," he said, sticking his arms out to me to steady himself. "Just hold on now."

"I'm holding, Curly."

"You told me... You walked into this bar tonight and you told me that you saw Tommy last night. But you couldn't have, or you would've known about the broken hands. That's some kind of dirty trick, mister..." He clenched the fists again like he was readying for a fight.

"Relax, pal. I saw Lawrence all right, that was no trick." I thought back to when I had faced him in the lineup and the light came on. "The parade rest."

"Who said anything about a parade?"

"Last night, at SevCom—"

"What's a sevcom?"

"It's—well, not now, I'll get to that. When I saw Thomas, he stood with his hands behind his back. I thought it strange, but it just seemed like part of the overly formal vibe he had going on. But yes, of course, that would've been the perfect excuse to make sure I never saw his hands." I felt the progress I had made last night melting away. Not totally, but substantially.

"Broke his hands," Curly said, his eyes heavy again. "Had to do it. For his own good. Had no choice."

For as proud and stubborn as he acted, there seemed a great sadness in him. Even during our short conversation, he tried over and over again to convince himself he had done the right thing. And maybe he had, but I didn't think his conscience saw it that way. Which maybe explained all the alcohol. From sad to sadder.

Curly wasn't too communicative after that, but I had promised to fill him in on what I had learned about Lawrence, so I kept my word, recapping the previous night's events. He nodded a lot, sometimes broke in with a one or two-word rejoinder, but I couldn't tell how much of it he really took in. Maybe that was for the best. I checked in with Janie again before I left, thanked her for the call, and made sure she would see that Curly got home safely.

It was after midnight by the time I left the Silver Rabbit. That same ghostly moon was still up there in the clear sky, and the winds hadn't gotten any more inviting since I had stepped inside the bar. The walk back to the bus stop was uneventful, the bus ride home doubly so. All I did during both was think. I thought about Janie and I thought about Curly, but mostly I thought about what Manticore would do to the painter who could no longer paint.

21

Terminus

Veronica came at just the time she said she would, and she had the full payment just the way she said she would, too. I tried to read her mood when she came in, but she had a pretty good poker face. Even when I handed her the bill with a number I considered substantial, it hardly registered on her expression.

"You're sure he's at this Manticore outpost? It occurred to me after we hung up that you don't really have any proof to share with me, do you?"

"I sure don't," I acknowledged. Caroline was a witness, but she had been through enough already. "I can tell you that he kept saying the work wasn't finished and he stood at attention like some kind of military subordinate the whole time I talked to him." There wasn't any sense in further upsetting her by mentioning anything about broken hands.

"That sounds right. I hate it, but that sounds right. What did that place do to him?"

"They promised him the chance to save the planet, the way they do with all their recruits. Maybe on some level he knows that's bunk by now, but he's too committed to let himself believe it. It's a lot easier to trick someone than it is to convince them they've been tricked."

Veronica took a seat across from me. "You think so? Yes, you might be right. Still..."

I stayed quiet and waited for her to finish her thought.

"Still... I think I should like to see him. You could bring me to him, couldn't you?"

"Hmm." I paused. "I don't think I could. I've got no sense of direction at all, as far as retracing the route. We followed Crossley, remember. He'll be going out there again next week, so I guess you could follow him just the way we did... But no, I don't think that's a good idea either. Not that I don't understand the Hail Mary impulse, I'm sure I'd do just the same. But I really believe he's gone. You won't find anything there but pain."

"You're probably right." She looked down at her hands. "But—"

"What's more, you're not thinking about what the consequences for your husband will be. I'm sure my little doomed rescue mission got him in even hotter water than he was already in. Now you want to make things worse yet for him? It just isn't smart. I have to advise head over heart here, Mrs. Lawrence."

The poker face was gone now and she looked at me with obvious despair in her eyes. "I just don't think I could live with myself if I gave up on him. Better to fail than to not have tried at all."

"You might be right," I conceded. I still thought her showing up at SevCom would bring nothing but trouble to Thomas, but I had to respect her agency in the matter.

"There remains the fact that I don't know how to find it. And upon further reflection, I don't think following Crossley will work a second time. He'll be extra paranoid now. Heck, he'll probably change up his schedule too."

"What about the man who drove you out there? Bill was it?"

"Billy, yeah." Try as I might, I really couldn't think of a good reason Tony wouldn't be able to find the place again. He was resourceful like that. "It's just that it was dark when we went, and raining, and—"

"But you'll try. I'll pay extra, I'm happy to, but you must take me there. Even if just to see Thomas one last time."

I sighed. "I'll take you. Let me get my guy on the phone."

At least convincing Tony to take another trip came easily. He made sure the money would be worth his time, but I think the bug of the case had bitten him as well. He and I piled into his car late that afternoon with Veronica Lawrence taking her turn in the backseat. Even given our dire circumstances, I couldn't help but smile at the sight of the well-dressed and exceedingly-dignified rich woman squeezing into the back of the old Dart.

"Eddie's a nice guy," Tony said, "but don't count on him to find his way out of a paper bag, hey Eddie?"

I didn't have much defense against that so I opted instead to change the subject. "Once again, I'd like to go on the record with this being a bad idea."

"Way to think positively," Tony said and punched me in the arm. "What's the plan here anyway?"

"You and I can't show our faces anywhere near anything to do with Manticore, that's obvious. Which leaves Mrs. Lawrence here." Addressing her, I said, "I'm sorry to say we can't do much more than get you to the door. It's all you from there."

"I understand."

"But we'll be outside waiting for you," Tony assured her. "And the moment you think it might turn bad, you come running out and they'll never catch us."

I stole a look in the backseat and noticed for the first time Veronica was wearing some formal-looking shoes, almost like high heels. The point was, they weren't anything she should be running in. "Leave the shoes. Could be the difference between escape or..." There wasn't any honest way to finish that sentence without scaring her.

"Aw, these people ain't so tough," Tony said. "Not after that wallop I laid on what's his name, hey?"

"That's exactly what worries me. We won't catch them off-guard this time." But Veronica had made her mind up, so there was no sense in me dwelling on the negatives, potential or otherwise. "All I'm saying is stay sharp in there."

"I will say my piece," she said, "and then Thomas will have to decide. That is all."

Tony navigated the Dart slowly up the dirt path towards the compound. I had been keeping an eye out for extra Manticore defenses or anything else out of the ordinary, but from what I could tell everything was just how we had left it a couple days ago.

"Stop here, Tony." That was the wrong name. I caught myself, but too late. Mrs. Lawrence noticed the contradiction from the backseat. "Old nickname," I said. "Long, uninteresting story." That was the first time all day either he or I had slipped on the alias tightrope. Pretty good to have made it faultless that far, I thought. I also thought that the stress was wearing on me and this would be an awful place to fall.

"It's about a hundred yards farther along this path," I said. "Heading up alone is your best bet. We'll pull the car in behind you and be ready to take off if needed." More like when needed. "I'll climb into the back and you can jump into the passenger seat."

Veronica nodded. "Thomas and I can sit together until we're able to stop safely."

She still clung to hope. "Sure," I said. "You ready?"

She took off her shoes as I had suggested and laid them gently on the floor of the car. She took a deep breath and nodded. "See you soon."

I crawled into the backseat and we watched her disappear in the direction of SevCom. Tony eased his foot off the brake so the car could creep along in the wake she had left.

"How do you think this plays out?" I asked.

"You said this guy is too far gone, hey? Guess I haven't known you to be wrong about that kind of thing before. Reading people or whatever you want to call it."

I stared forward, watching the greenery of the woods pass slowly by in my peripheral vision. "I'm worried about her. But she needs to be able to make her own decision, right?"

"I don't know." He shrugged. "But we will soon."

Soon was selling it short. We had barely arrived at the clearing when I saw the figure of Veronica Lawrence sprinting away from the house. Less of a sprint and more of someone who has never run in her life's idea of a sprint. But the wild urgency of her movements was unmistakable, like a squirrel who darted out in front of a car perhaps too late to escape the tires. When she got closer, I saw the panic in her eyes.

Behind her, someone came out of the doorway carrying

a hunting rifle. Not Charles this time, someone I didn't recognize. Then there were two of them. They raised their guns and fired in our direction. The shots passed by harmlessly, but that's not to say getting shot at doesn't serve as a unique sort of eye-opener. I leaned over the seat and threw open the passenger door while Tony spun the car around like a top in a quick 180. Veronica's pure hysteria compensated for her physical limitations and she threw herself into the car, slamming the door behind her.

"Go!" she ordered, and Tony did just that.

Bullets whizzed past us, closer now, leaving the sounds of the parted air behind them. I heard a loud crack from the back of the car and looked up to see a trail of red shards left behind us.

"My taillight!" cried Tony. He looked as if he had just seen his only child get carried off by a pack of wolves. "Not the taillight!"

We shot forward, the car tearing through the long grasses and kicking up tan clouds of dust behind us. Tony jerked the wheel violently as we went along, alternating between flooring the gas and hammering on the brakes. There was nothing pretty about it, but it was awfully effective, and soon the worry of anyone from SevCom catching up to us was nearly unthinkable.

Unfortunately, by that time Mrs. Lawrence was weeping inconsolably in the passenger seat next to him. When I regathered enough of my wits to speak, I tried to get to the bottom of what the hell had happened in there.

"What the hell happened in there?"

"I should never have come," she wailed. "You told me I shouldn't come, and I insisted, and—" The rest was tears.

I still wanted to know what she saw, but I also knew better than to press it just then. The Dart shot out of woods back onto a paved road, and a minute later SevCom was a memory again.

Tony didn't share my patience for delicate situations. "They kill him or what?" he asked after we had shaken the threat of a pursuit. "What with those guns and all that."

"I should have listened," Veronica said through the sobs. "I had to try, but I should have listened."

"You did what anyone would have done in your situation." I imagined that provided little comfort, but I had to say something.

"I didn't have to see what they did. Why did I have to come?"

Those weren't the tears of someone who had been predictably abandoned by a faithless spouse. They were tears of a deeper hurt. When I said before that Thomas was gone, I had not meant it in the physical sense. Now, with my hand on Veronica's heaving shoulder trying to ease her unceasing sobbing, I knew he was gone in the most corporeal respect as well. Apparently Manticore had decided the painter who could no longer paint and kept stirring up trouble through no fault of his own was more bother than he was worth. A money-grubbing organization of shysters was one thing, but a cult willing to kill to protect its interests was quite another.

We got onto the freeway and no one said much of anything for the rest of the ride. Somewhere along the way, Mrs. Lawrence composed herself enough that her parting words came through with perfect clarity, both in diction and intent. "This was that Jake Crossley." She let the car come to a stop, unbuckled her seat belt, and stepped outside. Before she closed the door she turned and said, "And I will have my revenge."

22

Death Arrives in Stereo

Tony dropped me off at home, still all kinds of broken up over his taillight that caught the bullet. I sank into the most comfortable chair I could find with the big whale book. I thought it would do me some good to get my mind off my own life for a while, but the goings-on of the *Pequod* couldn't hold my attention for any sustained length of time. I couldn't stop thinking about the tragic fate that had befallen poor Thomas Lawrence.

Gullible and stubborn though he was, there was never anything about him that suggested he was an especially bad man. His undying devotion to Manticore was almost admirable in a twisted sort of way, though the object of his affections could hardly have been less deserving. The forgery business wasn't the most upstanding career, true, but I had known a lot of people who did a lot worse for a lot less. What did I care about the difference between one painting and another that could never be distinguished by the naked eye? The world had far bigger problems to worry about.

On the other end of the scale, one had to weigh his requisite bravery, uncanny talent, and a wife who loved him, unflinchingly till the very end. Not that he had treated her very well, I reminded myself, and the scales swung back in the other direction. But people were complicated that way. I hadn't found one yet who was either all good or all bad, and I doubted I ever would. Any way you looked at it, he hadn't deserved to die. Especially not at the hands of someone like Crossley.

I told myself that wasn't my concern anymore. Veronica Lawrence's, sure, and I wasn't about to step in to defend Crossley from anything she had planned for him. But the case had taken its toll on me, physically, mentally, and more than a little spiritually. I was ready to leave it behind. I closed my eyes with Melville on my chest and drifted into as carefree a sleep as I had managed in some time.

That didn't last either. The shrill ringing of the phone cut into my dreaming and I answered it with a dry mouth and a sore head. I felt only half-aware of what I was even saying.

"Hello?"

I didn't recognize the gravelly voice on the other end of the line, but it asked me to verify my personal information. I was too tired to fight it, so I confirmed that he was speaking to whom he thought he was.

"This is Detective Jacob Baxter with the Summerport Police Department," he continued. "Homicide Division."

The last two words banished the remnants of sleep that had been clinging to me. Veronica couldn't have acted that quickly, right? I was fully awake now.

"Homicide?"

"I'm calling about Abe Hansen. That name mean anything to you?"

It sure didn't. "I've never heard the name in my life."

"Well, he sure seemed to know you."

"I don't understand."

"I'll try to make it short for you, sir. A body washed up on shore late last night, early this morning, however you want to look at it. Anyway, the cause of death hasn't been determined, but we found a business card in our guy's wallet. And I'm calling you because, if you haven't guessed yet, it was your business card."

Those business cards had been so recently printed, I had barely had any time or opportunities to give them out. "I see. Well, officer—sorry, detective—the truth is I've put a lot of those cards up all over town, tacked them onto billboards and the like, you know. Trying to spread the word about my business. I'm just starting out, see. This guy could've gotten that card from anywhere."

"Uh-huh," he said, unsatisfied with that explanation. "Except he couldn't have, because there's no hole at the top of this card. Meaning it wasn't tacked anywhere. Meaning I've got to believe you handed it to him personally."

The phone call was quickly bringing a discomfort in my chest. "Yes," I said, "I can follow your thinking there." There was only one business card I remembered handing out personally, the one I gave Curly the night we met at the Silver Rabbit. "Listen, what did he look like, this guy who washed up on shore?"

"Let me grab the notes here, give me a minute." I heard the sound of shuffling papers. "Ok, so he's male like I said, we put the age at about... fifties, I guess. Bald guy, goatee, no other features that stand out really." That about confirmed it was poor old Curly as far as I was concerned. "Ringing any bells?"

"No," I lied. I wasn't much interested in having the police poking around me given all the legal gray areas I'd found myself in as of late. "But I was passing those cards out all over town, like I said. Not all of them were tacked on billboards. Sometimes I just hand them out to strangers, to get them out in the world and hope they'd end up somewhere of use to me. That's pretty much their purpose, right? I guess this is the flip side of that. Eventually they were bound to end up somewhere else."

"I suppose so," Detective Baxter said. "Heck, it's probably nothing. Like I said, no cause of death or anything yet, could be the guy had too much to drink and fell off the pier. Happens more than you'd think. But I didn't have much else going on today, and it struck me as odd. Thought I'd follow the lead where it took me. I'm sure you know that feeling, you being a private investigator and all."

"All too well," I said. "One of the perils of the business, hey?"

The detective laughed. "Boy, if that ain't the truth. Well, you take care, sir. I'll get ahold of you if I need to follow up on anything, but I don't anticipate you'll be hearing from us again."

We said our affable goodbyes and I hung up the receiver. I let out a long exhale. Curly was a dead end now, in the most literal sense. Maybe the detective was right and his passing was from some kind of natural, or at least malice-free, cause. Or perhaps he had been murdered, perhaps even as a result of his connection to this mess with Thomas Lawrence, Warren Hyde, and the Manticore Cooperative.

I kicked myself, figuratively, for not leaving well enough

alone. If I had followed Tony's advice, I could have walked away from this thing with Thomas found, alive, and a big fat check for my troubles. But now Lawrence was dead, Veronica broken, Curly washed up on a lonely shore, and a homicide detective interested in me past a level I was comfortable with (which was to say at all). I guess sometimes you get to that point in your life where even your successes are just a different shade of failure. I mean to tell you, it was an altogether lousy development.

On the bright side, my next move was obvious: Stay the hell out of whatever this quagmire had become. Hannah and Caroline were safe, and already out of town if they knew what was good for them. Veronica's vendetta and Crossley's survival, or lack thereof, were no business of mine. Ditto the rest of the drones at Manticore. If I never saw any of them again, that was just fine with me. The case was solved and, therefore, closed.

And it stayed closed for several weeks after that. Work was slow during that time. A lead or three came my way, although nothing anywhere near as major as the Thomas Lawrence misadventure. But building a business is slow work, and lucky for me Veronica's generous payment bided me plenty of time to gather some professional momentum.

It was late October and the leaves that had been varying colors of bright red and gold now lay brittle and dead below the trees. They were blown out across the streets and piled up along curbs in sad, discolored piles. I gave them verveless little kicks as I walked along, a man without much destination most days. On Halloween I got the notion to visit the Silver Rabbit again, if only to see how their distinctive clientele celebrated the big day.

I shook hands with the bouncer as though we were old friends, and Bruce patted me on the back as he saw me come through the door.

"Janie working?"

"Yeah," he said, "she's around here somewhere. Been a long time. What brings you by?"

"Something in the air, I guess." I looked around and saw to my disappointment that the holiday had gone unacknowledged by the staff and patrons alike. Part of me was disappointed, but the larger part was happy I had decided against wearing the T-Rex costume. I didn't see Janie anywhere so I went ahead and set up at the place where Curly and I had had our initial confrontation. I ordered up a seven and seven for old time's sake and raised the glass to his memory; that part was just for my own sake.

A minute later I felt a squeeze on my shoulder. A woman's voice in my ear said, "Is that who I think it is?"

I turned around to see Janie. She looked happy to see me and I was happy to see her too. "Hey, Stranger."

"Hadn't heard from you in a while," she said. "Even tried calling a time or two, but you must have been out and there was no answer."

I nodded. "It's an imperfect system. Overdue for improving."

"I figured that meant the case was either going really well or really badly."

"Little of both, actually. Haven't seen Curly around here lately, have you?"

She shook her head. "Not since that night with you, I don't think. Does that have something to do with your case?"

"I don't even know anymore Janie," I said with a grim smile. A thought hit me. "What time do you get off tonight?"

"What is it now, about eleven? I can probably be out of

here in an hour. What's up?"

"Come find me then, yeah? I'll be hanging around this general area here for a while," I said with a wide wave of my hand.

"It's a free country." She gave me a smile then went off in some other direction.

I sipped my drink and ran over the events of the Lawrence case again in my head. I still didn't have a good explanation for how or why Curly ended up dead, and I still didn't know what became of Manticore after I had moved on. Both those things bothered me. I hoped talking it out with another person might get me a new perspective on things. Janie wasn't a detective, amateur or otherwise, but she was sharp. If nothing else, it felt like a nice way to spend a Halloween night.

Janie found me an hour later, as good as her word. "I could use a change of scenery," she said. "Follow me."

She took my hand and led me out a backdoor marked Emergency Exit. When I stepped outside, I saw a bonfire burning in a small fire pit. It was modest but warm, its glow cozy and welcoming against the black and starry sky above us.

"Not many people know this is even back here," she said. We settled into a couple chairs near the fire's edge and moved closer to the heat of the flames. "I like to come back here and think sometimes. No interruptions, you know?" The firelight cast twin reflections in her dark eyes. "Anyway, what's on your mind?"

"I thought I'd catch you up on the case," I said. "If you're interested."

"Well," she laughed, "I had been wondering a little how

that whole thing turned out."

"Ever heard of the Manticore Cooperative?" I started.

"Manticore... Yeah... Where have I heard that? Oh, that was where that guy got knocked off, isn't it?"

An involuntary puzzled look came over my face. How would she have known about the SevCom killing? "You heard about that? Thomas Lawrence?"

"No," she shook her head, "that wasn't the name. What was the name? It was in all the papers."

"What was?"

"The name of that man who got killed. Carpenter... Craston... You know who I mean Eddie, they had his picture too. Big bald guy."

"Crossley?"

"Crossley! Yes, that was it. Something Crossley. He was the head of this Manticore thing. They were, what, a marketing company or something?"

She was moving way too fast for me to follow. "Crossley's dead?"

"That's what you were talking about, right, Manticore? Jeez Eddie, it was all over the papers. Don't you read the papers?"

"No. Why would I read the—"

"Well, it was a pretty big story. That Crossley guy was apparently somebody important. The leader of that Manticore place they said, and the police found him dead one morning. A single bullet through the heart, I heard." She shivered in the cold and I followed suit. "Was that connected with your case somehow?"

So, Veronica got her revenge after all. "Who killed him?"

Janie shrugged. "Dead end case I guess. No evidence to go anywhere with, that's what they said. What does all this have to do with you?"

"You said Crossley was the leader of Manticore?"

"Well, I guess they didn't say 'leader.' President, owner, whatever the title was. They said he was the guy in charge anyway, is what I mean."

I nodded, watching the fire jump and recede against the dark, and tried to assimilate this new information with the old. "No mention of a Patrick Raymond? Or anybody by the name of Lawrence?"

"This was weeks ago Eddie, I don't know. Not like I remember all the names. Just that it was all over the papers for a while. Never named a suspect like I said though, and eventually everybody moved on to the next big story. That's how it always works, you know?" She paused, assimilating a few facts of her own. "You didn't kill him, did you, Eddie?"

"Of course not."

"But you think you know who did."

"I have a pretty good idea, yeah."

Janie took her eyes off the fire and looked over at me. "What are you going to do about it?"

I kept my gaze on the flames as they danced, flashing back to the widow Lawrence and the first day she came to me for help, then how she looked on our car ride back from SevCom. "Nothing."

The fire popped, sending a shower of sparks in the air. A silence followed.

"I guess you have your reasons," she said.

"I guess I do. You know what's funny about this case? I started with three persons of interest; one I never did find, and another turned out to be the propagandistic creation of a money-obsessed cult."

"What about the third one?"

"The third one was Crossley. He was the killer. But," and here is where it got hard to explain, "not at first. It ended up pretty complicated."

"So, you found your missing man, and you solved the case, and the killer got what he deserved." She moved her chair over closer and put her hand on my knee, reassuringly. "That sounds like a win."

"You think so? I'm less sure." I felt at the scar above my left eye, then reached down with my right arm and took her hand in mine. "But that's over now."

Epilogue

As for that streak on the window I had been wrestling with when Veronica Lawrence first showed up at my door (more of a smudge than a streak, really), I never could get rid of the thing. Instead, I thought about what the woman at the museum had said and decided on the next best thing. I got back up on my chair—my fee for the case afforded me a nicer, sturdier chair than the original—and erected a little frame around the blemish. The way I figured, that made it art, with the universe itself as the artist. Plus, that way I didn't have to clean it.

It was still there in the weeks following Halloween, when I received three letters.

The first bore a return address of simply "Kansas." That was as specific as it got. I knew the sender before I opened it. Hannah had sent the letter of course, and I couldn't help but smile the whole way through it. She and Caroline were doing just fine back home. Caroline still had bad days, and bad nights especially, but Hannah was sure those would become less frequent with time.

They both thanked me for being a literal lifesaver, though I think we all knew I would have been hopeless without Hannah's help. In closing, she told me to look them up if I was ever in Kansas. She didn't leave an address, not even a town, but she said that I was a real detective now, and I should be able to find that out by myself. And if I couldn't, the practice would be good for me. She also enclosed a small balsa plane, still in its package. I assembled it and placed it on my desk, where it still sits like a sentry.

The second letter came attached to a thin cardboard box that was a good two feet by three feet at least. I opened the envelope first and found another thank you letter inside. This one said that I was on my way to being a good detective too, with my first big case officially under my belt. Mrs. Lawrence thanked me for my work in finding her husband, and told me to thank my friend Billy too. She said she would never be able to come to terms with what my work had turned up, but as she had said all along, that was hardly my fault. And besides, she said, justice found Jake Crossley after all.

As for the box, she said she had been going through some of Thomas's old things and found a painting she thought I might like. *The Gulf Marseilles Seen From L'Estaque* it was called, by the painter whose name I had mispronounced as Caesar. I tried translating the French word, but my dictionary was no help there. It seemed like something Old Leonard would know though; I'd have to ask him the next time we crossed paths.

In the confusion of Thomas's disappearance, she wasn't sure whether this was one of his replicas yet to be switched or the genuine Cézanne itself. If I had it authenticated by an expert, she said, that would prove only that I was in possession of stolen property. She recommended I embrace the mystery of the forever-unknown and hang it on one of my walls, which, as she recalled, were frightfully bare. I fished a nail out of a drawer and did just that.

The third letter had no return address. I would like to present it in its entirety, so as to not muddle any of the facts in the paraphrasing or retelling. It said:

To Eddie London (if that is your real name, haha),

If you're any kind of detective at all, you know by now that Jake Crossley is dead. What you may not know is who did the honors, if you'll pardon my expression. He would have been all right if he had only been content to run his abominable little self-help scam and leave it at that. But his reach exceeded his grasp, the way it always does with those types. He wasn't satisfied as a king; he had to fashion himself into a god. I ask you Eddie, when has that ever ended well for anyone?

The fact of the matter is I keep my ear to the ground, as they say. From that, I hear things, and from that, I know things. The news (and circumstances) of Thomas's death reached me faster than you might think. I knew his wife only in passing, but even that was enough to know she wouldn't rest until either she or Crossley was in the ground. But Eddie, had she gone after him, it would have been her. I couldn't have both their deaths on my conscience, no matter how indirectly.

It occurred to me that I had taken the coward's way out earlier, breaking Thomas's hands to get him out of the Manticore racket. That was never going to suffice as long as Crossley was around. I should've cut the head off the snake in the first place, but time is a one-way street, isn't she? Anyway, never make the same mistake twice, I say. I wish I could've seen the mix of surprise and gratification on Veronica's face when she heard the news about Crossley, but I guess I'll have to settle for my imagination. I hope it brought her some peace; I know that's in short supply these days.

I enjoyed our chats, and in some ways I think you might make a not half-bad detective someday. Which brings me to the last thing I guess I should clear up. You simply cannot believe a man is dead because a stranger's voice on the telephone tells you so, Eddie. What was the name I used... Detective Jacob Baxter, I think. That and a disguised voice— not even much of a disguise, Eddie—was all I needed to operate with impunity. It bought me enough time anyhow to avenge my friend and then get the hell out of California.

Maybe you'll give this letter to the police, but I sure doubt it. There's nothing for them to track anyway. I thought you might even try to find me yourself, some bizarre sense of justice gnawing you into it, but no, I don't think you'll do that either. You knew the man Crossley was. With any luck, the whole ugly Cooperative will come crashing down without him, though I may be too optimistic in saying that.

Oh, one more thing (and it really must be one more thing as this has spilled over onto too many pages already). I worked hard not to be found, even cut off all my hair and grew out that silly beard, but it was lazy of me to stick around my old bar, wasn't it? I guess some habits die so hard they're practically immortal. And I never could shake that awful nickname. It always struck me so funny to be a Warren hiding in the Rabbit. It's usually just the reverse, Eddie.

Anyway, it was a pleasure to know you and you did not too bad a job, like I said before. Not good enough, but not too bad.

Your friend,

Warren Hyde

I allowed myself a wistful smile and set Warren's letter aside. So, I had closed my first real case, which made me feel like a success. Except the man at the center of it was dead, which made me feel like a failure. Then again, Hannah and Caroline got their happily ever after, and that was no small thing. Warren Hyde the killer was free in the wind, which was maybe better than he deserved. But nobody was paying me to think about things like what people deserved. I gave up trying to decide whether this counted as a good ending or a bad ending. It was an ending though—no doubt about that.

About the Author

Adam Dompierre is an award-winning author with a bachelor's degree in psychology from the University of Michigan and a master's degree in education from Augustana University. He works as an English teacher and won the Michigan Reading Association's Secondary Teacher Award in 2025.

Adam lives in the Upper Peninsula with his wife Riley and their dog Pilot. In his free time, he enjoys playing guitar and tennis, though not simultaneously. *Paint an Inch Thick* is his second novel.

You can connect with me at:

🌐 https://www.adamdompierre.com_

Subscribe to my free newsletter:

✉ https://www.adamdompierre.com/newsletter

Thank you for reading *Paint an Inch Thick*. If you enjoyed this book, please consider leaving a review on Amazon, Goodreads, or your platform of choice; it would really help me out. I appreciate your support!

All the best,

Adam